SHANE HEGARTY was the Arts Editor of *The Irish Times*, but is now a full-time writer. He lives on the east coast of Ireland, in a village not unlike Darkmouth. Only with no monsters. That he knows about.

Follow Shane on Twitter: @shanehegarty

Books by Shane Hegarty

DARKMOUTH

DARKMOUTH: WORLDS EXPLODE

DARKMOUTH

SHANE HEGARTY

Illustrated by James de la Rue

HarperCollins *Children's Books*

First published in hardback in Great Britain by HarperCollins *Children's Books* in 2015
This edition published in Great Britain by HarperCollins *Children's Books* in 2015
HarperCollins *Children's Books* is a division of HarperCollins*Publishers* Ltd,
1 London Bridge Street, London, SE1 9GF

The HarperCollins website address is: www.harpercollins.co.uk

1

Printed and bound in England by Clays Ltd, St Ives plc

MIX
**Paper from
responsible sources**

FSC
www.fsc.org **FSC™ C007454**

For Maeve, who made the adventure possible.

I

The town of Darkmouth appears on few maps because very few people want to find it. When it is marked on one, its location is always wrong. It'll be a bit north of where it's supposed to be, or a bit south. A little left or a little right. A bit off.

Always.

Which means that visitors to Darkmouth invariably arrive having taken a wrong turn, soon convinced they'll reach only a dead end. They drive through a canopy of trees, whose branches reach from either side to clasp ever tighter overhead, becoming thicker with every mile until the dappled light is choked off and the road is dark even on the brightest of days. Then, just as the wood is almost scraping the paint from their car, and it seems that the road itself is going to be suffocated, the visitors travel through a short tunnel and emerge on to a roundabout filled with blossoming flowers and featuring a sign that reads:

The next line has been updated by hand a couple of times:

On a wall lining the road there is large striking graffiti. It says only this:

Except the last S forms a serpent, with mouth wide and teeth jagged. Visitors peer at it and wonder, *Is that a...? Could it be a...?*

Yes, that snake really *is* swallowing a child.

The travellers – by now a bit desperate in their search – have finally reached Darkmouth. Their next thought is this: *Let's get out of here.*

So they go right round the roundabout and head back the way they came. Which is a shame, because if they were to stay they would realise that Darkmouth is actually quite a nice little place. It has a colourful little ice-cream shop on the harbour, benches dotted along the strand, picnic tables and fun climbing frames for the kids.

And no one has been eaten by a monster for some time.

In fact, they aren't really monsters at all. They might *look* monstrous, and the locals might refer to them as monsters, but, strictly speaking, they are Legends. Myths. Fables. They once shared the Earth with humans, only to grow envious, then violent, so that a war raged through the world's Blighted Villages for centuries.

Now Darkmouth is the last of these Blighted Villages. And Legends show up only occasionally.

This morning just happens to be one of those occasions.

2

Thinking back on it all later, Finn identified that morning as the time when things began to go badly wrong.

Thinking on it a little bit *more*, he realised he could identify just about any morning of his first twelve years as when things began to go wrong. At the time, though, he wasn't doing much thinking. Instead, he was running. As hard as he could. In a clanking armoured suit and heavy helmet. In the rain. Away from a Minotaur.

Five minutes earlier, everything had *seemed* to be going a bit more to plan, even if Finn wasn't entirely sure what that plan was.

Then it had been Finn doing the chasing, carrying a Desiccator, a fat silver rifle with a cylinder hanging in front of the trigger. He was the Hunter, lumbering through the maze of Darkmouth's backstreets in a black helmet and fighting suit – small dull squares of

metal knitted together
clumsily – so that
when he moved
it sounded like a
bag of forks falling
downstairs.

Desiccator

It was oversized because
his parents had told him he should leave room to grow
into it. It rattled because he had made it himself.

From somewhere in the near distance, about two
laneways away, he had heard the sound of glass being
mashed into stone, or maybe stone being pounded into
glass. Either way, it was followed by the scream of a car
alarm and the even louder scream of a person.

Darkmouth was a town of dead ends and blind alleys,
with high walls that were lined with broken glass, sharp
stones and blades. The layout was designed to confuse
Legends, block their progress, shepherd them towards
dead ends. But Finn knew where to go.

He followed the Legend's dusty trail, emerging on to
Broken Road, Darkmouth's main street, where vehicles
had screeched to a halt at wrong angles, and those
townspeople who hadn't scarpered were cowering in
still-closed shop doorways.

And at the top of the street, glancing over its shoulder, was the Minotaur. It was part human, part bull, all terrifying. Finn's heart skipped a beat, hammered three more in quick succession. He took a shuddering breath. He had spent his childhood looking at drawings of such creatures, which were always depicted as mighty, almost noble, Legends. Seeing one in the flesh, Finn realised they had captured its strength, but had not really conveyed any sense of just how rabid it looked.

From where its jutting, crooked horns met its great bull's head, it was covered in the mangy hair of a mongrel. As it looked back, slobber dripped from its great teeth

Minotaur

and ran through the contours of muscles bulging along its back, past its waist down to patches of skin as cracked as baked clay. It stood on two legs that tapered down to menacing claws instead of hooves.

The Minotaur was worse than Finn had ever imagined it could be. And he had imagined it to be pretty bad.

It was looking straight at him.

He ducked into a doorway. A woman was already hiding there, her back pressed against the door, a dog pulled close. Her face was tight with fear.

"Don't worry, Mrs Bright," Finn told her, his voice muffled by the helmet. "You and Yappy will soon be safe, won't you, boy?" He petted the dog, a basset hound, with his free hand. It sneezed on him.

The woman nodded with unconvincing gratitude, then paused. "Where's your father, young man? Shouldn't he be—?"

There was a smash further up the street. The Minotaur had disappeared round the turn at the top of Broken Road. Finn took another deep breath and moved on after it.

From the other side of a wall, there was a thud so forceful it sent a shudder from Finn's feet to his brain, which interpreted it as a signal to run screaming in the opposite direction.

But Finn didn't run. He had trained for this. He had been born into it. He knew what was expected of him, what he needed to do. Besides, if he ran now, his dad would be disappointed in him. Again.

I'll be there when you need me, Finn's father had told him that morning.

Pressing a radio button on the side of his helmet, Finn whispered, "Dad? Are you there?"

The only response was the uncaring crackle of static.

A dark, looming hulk crossed an intersecting laneway, tearing along its narrow walls. Finn raised his Desiccator and followed. At the corner, he crouched and peered round. The Minotaur had paused no more than twenty metres away. Its great shoulders heaved under angry, growling breaths as it figured out which way to go next.

It was all up to Finn now. He recalled his training. Focused on what he had been taught. Thought about his father's expert words. Carefully, he aimed his stocky silver weapon, steadied himself, exhaled.

At that exact moment, the Minotaur turned to face him, its eyes like black pools gouged beneath scarred horns. Froth dripped from chipped and jagged tusks. For a second, Finn was distracted by the way drool, blood and rain clung to a crystal ring wedged through the Legend's nose.

The Minotaur roared. Finn squeezed the trigger.

The force of the shot sent Finn tripping backwards. A sparkling, spinning blue ball flew from the barrel of the Desiccator, unfurling into a glowing net as it was propelled towards where the Minotaur had stood only a moment before… and wrapped itself round a parked car.

Finn groaned.

With a flash and a stifled *whooop*, half the car collapsed in on itself with the anguished scrunch of a ton of metal being sucked into a shape no bigger than a soda can.

Finn looked for the Minotaur. It was gone.

He pressed his radio switch. "Erm, Dad?"

Still nothing.

He paused, calmed his babbling mind as much as he could and moved off again through the laneways. Using the ancient methods handed down to him, Finn began carefully tracking the trail of the Minotaur.

He needn't have bothered. The Minotaur got to him first.

3

Naturally, Finn fled.

As he did, several thoughts went through his head, mainly to do with whether he should turn and shoot, or find a hiding spot, or whether he had time to stop and fling aside his clattering armour.

For its part, as it chased him, the Minotaur had only a single thought in its head. Finn was better off not knowing just how many times the word 'gouge' featured in it.

Finn ran down the laneway as fast as his rattling fighting suit would allow, his breath hot inside the helmet, his weapon flailing from a strap round his wrist. He spotted a gap and turned into it just before the Minotaur reached him. The creature smashed into a dead end, throwing up a cloud of brick, dust and drool.

Finn pushed on, darting across alleys, stumbling round corners, squeezing through gaps, until it occurred to him that the only sound he could hear above the noise of his suit was that of his own panting.

With some effort, he persuaded his legs to stop running.

Crouching at a corner, he looked around for any sign of the Minotaur. There was none. He sank down, feeling the rivulets of sweat running down his cheeks, the itchiness of the suit and the thump of his heart in his chest.

There was a rustle close by. The briefest flicker of a shadow.

"Dad?"

The Minotaur burst through a wall in front of Finn, collapsing with dreadful force into the laneway, its horns scraping and sparking off the concrete, before righting itself and looming over him. Finn raised his Desiccator, but the Minotaur reached out a huge arm and swiped it from his hands.

Backed up against the brick, Finn could taste the deathly sourness of the Minotaur's breath and see the deep blackness of its mouth. He was briefly mesmerised by the radiance of that fat diamond ring lodged in the Legend's nose.

Finn tried to think of a way out, of a fighting move his father had taught him, a plan, an escape route, anything other than just giving in to the inevitable pounding thought that he was about to die.

As it poised to strike, the Minotaur still had just one thought in its head, although it had evolved to include repeated use of the word 'maim'.

If this Legend had been a little less single-minded, however, it might have realised that the sliver of time it took to move in for the kill was long enough for a shadow to pass above it and the boy; for that shadow to grow larger, darker; for it to become solid as it bounded across the creature's great shoulders and landed behind it.

The Minotaur turned. The armour on this new human shimmered; it was hard to focus on. He seemed to be there yet not there. The figure carried a weapon similar to the boy's, but larger. And the Minotaur knew instantly who it now faced.

This was not *a* Legend Hunter. This was *the* Legend Hunter.

The Minotaur had moved barely a centimetre in attack before it was struck by the glowing net of the Legend Hunter's weapon. For the briefest of moments, it was frozen in an all-enveloping web of sparkling blue. Then, with a stifled *whooop*, the Minotaur imploded. All that was left was a solid, hairy sphere no bigger than a tennis ball.

The Legend Hunter remained steady, a thin wisp of blue smoke drifting from the barrel of his weapon. "Bullseye," he said, popping open his visor to reveal a face as solid as the helmet and an obvious delight at his quip.

Finn picked himself up off the ground and glared at him. "Where *were* you, Dad?"

L ike other Blighted Villages around the world – with names such as Worldsend, Hellsgate, Bloodrock, Leviatown and Carnage – Darkmouth had been home to generations of Legend Hunters, families who swore to protect the world against the unending attacks from what they called the Infested Side.

Except the attacks did end.

Mostly.

Each year had brought fewer reports of humans captured or killed by Legends – and of Legends captured or killed by Legend Hunters.

In Blighted Village after Blighted Village, the attacks had slowly died out. For the first time in thousands of years, our world appeared sealed off from the realm of Legends. After many generations of war, the Legend Hunters could stand down.

Except for one village. One family.

"You were fine," said Finn's dad, breezily. "I had you covered the whole time."

"That thing almost killed me."

"You know I would never let that happen."

"It didn't feel like that."

"Look, Finn, don't be so hard on yourself. You did well. A little loose in parts maybe, but you weren't exactly chasing after a chicken there. And don't be so sour. Most twelve-year-olds would die for a chance to run around chasing Legends."

"*Die?*" said Finn.

"You know what I mean."

Finn's father held his gaze for another moment before giving his son a gentle punch on the arm and picking up the desiccated remains of the Minotaur.

Wearily, Finn unhooked the container from his belt and entered a code into a keypad on its side. The lid hissed open, releasing a small cloud of blue gas and the faint tang of what smelled like orange juice. His father placed the round object in the box and pressed the lid shut. "It'll have a ball in there," he said.

Finn shook his head in mild disdain.

"Oh, suit yourself," said his dad as he grabbed the container and began to walk out of the alley. "Get out of that gear and I'll drive you to school."

"School? Seriously? How am I supposed to go to school after that? I'm not going. I'm just not."

But his dad didn't stop, so Finn reluctantly picked up his Desiccator and started to follow. A glint of light in the rubble caught his eye, a tight curve of crystal lying where the Minotaur had been desiccated. It looked like the diamond that had been in the creature's nose.

Odd.

Finn picked it up and examined its jagged beauty. He began to call after his father, but stopped himself. If he was being forced to go to school after all of that, then he wanted a reward.

He slipped the diamond into his pocket before jogging clumsily on, his suit clattering all the way.

They drove through Darkmouth, their car a large black metal block on wheels, its seats torn out to make room for lines of weapons and tools of various shapes and sizes and sharpness.

There were a few people on the streets now, though most had their heads buried in hoods, their faces down, protecting themselves from the drizzle, looking like the last place on Earth they wanted to be was the last place on Earth where Legends still invaded. It didn't exactly help their mood that Legends always brought rain with them.

"It's always the same when a gate opens," Finn's dad observed. "At least a small gateway means only a light shower. There was a time when the bigger gateways brought terrible storms. The old stories blamed them on the gods. As if, eh?"

Finn didn't answer. His father tutted. The car swung right.

Before jumping into the passenger seat, Finn had thrown his suit into the rear of the car. On his lap were his schoolbag and his Desiccator. He held the canister in front of his face and gave it a rattle.

"It never ceases to amaze me, that trick," said his father.

Finn felt a spark of sympathy for the creature trapped in there. From the outside, the only evidence that a Desiccator net's victim might once have been something living was the way the exterior of the resulting ball was coated in whatever the creature had been wrapped in originally: fur, scales, skin, leather trousers.

"Doesn't it seem a bit cruel to do this to them, Dad?"

"Maybe you'd prefer to tickle the next Minotaur into

submission. Or pet him and offer him a biscuit. Seriously, Finn." He glanced across at his son and noticed his scowl. "OK, so this morning didn't go too perfectly."

"Neither did the last time," said Finn, grimacing.

"Yes, but—"

"Or the time before that."

"My *point*, Finn, is that you are learning," said his dad. "I was the same when I was your age. Did I ever tell you about the time I—?"

"Yes," said Finn with a sigh.

"And the day I—?"

"That too. All I *ever* hear about are the great things you did when you were my age. You defeated this Legend. You invented that weapon. Unless you've a story that ends with you falling down a toilet or something, you're not going to make me feel any better right now."

The car pulled up at the school. Finn didn't move.

His father shifted a little, the armour of his fighting suit creaking in the car seat.

"It's not all bad news," he started.

"How is this not bad?" interrupted Finn, dismay in his voice. "My Completion Ceremony is only a year away, Dad."

"When did you turn twelve?"

"Two weeks ago."

"So, the ceremony is eleven and a half months away to be accurate, but plenty of time still."

"What about this morning – did you not see?" said Finn, shaking his head in disbelief.

"Finn, our family has defended Darkmouth for forty-two generations."

"Well, I haven't."

"But you will," said his dad. "You're going to be generation number forty-three."

"I won't be ready."

"Darkmouth is going to be your responsibility."

"It can't be," protested Finn.

"It *has* to be."

His father let a hush settle in the vehicle before continuing.

"Anyway, the Council of Twelve has been in touch," he said. "They have good news."

"Does it have to do with me?" asked Finn.

"No. Well, yes. Kind of." His father paused. "The Twelve have offered me a place on the Council. Forty-two generations, Finn, and not one of our family has ever been invited to become one of the leaders of the world's Legend Hunters. Sure, most of the world's Legend

Hunters are sitting at home getting fat right now, but still, it's a huge thing for us, a big honour, and—"

"Hold on," said Finn. "You'll be on the Council of Twelve?"

"Yes, isn't that excellent?"

"Aren't they based in—?"

"Liechtenstein. Small place with big mountains."

"So, you'll be out of Darkmouth?" asked Finn.

"Yes," said his dad. "Sometimes."

"And me?"

"No."

"Oh great," said Finn, feeling a great weight settling on his shoulders. "You'll be gone and the protection of Darkmouth will be up to—"

"You. Exactly. Won't that be cool?"

Finn stared at him as his brain tried to process that notion.

"It doesn't change anything, Finn," said his father. "Not much anyway. You're about to become the first true Legend Hunter to graduate in years. Darkmouth was always going to become your responsibility at some stage after that. And I won't be going straight away. The Twelve say there'll be a process, some checks."

"What kind of checks?"

His dad shrugged. "I don't know. Background stuff, subject to confirmation of rule 31, clause 14 of the whatever. You know, paperwork. The Twelve love their paperwork. Anyway, it's happening." He cleared his throat. "Just as soon as you become Complete."

"And what if I'm not ready?"

With a squeak of his fighting suit on the car seat's leather, his dad turned to look at him directly. "Finn, every Legend Hunter in this family had their Completion on their thirteenth birthday. Every single one, as far back as records go. They could have waited until they were fifteen or seventeen or even nineteen, like weaker families, but they didn't. So, our family – past, present and future – needs you to be ready. I need you to be ready. This town needs you to be ready. You *will* be ready."

Finn pushed open the car door and stepped out. "I feel so much better. Thanks, Dad."

As he swung the door shut, Finn saw his reflection in the window. His hair was damp, his skin flushed. He opened his mouth to protest again about having to go to school, but his father cut him off. "We'll talk about it later."

Finn stood at the kerb with his bag slung over his shoulder, listening to the low growl of the car as it drove away. The drizzle tickled his forehead.

In his pocket, he felt the buzz of his phone. There was a message from his mother.

DEEP BREATHS. LOVE YOU.

He took a deep breath, then another, steeling himself for the next challenge.

School.

5

Finn was late. And he was sure that everyone knew why.

As he trudged up the corridor, Finn sensed a rising giddiness from each class he passed, lessons stopping so teachers and pupils could watch him.

"Was that a big fella this morning?" a voice called down the corridor after him.

"Any chance you got rid of them all this time, Finn?" asked another.

He ignored it all until he reached his own classroom, his arrival greeted with a frisson of excitement. He mumbled an apology to Mrs McDaid for being late and headed for the last available seat. Unfortunately, it was between Conn and Manus Savage, identical twin brothers except for one chewed-up ear on Conn, which he had always claimed was the result of a fight with a Dobermann. He also claimed that the dog had lost.

Finn wriggled into the seat between them, the metal legs screeching across the floor.

The twins looked a little confused for a moment as they grew aware of the ripe stench of sweat.

"Hey, monster boy," whispered Conn out of the side of his mouth, "you forgot to change your nappy this morning."

"Miss?" Manus asked the teacher. "Can we open a window?"

"Better make it two," suggested his brother.

Finn wouldn't ordinarily have been too bothered by them. He knew his place. As a Legend Hunter in training, he couldn't really have friends. He practised with his dad. He studied. He ate. He slept. He didn't have birthday parties or sleepovers. He didn't have other kids just calling in. He didn't get a chance to answer their awkward questions about, say, that three-headed dog his dad had just brought home. He was never able to say, in a casual, it's-no-big-deal manner, "Oh, just ignore the Cerberus; its bark is worse than its bite." Darkmouth's parents were understandably not too keen to let their precious children run around a house like Finn's.

His family had been in town for forty-two generations, but Finn would always be an outsider. There would always be whispers swirling around him. Questions with a hint of resentment. Rumours. Why Darkmouth was the only Blighted Village left in which Legends still attacked. Why more wasn't being done to stop them.

He tuned out of it as much as he could, but it was hard to do that when it was coming at him in stereo.

"What did you do to scare the monster away this morning?" muttered Conn. "Breathe on him?"

"If you just waved your socks at them, maybe you'd finally get rid of them all," added Manus.

Finn began to feel irritated. It was one thing being different because of what he was – that was part of his life, something he'd learned to live with. It was another to be picked on after trying to protect these people from being mauled by a mythical creature.

But he didn't say anything. The Savage twins were more intimidating than some Legends. He did, however, make a mental note to stash some deodorant and soap in his bag from now on.

Mrs McDaid had resumed teaching and most of the class was paying attention to her again. Finn noticed there was a new girl sitting in the back corner, staring at him through a curtain of deep red hair.

A new girl? But there was never anyone new. You were

either born here or you visited by mistake and didn't come back again. No one *moved* to Darkmouth. Ever.

And yet there she was.

From behind her fringe, the new girl gave Finn the tiniest hint of a smile. Finn looked away. When he glanced back at her, her eyes were on the teacher.

Conn leaned in. "Fancy the new girl already?" he whispered.

"You never know," added Manus in Finn's other ear. "Maybe she likes Eau de Armpit."

Finn imagined the twins being chased by the Minotaur, the looks of horror frozen on their faces as its claws lopped their heads clean off their necks. The image cheered him for about half a second until he slumped down for what he knew would be a thoroughly miserable day. Which it was. Thoroughly.

6

Finn walked home, the hood of his jacket pulled up to hide his face. The drizzle had cleared and the town was returning to normality – its own sort of normality at least. Not for the first time, Finn felt the pressure that came from knowing that the safety of this town would one day be entirely his responsibility.

Except now he'd been told the 'one day' was less than a year away, when his father would leave to join the Council. That revelation made it hard for Finn to even breathe.

He had grown up hearing stories of the world's Legend Hunters, the defenders of each Blighted Village. The families in each town had passed down knowledge, techniques and weapons through generation after generation, each swearing to protect the people.

Except the world's Legend Hunters weren't needed any more. Their villages had grown quiet. The Hunters remained in their once Blighted Villages as a precaution – some even continued to train themselves and their children just in case – but most had moved on to other careers. That man stamping your ticket at the train station could be from a long line of Legend Hunters. So could that dance teacher, that weather presenter, that guy who's come to fix your TV.

But not in Darkmouth. Finn's family had been Legend Hunters as far back as the histories went. And as long as the Legends kept coming through, as long as they continued to attack Darkmouth, his family would be needed. As long as he was the only child of the only Legend Hunter, then Finn would be needed. And now that his father was moving up to the Council of Twelve, he would be needed to protect Darkmouth *on his own*.

Every bit of that responsibility weighed on him as he sulked home.

What made it worse was that he *wasn't ready*. He had needed rescuing. Again. His third time on a hunt with his father. His third failure.

The first hunt, a few weeks ago, had been pure humiliation. The Legend in question had been a Basilisk, a particularly stupid, fat reptile with a beak. Basilisks were brought up to believe that a single stare was enough to kill a human being. When cornered, they would stop, open their eyes wide and glare at an oncoming human. The only problem was that their stare was marginally less threatening than a baby's giggle. A Hunter wouldn't even break stride.

Only a particularly inexperienced or inept Legend Hunter could fail to capture such a creature. Finn happened to fit into both of those categories.

His father had strung the hunt out to show Finn how best to track a Legend using his own skills rather than any technology. "When their world meets our world, it creates a dust. Even the rain won't wash it away. Follow those dust tracks. Know the streets. Go at an even pace..."

It was then that he noticed Finn wasn't in his shadow any more. Instead, after quickly bagging the Basilisk, he found his son two lanes away, on his back, kicking his legs in the air like a stranded turtle. His dad's fear had been that a Legend would fell Finn; instead, his son had been undone by the awkwardness of his own fighting suit and the not-exactly-famous fighting skills of a pavement.

There was an uncomfortable silence on the walk home.

The second hunt, just the previous week, had started well enough. Following a few modifications to his armour, Finn was even given his own Desiccator. His father stayed with him as they hunted the intruder. It was a small Manticore, with the body of a lion, the stubby wings of a dragon, a scorpion tail lined with poisonous darts and, most dangerous of all, an inability to shut up.

They moved quickly, Finn tracking the dust from the Infested Side, just as he had learned, until he cornered the Manticore in an alleyway. Then it all went wrong. When Finn tried to get his Desiccator from the holster at his waist, he snagged his

Manticore

glove on his armour and couldn't even raise his arm.

"Hold on a second," he said to the Manticore.

This was a big mistake.

The first thing Legend Hunters in training are told about Manticores is: *Never engage them in conversation.* The Manticore will keep you there all day, talking almost exclusively in riddles. Bad riddles. You will eventually go quite mad.

Luckily, as the Legend opened its mouth to respond with a particularly devastating riddle, Finn's father desiccated it

He and Finn again walked home in a deeply awkward silence.

And then, of course, there was today.

In less than a year, Finn would be expected to Complete and become a full Legend Hunter. Among the criteria to even be *considered* were three verified, successful Legend hunts. Being cornered by the Minotaur that morning had instead completed a hat-trick of calamities.

He had caught the look on his father's face as he got out of the car outside school, the disappointment furrowing his brow. Now, as Finn walked home, he had a greater understanding of how deep that disappointment ran. He faced two possibilities.

Either he would fail so spectacularly that he couldn't become Complete, thereby preventing his father from being the only Darkmouth Legend Hunter in forty-two generations to bag every Legend Hunter's dream job.

Or he would somehow succeed and be left with the responsibility of defending Darkmouth, and every soul in it, alone. Finn couldn't decide which was the best outcome.

Or, more accurately, the worst.

Finn turned on to a street that featured a row of apparently derelict houses on one side, windows bricked up or boarded, some painted with childish images of flower boxes in an attempt to brighten them up a bit. A couple of trees sprouting from the pavement softened it a little, but a long blank wall on the other side of the street gave everything an inescapably austere look.

In a town with street names that spoke of Darkmouth's violent past, this one had no name. Finn's house was the last in the row, ordinary-looking and unremarkable.

As he approached, Finn could see a police car parked just behind his father's. The front door to the house was open and he could make out the figure of the local sergeant just inside.

Finn scurried to the low wall that hemmed in the small patch of garden outside his house. Out of sight, he crouched and listened.

"You know we appreciate what you do, Hugo," Sergeant Doyle was saying. "And we know you've got to teach the boy." The sergeant was a large man who used to be barrel-chested, but that barrel had slumped into his belly with age. "But this is the third time in only a few weeks." There was a pause. Finn peered over the wall into the open doorway and saw Sergeant Doyle flip open a notepad and begin reading. "Two walls pulverised in Fillet Lane. A car half destroyed by your boy at the Charmless Gap—"

"OK, Sergeant," said Finn's dad, raising his hands. "We'll be sure to..."

"Two people treated for shock."

"We can cover whatever costs..."

"The real cost is to you, Hugo. The people here are already scared stiff of the monsters; they don't need to fear the people who are supposed to be protecting them." Sergeant Doyle never looked pleased to be in Darkmouth. This day was no different.

"I have to train him, Sergeant—" began Finn's dad.

"We *know* you need to teach the boy, but there must be a better way than giving him a weapon and letting him loose," said Sergeant Doyle, stepping away from the door. Pressed against the wall, Finn felt the heat rise in his face.

The sergeant walked right past Finn without noticing him, got into his car and rolled down the window. "Hugo, you and I both know people here wonder why Darkmouth is the last place left where these attacks still happen. They're beginning to blame you. Some of them are even asking if you keep letting the monsters in deliberately to keep your job."

"Ah now, Sergeant...."

"There are people in Darkmouth who wonder if they might be better off dealing with this themselves. It's the twenty-first century, Hugo. They think they can buy monster-killing kits on the internet."

Finn's dad sighed. "They're called Legends."

"What?"

"See you, Sergeant."

Sergeant Doyle drove off. Finn's dad watched him go. "Close the door on your way in, Finn," he remarked as he re-entered the house.

Finn groaned. He should have known it was pretty much impossible for him to snoop on his dad. Even his childhood games of hide-and-seek had been ruined by his father's inability to even *pretend* he didn't know where his son was.

As Finn started towards his front door, he saw

something out of the corner of his eye, a blur further back along the street, moving quickly from one doorway to another. It was smaller than him, but tall enough, and he caught a glimpse of what might be fur. Red, flaming fur. Either that or…

Finn hesitated, opened his mouth to call his dad, then decided against it.

He held his palm out but felt no rain, turned his head towards home but heard no alarm.

He looked at his house, then back towards the figure. Quick and deft, it disappeared round the corner.

This was one chase Finn needed to do himself.

He followed it.

8

As he turned the corner, Finn got a better glimpse of the figure he was pursuing.

He felt a shot of relief as it confirmed what he had hoped from the moment he saw it. He was confident now that he would not need any help, any armour, any weapon. Nor would he need any of the courage his father kept insisting he would one day find.

It wasn't a Legend but a person. And, if a person was going to be sneaking around, a mass of blazing red hair wasn't much use for blending in.

Arriving on to the next street, he saw her straight away. She hadn't even attempted to hide, but instead appeared to be waiting for him, leaning against a wall, her eyes only half visible behind her hair. Finn had felt those eyes trained on the back of his head throughout the school day, but whenever he had glanced back at her she hadn't been looking at him.

"What do you want?" he asked, realising he didn't know the new girl's name.

"You're Finn, aren't you?"

"Yeah," said Finn crossly. "And you are...?"

She didn't answer.

"Why are you following me?" said Finn. "I mean, have you seen my street? We don't exactly get many visitors."

"That's not what I heard."

"Then you should know that you're better off staying away." He took a deep breath so he could stand a bit taller. "I deal with a lot of things far worse than you every day of the week, and it usually doesn't work out well for them."

"That's not what I heard either."

Finn immediately deflated. "You seem to have heard everything then," he said, betrayed by a squeak of hurt in his voice. "Now leave me alone."

He turned and started marching away.

"Emmie!" she shouted after him. "My name's Emmie. Sorry. I didn't mean to be rude. First-day nerves, I guess."

"Yeah, well..." Finn paused, but he still didn't know what to say.

"I mean, my dad moved here because of his job and I never thought I'd end up in a small town because, you know, I grew up in the city and I've never had to be the *new* girl, not that I had that many friends back home anyway, but I had a few and now they're there and I'm here and this town is kind of weird because, you know, I wasn't even allowed to bring Silver with us because he'd get hurt just climbing the walls because – oh, Silver's my cat by the way – because of all the glass on them. I mean, what is the story with this place and its high walls and all the glass and these narrow mazy lanes? Do people actually like living like this? Because it seems like, I don't know, kind of depressing. I mean, another few weeks and I'll probably just go completely..."

Emmie stopped, suddenly aware of how much she had blurted at him.

Having been blurted *at*, Finn was a little stunned.

"Oh yeah," she said. "It's to stop those, erm, things, isn't it? I heard all about it. In school."

She stepped forward, her hair parting a little to reveal green eyes that were wide with enthusiasm. "Tell me, do you see many of them? Did you see one this morning? Are they dangerous? What are they like? Have you ever *killed* one?"

Self-awareness reasserted itself and she stepped back, tucking her head down so that her face again retreated behind her hair. "Sorry. I shouldn't be so nosy," she said.

"It's just, well, it's kind of *cool*."

A flush burst across Finn's cheeks. Emmie looked around, seeming a little uncomfortable. "I've blabbered on too much. I'd better go."

"Oh," said Finn, still a bit dazed by all of this.

"I'll see you tomorrow," she said brightly.

"Whatever. At school, I suppose."

"I'll see you before that, on the way there."

Emmie opened the door of the house they were standing in front of and disappeared inside.

Finn remained where he was, somewhat bemused by the encounter. He looked at the house for a few seconds. It was a standard mid-terrace, nothing special. His house was similar, of course – from the outside at least – so he knew how deceptive looks could be, but Emmie's was on an ordinary street, lined with busy houses and cars and a sense of life. It wasn't the ruin that his street appeared to be. He envied that.

Finn turned to make his way home. As he did, he noticed the twitch of a curtain in the downstairs window, but whoever was there was gone just as quickly.

9

Finn sat at the desk in his bedroom, below a windowsill cluttered with coins, batteries, broken bits of an old phone, and a frayed cuddly toy with eight arms and soft fangs that he'd never been able to bring himself to throw out. His goldfish, Bubbles, picked about the stones in his tank, occasionally darting in fright at his own reflection.

In front of him was a large hardback book: *The Most Great Lives of the Legend Hunters, From Ancient Times to the Modern Day (Vol. 18: 'From Rupert the Unwise to Sven Iron-Tooth')*. Finn was meant to be studying it, but his eyes were not on the book. Instead, they were on the now dark, quiet street outside, which still glistened with the wet of the day's rain.

His *mind* was somewhere else entirely.

It was replaying the sight of the car that morning, crumpling like a tin can. The disappointment on his father's face. The moment when the Minotaur had cornered him. The smell of its breath still clung to Finn's nostrils, forcing him to run the scene over and over in his head, and he felt his shame grow with every replay until it formed a large knot in his chest.

From deep within the house, he could hear dull thuds and whirrs. His father had been making something for weeks now, sometimes long into the night. Since returning home, Finn had seen him only briefly – when he walked into the kitchen while Finn was doing his homework, telling him what section of *The Most Great Lives* he had to read that night, while prising a blade from the food blender before leaving again without explanation.

There was a thump so loud it sent a shiver through the house and shook Finn out of his self-pity. Then silence.

Finn glanced outside, trying to clear his mind. Reaching into his pocket, he pulled out the curved, diamond-like object that had been in the Minotaur's nose and held it up to let the street light catch its edges. Before he could study it further, his door opened. Finn quickly threw the crystal into an open drawer.

"Mam! You're supposed to knock before coming in."

"Sorry, Finn," his mother said, entering the room. "I was just worried about you. I heard you had a tough day."

They sat on the edge of his bed together. "How was work?" he asked her. His mother was a dentist and, as she did most days, she had brought home a faint odour of chemicals and ground teeth. This was more comforting to Finn than he had ever stopped to consider.

"Not as exciting as your day thankfully. Although everyone was talking about the Legend that came through this morning. Luckily, all I had to do was wave the drill at them and they shut up pretty quickly." She put her arm round Finn and went to give him a kiss on the top of his head.

Finn smiled, but squirmed away. "I'm not a baby, Mam."

"You're still *my* baby," she replied quietly.

He groaned in protest. He didn't want to admit that it warmed him when she said that.

There was a *phwump* from deep in the house, followed by the long *squeeee* of a drill. "I wish he'd hurry up and finish whatever it is he's building down there," said Finn's mam. There was another thud. "Have you talked to him? About… this morning?"

"Not much. It's fine, really. Stop worrying."

Finn's mam looked at him. "I knew what I was getting into when I met your father. You never had that choice."

"Sometimes, I wish you were a Hunter too," said Finn. "You'd be a really good one."

Finn's mam grinned. "I don't think my parents would have let me marry your dad if I'd been expected to do *that*. I don't think *I* would have married him. Anyway, you know the rules. Civilians can't become Legend Hunters, Finn. You've got to be born into it."

Finn and his mother were quiet for a few moments, the only sound the goldfish pecking at pebbles.

"I mean it, though, Mam. You'd be a great Hunter."

"I could give them a good flossing until they succumbed. Or threaten them with a root canal."

Finn smiled weakly, sending another trickle of warmth through his chest, loosening the knot a little.

"I'll talk to your dad," his mother said, standing up. "Get him to go a bit easier on you."

"No!" snapped Finn, before quickly calming down. "Please don't. I'm trying really hard, it's just…"

"I understand." His mam gave him another kiss on the head before she left. This time he didn't squirm so much.

Finn got up and locked the door after her, then went back to his desk and took the diamond from its hiding place. He heard the front door of the house open and looked out of the window to see light spilling on to the pavement.

His father's long shadow knifed across the street. Finn could see that his attention was focused on the far end of the street, where a parked van started up its engine and, without even turning on its lights, slowly pulled away.

His father turned back to the house and there was the heavy sound of the front door being bolted.

Finn wrapped the diamond in an old pair of pants and placed it at the back of his underwear drawer where it would be safe. He didn't know what he was doing with it, only that it felt too late to admit to having picked it up in the first place. It was his souvenir. No one would need to know.

He sat back down at his desk and flipped through *The Most Great Lives*, only half registering the text, until, from beneath it, he pulled out a smaller thinner book. On its cover was a man in blue medical overalls holding a dog by the jaw. It mightn't have been too clear if he was about to help the dog or punch it except for the title, half obscured by a school library stamp: *So You Want to Be a Veterinarian*.

Finn read a few pages, poring over the images of dogs, cats, birds and lizards, with instruments pointed at their ears, or holding down their tongues, combing through their fur, feathers or skin, each in the hands of a confident-looking person in scrubs. He imagined himself in those scrubs rather than a fighting suit. He closed his eyes and saw himself tending to an animal rather than blasting one, healing creatures rather than shrinking them into little balls.

His daydream was interrupted by the sounds again, deep in the house. Finn placed his head on the desk, the page of the book cool on his cheek, and listened to the noises, feeling the vibration tickle his face. *Khrump, khrump, khrump.* Silence. *Squeeee.*

They didn't stop him from quickly falling into a deep sleep.

From *A Concise Guide to the Legend Hunter World, Vol. 2,* Chapter 65: 'The Infested Side: A Guide to What We Know and What We Don't' (published by Plurimus, Magesterius, Fortimus & Murphy).

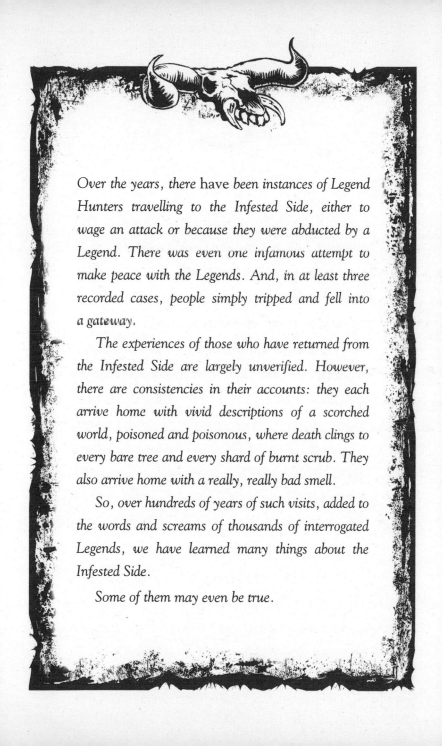

Over the years, there have been instances of Legend Hunters travelling to the Infested Side, either to wage an attack or because they were abducted by a Legend. There was even one infamous attempt to make peace with the Legends. And, in at least three recorded cases, people simply tripped and fell into a gateway.

The experiences of those who have returned from the Infested Side are largely unverified. However, there are consistencies in their accounts: they each arrive home with vivid descriptions of a scorched world, poisoned and poisonous, where death clings to every bare tree and every shard of burnt scrub. They also arrive home with a really, really bad smell.

So, over hundreds of years of such visits, added to the words and screams of thousands of interrogated Legends, we have learned many things about the Infested Side.

Some of them may even be true.

10

Broonie did not know where he was being dragged to, but the simple fact that he had a bag over his head, and his arms were tied, gave him reason to suspect that it was not anywhere pleasant.

At first, he had thought it was a practical joke played on him by the Hogboons who lived three mounds over and with whom Broonie had been engaged in a battle of pranks for a few months now. The most recent gag played on Broonie had involved a small rodent being released into his home, which in itself wouldn't have been so remarkable if the small rodent hadn't been on fire at the time.

It was, Broonie reckoned, a fair response to his own clever and complex jape involving ivy, sharpened sticks, a large hole and a bag full of beetles.

So, when he was woken rudely from his standard all-day nap by a bag being placed over his head, he was certain it was just another revenge prank. "Oh right, lads, very funny," he'd said as his arms were being tied. "But wasn't it my turn to play the joke?"

That was when he got punched in the head for the first time.

Even through a minor concussion, he could tell that there were two assailants and they were big. They clearly weren't Hogboons like him, because Hogboons were a short, spindle-limbed race, though what they lacked in physical stature they made up for in length of ears, crookedness of teeth, greenness of skin and general mischief.

"Stay still, you ugly little thug, or I'll snap your arms off and use them to break your legs," one of the assailants roared as Broonie found some energy to struggle.

"You're calling *me* ugly?" exclaimed Broonie. "I can see your feet through the bottom of this bag. Do you mind me asking, are all of those warts yours or did you borrow some for this special occasion?"

Hogboon

61

That was when he got punch number two. It knocked him out.

When Broonie came to, he was being dragged up a slope of some sort. It was steep and brutal underfoot. Actually, brutal underfoot would have been a luxury to Broonie right then. As he was dragged along, it was brutal under his toes, brutal under his shins and particularly brutal under his knees.

Worse than that was the stench in the air. It seeped through the canvas of the bag until he could feel it burning his throat. He had heard about this intense smell from other travellers, or at least from those who claimed to have survived it.

"If you were to leave a bag of fish to rot inside a corpse stuffed with already rotten fish, that would be sweet perfume compared to the stench of this place," one traveller had insisted.

"I burned every item of clothing I owned to get rid of its foulness. Even then it wasn't enough," whispered another. "In the end, I had to shave every last fibre of fur from my body, pluck every hair from my nostrils, pull every lash from my eyes, to free myself of it. Yet, even now, if the wind blows in a particular direction..."

The air seemed to grow more putrid with every step Broonie's captors took, with every bump and scrape his body absorbed. He understood now where he was being taken. It was to a place of death. Most probably his.

Eventually, the climb evened out, the ground becoming flat, hard stone. It was warmer and the echoes of his captors' footsteps told Broonie he was indoors.

A door groaned open and heat smacked Broonie hard. They stopped. Broonie was flung to the floor. As he pushed himself up, one of his kidnappers yanked the bag from his head. The Hogboon was briefly blinded by numerous fires, burning tall in huge cauldrons that lined the large stone room. In front of him, the largest of them popped and crackled and leaped high towards the ceiling.

His captors shuffled their hulking bodies away. Broonie realised now that they were Fomorians, brutal, merciless giants who were all either very intelligent or spectacularly dumb, with nothing in between. He wasn't entirely sure which type was better to encounter.

His eyes adjusted quickly and he saw, stomping towards him from the far side of the room, a figure Broonie had dearly hoped he would never have to lay eyes on.

Gantrua's massive bulk was turned away from Broonie and, when he spoke, he turned his head only slightly towards him, just enough to reveal the curved edge of great fierce horns that sprouted from his forehead.

The light of the flames danced off armour that ran from his waist up to a jagged grille across his mouth. Even in the uncertain light, Broonie could see that it was made up of many individual teeth fixed on to a metal rim.

"Do you know who I am, Hogboon?" Gantrua's voice was so deep Broonie felt it quiver through the stone at his knees.

"Yes, Your Greatness. The whole land trembles at your very name."

"Do you know why you're here?"

Broonie did not. So he took a guess. "Is it the beetles? It was only a bag of them, Your Lordship, and no one was eating them at the time. If they were yours, I am truly sorry. I had intended to sweep them all up and return them, but, you know how it is, Your Powerfulness, there were other things to do, and—"

"Quiet," commanded Gantrua with an authority that terrified Broonie so effectively he briefly lost his balance. "I don't care about your pathetic thieving. If you had decided to steal from *me*, you would have been struck down before the thought had even entered your head."

Broonie's head drooped from exhaustion and humiliation. His body ached from the violent journey. His head hurt from trying to figure out why he was here in the first place.

He lifted his head again to see that Gantrua was ignoring him now, engaged instead in a conversation with a smaller hooded figure in the shadows. Gantrua signalled to this other creature to wait, then turned fully and loomed over Broonie.

In the flickering light, Broonie could make out the scars that marked Gantrua's skin, valleys sliced across his arms, rivers of wounds crossing at his shoulders.

"You are trained?" asked Gantrua.

Broonie had not expected that question. "We all were, Your Greatness. A long time ago now. Before the sky closed."

"You had better search your memory for those lessons. The sky has not closed entirely."

So the rumours are true, thought Broonie. *There are still gateways to the Promised World.* There had been talk among the armies of this, but he had never heard it confirmed. It had been a long, long time since he had heard of anyone going through and coming back.

"We are on the verge of a great invasion of the humans' world," continued Gantrua. "It must succeed or the way through could be locked for eternity and we will be trapped. Forever. In *this* place."

He spat into the flames, shocking them into chaos. He composed himself again as the fire settled into its normal dance. "You, Hogboon, shall go to the Promised World."

"I'm flattered, Your Worship. Really. I am greatly honoured. But, Your Masterfulness, I have not trained for many years. I fear I'll get captured as soon as I step through the gateway."

Gantrua leaned forward so that the flames licked the metal guard at his chin. "I am counting on it."

He stood back, acknowledging a whisper from the hooded figure who was still lurking in the shadows. Then Gantrua addressed Broonie again. "The boy will be there."

"The boy?"

"Do not act dumb, Hogboon. I know what they talk about beyond these walls. I know they talk about the boy. They wonder if it is true, if he is real. Well, he *is* real. You will meet him and you will take with you two things for him. One is a message. The other is a gift. My guards will give you both."

One of the Fomorians removed a pair of tongs from his

belt and approached a cauldron. Ignoring its angry flames, the guard plunged his tongs into the fire and pulled out a long clear crystal. He brought it over to Broonie.

"The miners work day and night to find the meagre supply of these crystals," growled Gantrua. "Each has the power to open up a path between the worlds. We need to send one to the Promised World, but it will only retain its power through a sacrifice. I suppose I should tell you that yours will be a noble one, but I doubt very much nobility would ever stoop to be an acquaintance of yours, so we shall just get on with it."

Gantrua turned away to exit from the far side of the plinth, then paused mid-step. "Which of your fingers is least precious to you, Hogboon?"

"Erm, they're all kind of useful to me, Your Superlativeness. I'd find it hard to choose."

"They all say that," snarled Gantrua, then disappeared off the far side of the plinth.

The guard holding the crystal came closer. From his waist dangled a rather bloody-looking pair of pliers. The second Fomorian grabbed the Hogboon by one arm and pinned him to the ground.

Broonie had held out for this long, but he decided it was finally a good time to scream.

At breakfast, Finn's father came into the kitchen and began rummaging through a drawer.

"How are you feeling this morning, Finn?"

Finn had a mouth full of cereal and couldn't quite get an answer out.

"Good stuff. Listen, I've been thinking about what happened yesterday," said his father, now searching through a cupboard. "It's a lack of live Legend practice that's held you back. My fault really. We'll remedy that. Get hold of a Legend for you to fight."

Finn swallowed his cereal. "Um... is that what you're looking for now?"

His father had moved to another cupboard, his head stuck in it as he searched for something. "It's all very exciting, Finn. You becoming Complete, me joining the Council. No other family in the world has that to look forward to. It's really something."

He emerged empty-handed, then stood up straight while looking around intently. "That's going to have to do," he said, grabbing a knife and moving towards Finn, who dodged as his father made for the toaster behind him. Using the knife, he forced off the toaster's handle and left the room with it.

A few seconds later, Finn's mother arrived in the kitchen. "Hello, sunshine," she said, grabbing a couple of slices of bread and putting them in the toaster. She paused, realising what was missing. "Hugo!"

Finn left the house for school, and Emmie appeared just as he passed the corner where their streets met.

"What's happening?" she asked, stepping in beside him as if the two of them had known each other forever.

"Erm, eh..." was Finn's reply. It occurred to him that he should be a little more articulate from now on.

As it turned out, he didn't need to worry too much because Emmie did most of the talking. She generally seemed to treat silence like an enemy. And what she mostly liked talking about was Darkmouth. While most newcomers found themselves compelled to run out of the place as fast as they could, Emmie was fascinated by almost every detail.

She had noticed there were bars on the windows of many homes and businesses. "Even the church looks like a prison. What if you had an actual prison here, would they put bars on the bars?"

Then there was the way the people greeted every drop of rain warily, as if it might be a deluge of blood, not water. "If they're afraid of rain," observed Emmie, "Ireland isn't a great place to live, is it?"

She greeted every dent in a lamp-post and every crack in the pavement as possible damage from a Legend attack, and was disappointed when Finn dismissed each one as just another dent caused by someone not watching where they were backing up their car or yet more cracks that hadn't been fixed.

Finn hadn't given a tour of Darkmouth to a newcomer before and he could see how much Emmie longed to hear of adventure. So, as they walked along the seafront, he pointed to the large weathered rock jutting straight up some distance off shore. "That's called Doom's Perch. A Legend threw that there. It's called Doom's Perch because, about a hundred years ago, a local man escaped a Legend attack by stealing a boat and taking it out to that rock."

Under her fringe, Emmie's eyes encouraged him to continue.

"He climbed to the top, assuming that it would be a good place to hide out, and waited for the Legend to pass. Once the attack was over and everything looked safe, he went to climb back down to the boat."

"Did he get eaten on the way down?"

"No, he slipped on seaweed, fell into the sea and was never seen again. They've called it Doom's Perch ever since."

Emmie screwed her face into a taut grin. "Yeah, nice one. Try and fool the city girl. You'll have to do better than that."

Finn felt a bit defeated by that. The story was pretty much true, although he might have made up the part about the boat being stolen.

Because they had dallied on the walk to school, they were late and Finn was again forced to take the last empty seat. As he sat down, he saw a half-melted toy car on the desk. The Savage twins were sniggering from the back, Conn Savage fiddling menacingly with his misshapen ear and Manus rubbing his knuckles beneath his eyes. *Boohoo.*

Over the next few days, Emmie asked Finn a lot of questions about Darkmouth and about his life, and the thing that came up most was this: she wanted to see inside his house. She was quite persistent.

"Maybe I could come to your house instead," he'd suggested.

"Nah," she responded.

She did this a lot, and it worked as a verbal weapon of sorts, a swift stab of a needle that punctured any talk she didn't want to carry on. Finn had learned little about Emmie, other than that her father had come here to work because of a contract on the phone lines, and he planned to go back to the city once his job was done. She had met all Finn's other enquiries with a wall of *Nahs*.

"Will your friends come and visit you here?"

"Nah."

"Do you have a nice house back in the city?"

"Nah."

"I suppose the city was really exciting to live in."

"Nah."

"Do you miss your cat? I'd like to have a cat, but my dad's not big into pets."

"Oh, I'd love it if Silver was here, but I couldn't bring him."

"Is a friend minding him?"

"Nah."

But, when it came to Finn's house, the words poured out like water from a burst pipe.

"Why can't I come in? I won't touch anything I'm not supposed to. I just *have* to see what it's like in your house because I can't imagine what kind of place it is, when your father's job is, you know, *what it is*, and the way everyone talks about your family and how you've spent, like, *centuries* doing this so there must be *amazing* things lying around, because of all that time and all those Legends—"

"*Legends?*" interrupted Finn.

"What?" asked Emmie. "Isn't that what they're called?"

"Yes," said Finn, frowning. "But people don't usually get it right. They call them monsters instead. Did you know about Darkmouth before you came here?"

"Nah."

It also became clear, over the following few days, that Emmie wasn't particularly interested in getting to know anyone else in the school, only Finn. He didn't quite know what to make of it, but he was glad she did most of the talking because it stopped him saying anything stupid.

That Friday afternoon, as they walked home, Emmie asked yet again if she could come to see his house, and his resistance broke so suddenly he could almost hear it snap.

"OK."

That stopped Emmie dead on the street. Finn kept going, quietly satisfied with having said the right thing, and keeping his mouth closed in case he followed up by saying the wrong thing.

12

They walked past the derelict house fronts on Finn's street, Emmie staying quiet the whole way. When they finally reached Finn's front door, he opened it and walked in, Emmie close on his heels. But, as she stood in the narrow entrance hall, Finn could see her struggling to hide her massive disappointment as she realised the Legend Hunter's home was as ordinary as any other house.

The coat hooks weren't made of serpent skeletons.

The wallpaper wasn't made of dragon leather.

The pictures of Finn and his family showed them sitting, eating picnics and generally doing anything but wrestling beasts from another realm.

"This is the sitting room," Finn said as he opened its door. He could see how crestfallen Emmie was to realise that it was, indeed, a sitting room. Nothing more, nothing less. The same with the dining room, with its dining chairs and dining table. And the kitchen. And the utility room, with its ironing board and an iron that could, at a pinch, be thrown at an onrushing Legend, although this clearly wasn't its primary purpose.

He could almost see what Emmie was thinking. *This could have been any house. On any street. In any town.*

Finn couldn't help feeling a bit sorry for her. "There is something else…" he said, going to a small door squeezed between the kitchen and dining room. A stranger might think it was a cupboard because there was seemingly no space for anything larger.

The door had a handle, but Finn ignored that and instead pressed each of the door's four panels in a practised sequence. He made a bit of a show of it, enjoying this rare dose of power he felt from knowing he'd kept the best for last.

"Ta-da!" he said with a flourish he immediately felt silly about.

There was the clunk of a lock opening. With a little effort, he pushed the door open with his shoulder and stood back so Emmie could enter first. She stepped through, peering into the deep dark that greeted her.

Finn flicked a switch and a single bulb flickered just over their heads. Then light raced along the ceiling away from them, illuminating bulb after bulb after bulb. It was not a room at all. It most certainly was not a cupboard.

"This corridor," Emmie gasped. "It's *huge*! It must take up a few of the houses next door."

Finn gave her a look, and she frowned for a moment, then gasped.

"The whole street? Your house takes up the *whole street*? That's insane!" She gave him a shove in delighted disbelief.

The hallway was narrow with a high ceiling. The lights bathed the faded brickwork, which changed in colour and texture every few metres, the street having been built one house at a time over many, many years. The entrance appeared to be the oldest part. "We just call it the Long Hall. It was like this long before I was even born," explained Finn. "Our ancestors started off with our house where we still live, and over the years took over one house at a time, until we were the only ones here."

Running along the length of the corridor's right-hand side were closed doors, some wooden, some steel, and each marked with letters and numbers that would mean nothing to anyone who wasn't a member of the family: the first was T4; the second E1; the third S3.

The left wall was lined with large portraits, some

reaching from floor to ceiling. The first few were dark and faded. In them, the people wore metal armour topped off with shoulder spikes, helmets with antlers attached, and they carried basic but fierce weapons: double-bladed swords, nets rimmed with steel, shields studded with blades.

As Finn and Emmie moved slowly along the great corridor, the armour in the portraits grew increasingly modern and sleek, and the weapons changed from sharp instruments to guns.

The paintings were mostly of men, but women began to feature as the paintings became more obviously recent. Each had a nameplate: Sean the Brave, Hugh the Stone-Headed, Ragnall Iron Trousers, Aisling the Powerful, Conor Red Skull, William the Surprised, Rachel the Stubborn, Rory the Esteemed.

Each bore a striking resemblance to Finn.

"My ancestors," he said.

Emmie looked at the portraits. "Weird names."

"We don't get a surname at birth," Finn explained. "We gain one. Each of these people is named because of something they did or their personality."

"What's yours then?" asked Emmie.

"I don't have one yet."

"So you're just Finn?"

"Until I get my Legend Hunter name. Everyone at school thinks it's a bit strange not to have a surname, but it would feel strange to me to *have* one. Finn Smith, Legend Hunter. Doesn't quite work, does it?"

"Suppose not," said Emmie quietly.

It occurred to Finn that he had never asked her an obvious question. "What's your surname anyway?"

"Er, Smith."

"Oh." Finn felt heat flush through his face.

"Don't worry about it. I can blame my dad for that one," said Emmie, who didn't seem too bothered and was already scanning paragraphs of text framed beneath each painting.

She read from one.

"Conor Red Skull, Darkmouth, Ireland. Active during the late seventeenth century, he once went four days without sleep while tracking down and slaying two dozen Legends who had entered through three simultaneous gateways. It is said that he was so stained with blood it never properly washed off his skin. He earned his Hunter name due to his inability to spend any time in the sun without getting burned."

"Each portrait has an entry like that," said Finn. "It's

taken from *The Most Great Lives*, which is this book we have to read while training to become a Legend Hunter. *Books* actually. There's a lot of them and they're about all of the Legend Hunters throughout history."

"Does that mean you'll be in a book one day?"

"Um. Yeah, maybe. When I become a proper Legend Hunter," said Finn.

"Cool."

Finn flushed again, the heat prickling his face. Emmie moved on, eventually stopping at the second to last portrait. It was of a man who looked about as furious as it was possible to get. Across his lap was a simple rifle and behind him was a row of shelves lined with jars, whose labels the artist hadn't bothered to add detail to. On a small table beside him was a miniature tree, leaning away from him at a sharp angle.

The nameplate on the frame read *Gerald the Disappointed* and the text below was particularly lengthy, going into some detail about the many adventures of his early life, including his rescue of a family of Legend Hunters hemmed in on the Scottish island of Iona; the year in which he staved off 154 Legend invasions of Darkmouth; his world-renowned bonsai collection; and how he once single-handedly felled a massive three-headed Cerberus, armed with just a single rock ("...albeit a very pointy rock," *The Most Great Lives* clarified).

Finn hovered patiently while Emmie read. Finally, she spoke. "Nice nickname. Suits the face."

"That was my great-grandfather," replied Finn. "I never knew him."

"Bet he was a barrel of laughs."

"He trained my father. My dad says he was pretty fierce."

"Why did he have to train your father? What happened to your grandfather?"

Finn gestured towards the last portrait. This man wore armour but no helmet, and was the only one in any of the portraits who was not holding a weapon. Instead, he was surrounded by scientific instruments and scraps of paper. He didn't look particularly confident or aggressive. His chin wasn't held high

82

and his eyes were pointed down, as if he was meek or maybe even a little afraid.

"That was my granddad, my dad's father."

"Niall Blacktongue! Excellent name."

"Not really," said Finn, downbeat.

Emmie read the entry aloud. "Niall Blacktongue was the first Legend Hunter to try and talk to the Legends, to reason with them and attempt to understand why they wanted to come into this world. He died. No one likes to talk about it."

That was it. Nothing else.

"I don't get it. What happened to him?" asked Emmie.

"He died," Finn responded haltingly. "No one likes to talk about it."

There were two empty frames at the end of the row, with nameplates ready and waiting, but nothing engraved on them just yet.

"Who are those for?" asked Emmie.

"They are to remind us of our responsibilities to all of the Hunters who have gone before, all of these people along the wall. You only get a portrait when you've passed the role of Legend Hunter to someone else or if you, eh, well, die."

"Wow, that must be pretty scary."

"Well, you know, it's our way of life, I suppose. That first empty frame's for my dad."

"What's your dad's nickname then?"

Finn paused before answering. "Hugo the, erm, Great."

"The Great?"

"Yeah," Finn mumbled. "He did a couple of things when he was younger. Kind of great sorts of things."

"What, like fighting Legends?"

"That. And more. He never shuts up about it."

"So, when will you get your nickname?" asked Emmie.

Finn's hands were rammed into his pockets, his shoulders tight. "I have to do a thing called a Completion first. It's a big ceremony."

"When?"

Finn didn't respond, but instead walked on towards the very end of the long corridor, the wall now empty of portraits on one side, but with doors still lining the other (T1, A4). Emmie tried one, but it was locked. At the end of the corridor was a large steel door with a wooden sign that read 'Library'. Finn hesitated for a moment and turned to head back the way they'd come. "And this concludes our tour," he said, with forced jauntiness.

"What's in there?" asked Emmie, still standing at the library door.

"Nothing much," said Finn unconvincingly. "Let's go and see what food's in the kitchen. I'm starving."

Emmie hovered there a couple of moments longer. Finn watched her, listening to the noises from inside. The faint sounds of feet moving around, the squeak of a chair. She moved a little closer. From deep within came what sounded like a shriek.

"Come on. Race you to the kitchen," said Finn.

Emmie hurried after him.

13

"**H**it me."

Finn punched his father in the face.

"Hit me again."

He hit him again.

"Put some anger into it."

Finn had anger in reserve, but he had to drill deep below his exhaustion to get to it. He concentrated hard, summoning it from the depths, and swung again. His father hardly flinched. Instead, he pulled off his soft padded headgear.

"Come on, Finn, this is only training. When I was your age, I was—"

"—already fighting Legends five times my size," Finn panted. "You've mentioned it once or twice before."

He dropped his tired arms. His father gave him a dig to the chest.

"Hey!" Finn protested.

"Don't drop your guard. Now kick me. Aim for the crotch."

Every Friday night, one of the rooms off the long corridor would host Finn's often futile attempts to learn how to roll over and get up again; or to shoot at a target; or to leap; or to dodge; or to leap while dodging. This room was T2, a training room bare but for the soft mats on its floor, a mirror running the length of one wall and a box of simple gym equipment containing various items of padded gear that allowed Finn to hit his father wherever he was ordered to.

He stretched out and kicked. His father grabbed his leg and wouldn't let go, so that Finn was left hopping on one foot, completely at his father's mercy.

"I've seen ducks kick harder than that," said his dad.

Finn had been training since he was very young, so it wasn't that he couldn't do any of these things. It was worse: he could *almost* do most of them. He could half roll, and just about jump to his feet. He could kind of shoot, nearly leap, more or less punch and semi-dodge. He had strengths; it just happened that they were usually closely followed by his weaknesses.

"Let's try the Wrigley Manoeuvre, Finn. It's a simple

way of not just avoiding an onrushing Legend, but of turning defence into offence."

"That's the same guy who ended up being known as Wrigley the Headless, right?"

"Yes, and that's why we have to make sure to do it right. Now take this seriously, Finn. It might save your life."

His father demonstrated the move, darting across the room, then sliding and returning to his feet, facing Finn, with his hands raised in an attack position. "Now you try it."

Finn followed his dad's lead, but compared to him he had the dexterity of a giraffe on ice. "I see what you're doing. I get it," he protested, breathing hard. "I'm just tired now."

"Twelve-year-olds don't get tired. When I was twelve..."

"That must have been some year. Did you save anything for when you were thirteen?"

"Look, Finn. In the classroom, you've the potential to be a very good Legend Hunter—"

"Well, bring the Legends to the classroom and I can tackle them there," said Finn.

"If you were as quick with your hands as you are with your mouth, this wouldn't be so difficult," his father replied.

Finn sat on the ground, breathing hard.

"Stay fresh," said his dad. "You can read a couple of entries in *The Most Great Lives* when we're done here."

"Ah, Dad, really?"

"You'll be in there yourself some day."

"So you keep saying. There won't be much to say about me," said Finn.

"That hasn't stopped them before. Besides, they're desperate for you to come through. No Completions, and no true Legend Hunter in years, mean no new edition of the book. No new edition, no profits. They're badly in need of an update."

Finn was well aware of this already, thanks to the publisher's repeated letters.

"Looking forward to your Completion," Plurimus, Magesterius, Fortimus & Murphy wrote. "How's the training going?" they asked. "We don't mean to rush you, but..." and so on. Finn spent a lot of time trying not to think about the queue of people lining up to be disappointed if he didn't Complete. Nevertheless, his conversation with Emmie had reminded him he wouldn't be the first family problem.

"Dad, what really happened to Granddad Niall?"

"No one likes to talk about it, you know that."

"*I want to talk about it.*"

"And I don't. Now quit stalling and get up."

Finn had almost got his breath back, but kept up the heavy panting to get a couple more moments' rest.

"Maybe I won't fight them when my time comes," he said.

"What?"

"Maybe it's the fighting that keeps the Legends coming, you know," said Finn, a clamminess rising in him as he realised he was treading on thin ice. "Maybe talking to them isn't such a bad idea."

"Which bit of the 'no one likes to talk about it' is hard for you to understand?"

"Maybe we can learn something from it."

His dad squatted down to stare directly at Finn, holding his gaze until Finn's eyes began to want to jump out of their sockets and run away. Finally, his father spoke. "What my father did is not something I will ever be allowed to forget, no matter how hard I try. That's all the lesson we need to learn." He offered Finn a hand up. "Now let's get fighting again."

"Is this going to be needed, though?" asked Finn. "The gateways are dying out. They'll be gone from here too eventually. Besides, we have Desiccators. Why do I need to learn this stuff?"

"You might have noticed that the Legends aren't gone yet."

"Then why do they keep attacking here and nowhere else?"

"I don't know. What do you think?"

Finn took a moment to ponder this. "I think I've scared the bigger ones away."

His father grinned at that, held out a hand and helped Finn to his feet. Then he jumped back. "OK, buster, wrestle me."

Finn's sigh of annoyance was lost in the clatter of an alarm rattling through the building. That noise had been the soundtrack to Finn's life – the signal that a gateway had opened somewhere in Darkmouth.

"Excellent," said his father, perking up immediately. "Who needs training when we have a live Legend to help us out? Besides, if we get into trouble, you can just give the Legend the look you're giving me now. That'll scare it."

Finn bit hard on his lower lip.

His father grinned. "Yep, that's the one."

14

Broonie walked through the gate and emerged into a world of rain.

What he noticed first was not the scenery, but the air. It had a purity that was invigorating. At least it had a purity once he sniffed his way past the many impurities that were layered over it: fatty foods, burnt fuels, seaweed, decaying flowers, all overlaid by tons of perfume-doused sweat. It carried in the breeze and through the light rain.

But, underneath all that, the air was so fresh that he wanted to drink it.

Everywhere he looked there was a vibrancy that he had never experienced. Each colour was divided into shade upon shade – even the greys exploded across a spectrum.

This was the Promised World. This was what centuries of war had been waged over. He understood it now.

He was on a Darkmouth street. *So orderly*, he thought. *Flowers growing from baskets in the air: novel. Numbers on doors: curious. The ground is painted with rectangles and vehicles are abandoned in them. Odd.*

Broonie felt grubby in his dull rags crusted with his own blood. He saw that he was covered in a fine layer of dust that seemed resistant to the rain. Instead, it shed from him as he nervously shuffled on the spot, trying to decide what he had to do next. He had been told his mission. He still didn't understand exactly what it was.

"When you see them, you can attack," the Fomorians had said.

"Attack?"

"Attack."

"Shouldn't I take a bigger weapon with me?" he had asked, holding up the small knife they had given him.

"Your best weapon is your ingenuity," they told him.

"While I appreciate the compliment, I'm not sure it will be entirely sufficient to—"

At which point a boot kicked him through the rippling gateway.

There was an incessant ache where his finger had been removed and clumsily replaced with a new digit made of crystal. It already felt loose at the knuckle. Even in his disbelief and pain, he was annoyed at the Fomorians' shoddy workmanship.

An older human in a headscarf crossed his path, pulling some kind of square bag filled with provisions. When she saw him, she screamed and scuttled away, leaving her bag to spill at his feet. Broonie rummaged through its contents. He was desperately hungry, and slurped from a carton of milk, then bit into an egg and sucked its contents. They tasted so fresh he shuddered in delight. He rifled through the bag some more and recoiled. Inside a clear package was meat. Bloody. Sliced neatly.

These people must be more vicious than it is taught. Even the elders carry the raw parts of their prey.

It was time to run.

He struggled through Darkmouth's maze of dead ends and blind alleys, continually failing to find a clear path.

Turning on to a wide street, he ran into a bustle of humans moving through the town. One noticed him and his shriek alerted the others. A small hairy animal at the end of a leash went wild, straining and snarling until Broonie thrust his knife at it, pricking the creature in the paw so that it squealed and withdrew, bleeding.

Its owner kicked at him and Broonie stabbed impulsively at him too, nicking his ankle, before jumping backwards on to the road where there was a horrible squeal of machinery as an oncoming metal vehicle braked only an ear-hair's width from his face.

Adrenalin coursing through his raised black veins, Broonie darted through the nearest doorway to crouch inside its large window while he tried to figure out an escape route. Outside, the scene was chaotic. Some ran off straight away, while others stopped first to stare at him with mounting disgust before following the others.

Broonie became aware of something above him. And behind him. And around him.

Carcasses, stripped down to their flesh, hung on sharp hooks. Torn and cut and placed on display. Ribs, livers, tongues, all manner of sliced hunks of animals were neatly laid out behind a glass compartment. Broonie guessed they must be the fresh kills of the fat human currently standing behind the glass counter in a bloodstained overall, with one hand on a large cleaver and the other on a half-sliced body laid out on a table beside him.

If Broonie had opened his eyes any wider, they would have popped out and rolled across the floor to the butcher's feet.

On the street, there was the squeal of metal, a great roar and another vehicle arrived through the crowd of humans that was heading in the opposite direction. A figure emerged from it, tall and imposing, fully armoured and wielding a gun.

Broonie immediately knew who this was. The Legend Hunter.

"A Hogboon," he heard the Hunter say clearly. "Hardly a challenge, especially if it's carrying little more than an apple peeler."

Broonie sprang at the butcher, wincing at the blood smeared on his clothes, and wrapped himself tightly round his head, grasping firmly at the man's face until he dropped the cleaver with a clang. Broonie then slid down on to the human's shoulders, holding his bloodied knife to the butcher's neck as the Legend Hunter burst into the shop, gun raised.

"Hugo..." whimpered the butcher.

"Don't worry, Leo, we'll soon have this sorted."

From his dry throat, Broonie summoned the best rasp he could. "You're a cruel species. Let me go or I will show you how cruel I can be too."

"You want me to drop this Desiccator?"

"Now," said Broonie, pulling tighter on the knife. His fear of having to carry through with his threat was outweighed by the thought of his insides hanging in this window while his outsides spent the rest of eternity as a comfortable pair of shoes.

"If I put it down, you won't hurt this man?" asked the Legend Hunter.

"On the rotting soul of my uncle."

"I'll drop my weapon." He bent down and placed it on the ground. "But on one condition."

"Which is?"

"That you look behind you."

Broonie glanced round. There, at a back door, was another armoured human, much smaller, far less imposing, but with a weapon pointed right at his head.

"The boy?" muttered the Hogboon just as a large piece of meat struck him in the side of the head and sent him crashing to the ground, the knife slipping from his grasp. The butcher barged out of the door to safety.

The Legend Hunter stood over Broonie, Desiccator pointed at him.

There was a blip from somewhere. Then another. *Blip. Blip.*

Realising the sound was coming from somewhere on him, the Legend Hunter patted his fighting suit until he found a pocket containing a rectangular device, which he pulled out and examined.

"The scanner's identified another open gateway, over by the harbour." Silence. No blip. "Hold on, it's gone again. Odd. Anyway, where were we?"

The boy joined the Legend Hunter, standing over Broonie too, lifting his visor for a better look.

"He looks hurt, Dad."

"Of course he's hurt, Finn."

"Should we help him?"

"Help him? *Help him?* We shoot him," insisted the Legend Hunter, sounding exasperated.

"But he's just lying there," said the boy.

"So, what, we bring him home for tea and biscuits? No, we desiccate him. *You* desiccate him. Here's your chance for a first confirmed hunt."

The boy looked pained. "That just doesn't feel right."

"Stop babbling, Finn, and do it."

"Wait!" interjected Broonie.

The humans focused on him. Broonie pointed at the boy, calmed himself and recited the words he had been given. "I have a message," he said. "The Legends are rising. The boy shall fall."

Then the Legend Hunter shot him.

15

Finn saw it at the same time his father did. A diamond, spinning to a stop beside the hard leather ball that had only seconds before been a Hogboon. This one was smaller than the one Finn had picked up after his encounter with the Minotaur, but sharper.

His father casually tossed the ball of Legend to Finn, who juggled it before getting a hold against his chest, then punched in the code for a container he was holding and placed it inside. In the meantime, his father had picked up the diamond and was quietly examining it.

"What was that?" asked Finn.

"Some kind of diamond," his father replied slowly.

"No. I mean, what did he say? About me?"

"He didn't say anything about you."

"Yes, he did. He looked at me and said 'the boy'. He wasn't looking at you at the time. It was definitely me. And he said I would fall."

"It was about all of us."

"No, it was as if he recognised me."

"Maybe you're a big celebrity on the Infested Side," said his dad. "He probably got you in the Legend Hunters collector cards. It was just a trick, Finn. A delaying tactic. Give these Legends a hand and they'll take an arm."

They both knew this was literally so in the infamous case of Graham the One-Armed.

Broonie's knife – a harmless piece, barely capable of slicing paper – remained where it had fallen. Finn picked it up and handed it to his father, who was hardly interested in it.

"That doesn't matter. This crystal is more important," his father said, studying it. "You saw the Desiccator swallow him pretty well, didn't you? So why was this left behind?"

"He must have dodged at the last moment."

"I couldn't have been closer to him. He didn't move."

Finn shrugged, dropped his gaze, tried not to betray what he already knew. The Minotaur had been hit full on by the Desiccator and a crystal had been left behind there too. He should have told his dad at the time. He should tell him now. But he reckoned his father would desiccate him on the spot if he knew he'd been hiding a precious stone from the Infested Side in his underpants drawer.

"This," his dad continued, still focusing on the jewel, "is the first thing I've ever seen survive the Desiccator net intact. It was definitely on his hand. I spotted it, where his little finger should have been, but just presumed it was some sort of decoration. Hogboons are thieving little beggars. He must have lost the finger at some point and used this as an artificial one."

"You're sure it's a diamond?" asked Finn.

His father turned it over in his hand.

"I don't know, Finn. But there's someone who will."

16

The shop was hidden down one of Darkmouth's narrowest lanceways. Finn had been there before, but not since he was younger when he would be brought along by his dad and left to wait outside on the step, where weathered paint peeled from the shopfront in sharp, fat flakes. Finn had never been inside.

The red lettering on the sign over the door was almost, but not entirely, faded. It read:

Specialities? Nothing about the shop looked special from the outside. Its window was caked with grime and anyone peering inside could see that the store was overflowing with odds and ends: parts of old electronics; guts of televisions; remnants of toasters; gaping insides of CD players. The clutter spilled on to the laneway at the front of the shop, cardboard boxes filled to the brim with tiny fuses, plugs trailing cords, old and worn radios and ancient phones.

Finn's father paused at the door, crouching down to pick through a box. "I love this shop," he said as he stood up with what looked like a dusty old computer game in his hands. "You don't get their sort any more."

"I wonder why," said Finn with as much sarcasm as possible in case it wasn't obvious enough.

"You'll be surprised what you can find if you know where to look," his dad replied, a touch of glee in his voice. He tossed the game at Finn. "Come on. It's about time you were properly introduced to my old friend."

Finn felt a flash of excitement as he followed his dad. He had never before crossed the threshold – instead, his memories were all of sitting on the pavement outside, or playing along the lane, barely seen silhouettes shuffling about inside. His father greeting another man, a mumbled discussion, the occasional glance towards Finn before they disappeared.

Now, finally inside, his excitement turned to

disappointment. He could see the place was as messy as the exterior had promised it would be. Wire hoops hung from the walls, disembodied screens dangled from the ceiling and towers of dusty DVD players teetered on the floor.

"What do you want for one of those old Space Invaders games?" Finn's dad called out.

"Some bread would be nice," came the reply. A man appeared behind a counter. Finn hadn't noticed him amid the clutter. He hadn't even noticed the counter.

"Business that bad, old man?" continued Finn's father.

The shopkeeper grunted. He looked as worn out as the electronics scattered about the place. His dark, unkempt hair hung like black spaghetti past his ears, his suit was frayed at the edges and his fingers were the yellow of old newspapers.

"Well, I might have something interesting for you, Glad," said Finn's dad, gently placing the diamond on the countertop.

Mr Glad didn't acknowledge it, but instead fixed his glare on Finn.

"Your boy has grown, Hugo. I haven't seen him since he was small, waiting on that step outside. Well, since he was smaller that is. Let me have a look at him."

Stretching out both hands, he grabbed Finn by the

back of the skull. Startled, Finn wasn't sure if he was under threat, but wasn't in a position to wriggle free anyway. Mr Glad turned Finn's head one way, then the other, examining him like a vet might search a dog for fleas.

"Will he be Complete?" he asked as if Finn didn't have a voice of his own.

Finn's father pushed up his lower lip in an attempt to exude confidence.

"Three successful hunts done yet?"

Finn's dad waggled a hand in a not-quite-there gesture.

Mr Glad kept hold of Finn for a few more seconds. Under his grip, Finn thought his head might crack open like an egg, letting his brain ooze out. It would be a welcome release.

"He'll have to do, I suppose." Mr Glad snorted in a way that didn't convey much satisfaction, then released Finn, who rubbed the back of his skull where a bruise was already heating up.

"Now what's this you have for me?" asked Mr Glad, picking up the object and examining it.

"I'm not sure," said Finn's dad. "But it looks like a diamond. A Hogboon came through a gate a short while ago and left it behind."

"Where's this Hogboon now?"

"In the car, doing a good impression of a stone."

"And did he say anything?"

"He didn't get the chance."

"He's some man, your father," said Mr Glad, addressing Finn. "I've known him since we were boys. And your mother too. We all grew up in this godforsaken town. He went his way, I went mine."

Finn hid his surprise that his parents and Mr Glad were the same age. Time had treated them quite differently.

"Your father did some extraordinary things, even when we were young," said Mr Glad. "Has he told you about the day he fought—?"

"Yes," said Finn wearily, because he had heard the same stories over and over.

"And the time he invented—?"

"That too."

"Well then, we're in agreement." Mr Glad turned and passed through a curtain of beads behind him.

Before following, Finn's father stopped and bent down to Finn. "You want to know what those 'specialities' are? You're about to find out."

He pushed aside the beads, beckoning Finn through. In the back room, much to Finn's surprise, there was... order.

It was not necessarily neat, nor was it any brighter or more cheerful than the shop, yet as Finn looked closer he began to see a strong semblance of organisation. The floor could be seen and actually walked on without fear of tripping over a fossilised tape recorder. There was even a bed, roughly made, in the corner.

But it was the equipment that most caught Finn's attention.

One wall was lined with shields of various sizes, some with spikes arranged round the rim or protruding from the middle. On another hung parts of armour – a breastplate, a pair of iron trousers and a steel cup that Finn knew was particularly important for protecting the vital bits of male Legend Hunters. On the shelves were a variety of objects, including triggers, handles, tubes, small boxes with fat wires and fat boxes with small wires.

Specialities, thought Finn.

His attention was caught by what looked like a long fork, with two prongs and a smaller blade jutting between them. Mr Glad seemed to notice his interest and handed it to him for a closer look.

"It's a Tooth Extractor," he said. "If you get bitten by a Legend, you don't want to leave any stray teeth in there. Poison, you see. It'll gradually worm its way into your skin and seep deep into the tissue. Then it'll turn rotten and eat away at your flesh so that you're left in terrible agony for hours, or days, unless..." Mr Glad leaned in to Finn. "*Schlupp!* You pop it out with one of these. It's a proper relief when you do. Trust me."

He tucked his hair behind his right ear. Finn could just make out the edges of a scar on his temple. It was deep and circular, with two small punctures on either side. He looked at the prongs of the Tooth Extractor, then back at the scar.

Mr Glad let his hair fall back over his ear and moved away.

Finn glanced at his father and raised his eyebrows in a silent question.

"Mr Glad is what is known as a Fixer," said his dad.

"What do you fix?" Finn asked.

"Whatever it is you need," answered Mr Glad conspiratorially.

"Mr Glad has been a Fixer for a long time, Finn," said his father. "He's one of the best."

"And one of the last," interjected Mr Glad, sitting down on a rusted seat at a large desk by the wall. "Civilians can't become Legend Hunters, but some of us have found other ways to become useful. Travelling the

Blighted Villages, making weapons, fixing equipment, sourcing materials. It's not what you'd call an official role. The Twelve like to keep us hidden, as you can see." He gestured at his surroundings.

Finn stared at Mr Glad, trying to figure out how to react. He felt his dad watching him, waiting for his reaction, willing it to be positive. "Interesting," said Finn because he reckoned he should say something.

Mr Glad opened a wooden drawer and lifted out a brass microscope. He placed it on his desk and opened a cap on its lens, before giving it a once-over. "I used to move about a bit. It was the best of times, it was the bloodiest of times, and all that," he said. "Soon neither of us might be needed by anyone. Unless *you* plan to keep us in business."

He paused for a moment, before slapping his knees in an unexpectedly cheery gesture. "But such is the small price of a great victory! Now let's take a look at this diamond, or whatever it might be, before we get chewed up by nostalgia."

Mr Glad placed an edge of the crystal just below the lens. The only sound was the rattle of his breath as he examined it.

"Well, it's not a diamond, I can tell you that straight

away," he announced, sitting back and inviting Finn's father to have a look. "I don't believe that diamonds dance like that, do you?"

Finn's father squinted into the lens and then beckoned Finn over so that he too could peer in.

Deep within the edge of the crystal, Finn could see strands of a pure white light dashing gracefully across the lens. It was quite beautiful.

"I don't know for sure what it is, but it's new to Darkmouth," said Mr Glad.

"New?" said Hugo as if the word tasted bad. "When it comes to Legends, new is never good."

"Never. Most of the time," said Mr Glad.

Finn looked down at his feet, thinking about the first crystal he had found, the one that was currently tucked away in his underpants drawer.

"Is this the only one that's come through, Hugo?" Mr Glad asked as Finn's father took another look.

"Yes."

"You sure?" Mr Glad was looking at Finn, who felt a

flush of guilt. Mr Glad's eyes were like a microscope on his conscience.

"Yes," Finn answered, trying not to let his voice squeak in betrayal.

"Well then," Mr Glad said, slowly breaking eye contact with Finn, "I'll hold on to it, if that's OK with you, Hugo, and run a few tests."

"Fine with me," Finn's dad answered, his fist pressed into his chin as he thought through this unwelcome twist in what should have been a standard hunt. "There was something else too. Another gateway."

"What do you mean?" asked Mr Glad.

"A second gateway while we were dealing with the Hogboon. It was just a small one, judging by the scanner, and wasn't open for more than a few seconds. No Legend could have come through."

Mr Glad rubbed the wisp of his beard with the back of his hand. "They might have been trying to get in another way, but something went wrong. We haven't seen too much of that recently, but it isn't unheard of for more than one gateway to open at the same time. Remember that plague year we had?"

"Of course. I'm still getting the stains out of my fighting suit," said Hugo. "But it's been years since that kind of thing happened in Darkmouth."

A hush fell over the room, broken only by the clang of swaying implements hanging in the shop out front.

"Oh, one other thing, Glad," said Finn's father, seeming to suddenly remember something of importance. "There are a few bits and pieces I need to get from you for a project I've been meaning to talk to you about. Finn, you have a look around. I'll just be a minute."

Finn wandered the room while his father and Mr Glad got on with their business. He pretended not to be interested in what they were talking about, but kept an ear on the conversation. Unfortunately, he could only hear snatches.

"...progress..." he heard his father say.

"...energy source..." he heard Mr Glad say.

"...close it permanently..."

"...highly dangerous..."

"...donkey cabbages..."

Finn wondered if he might have misheard that last one.

He continued to explore the room. In the corner were a couple of long pikes that he recognised from the more faded paintings in the Long Hall at home. At the foot of the wall, peeking out from behind the pikes, Finn noticed a framed wooden certificate on which he could only make out the words 'of the Hidden Realm'.

Finn ran his hands over a long countertop that was busy with objects he didn't recognise. He picked up a green metallic one shaped like an egg and gave it a bit of a shake.

"Look but don't touch," cautioned Mr Glad, suddenly appearing beside him and grabbing the object from Finn's hand. "You don't want to leave here with fewer fingers than you arrived with, and I don't want to have to clean up the mess after you. This is called a Fingerless Grenade."

He gave it a squeeze and rows of small jagged blades popped out of either end, one of them pushing a pin out of the top. "It's called that because you're the one who ends up fingerless if you hold it wrong. Give that about ten seconds and it will explode too." He pushed the pin back in before it did. "Maybe your parents will get you one for Christmas. How is your mother anyway?"

"Clara's fine, thanks for asking," interrupted Finn's dad.

"We go way back too, young man," Mr Glad told Finn, then winked. "Further back than your father."

Finn wanted to go home now.

They left, with Finn's father holding a couple of

machine parts. He threw them in the back of the car alongside the desiccated Legend.

"Shouldn't we just ask the Hogboon what the diamond is for?" asked Finn.

"It's not a diamond and he's not to be trusted."

Finn felt jittery. The Hogboon's apparent recognition of him still nagged, but he also felt a growing sense of obligation to tell his father that there was another crystal – presumably with the same curious properties as the Hogboon's – currently sitting in his bedroom.

"What do you think of Mr Glad?" his father asked him as they drove home.

Finn grimaced. "I think I'll be feeling his thick fingers on the back of my head for another week."

"He's a good man, something of a legend in his own right. Did you see that plaque in his room? That's the Honorary Sub-Knight of the Hidden Realm, the highest honour a civilian can be given by the Council of Twelve. He didn't get that for a lifelong dedication to fixing Legend Hunters' toasters. He earned it, just like he earned that scar."

They pulled on to their street as his father continued.

"When you need something, he always has it or knows how to get it. And you'll *always* need something, Finn."

The car approached their house and, as they got closer, they both saw the writing at the same time. There had been visitors while they were out. And they'd delivered a message.

Finn's dad slowed the car, slid down its window so they could examine it.

On the wall directly across the road from their front door, under the orange illumination of the street light, was a line of two-metre-high graffiti. It was fresh enough that its letters still dripped slowly down the concrete. It read:

STOP THE MONSTERS

They got out of the car and stood in front of the house, hands on hips. Finn saw that his father's gaze wasn't on the graffiti, but somewhere above the wall and beyond.

"Finn, do you ever get the feeling...?"

He didn't finish the sentence. Instead, he took the Desiccator canister and his newly acquired spare parts into the house, then returned with a tin of white paint and two brushes. Handing one to Finn, they got to work covering over the graffiti.

From *A Concise Guide to the
Legend Hunter World, Vol. 3:
'Blighted Villages, Known and
Unknown', 16th Edition*

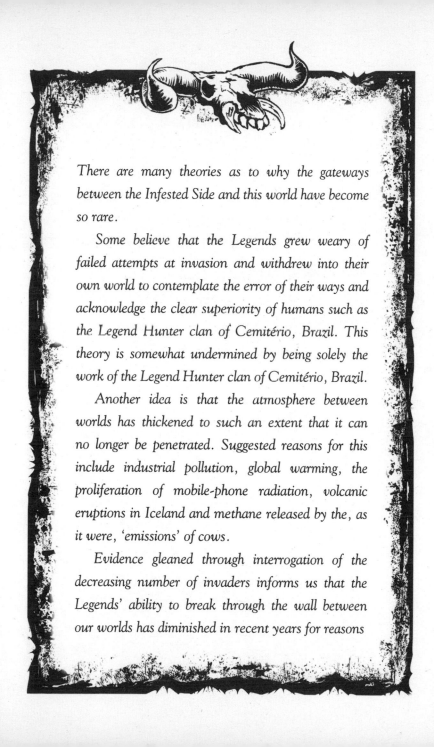

There are many theories as to why the gateways between the Infested Side and this world have become so rare.

Some believe that the Legends grew weary of failed attempts at invasion and withdrew into their own world to contemplate the error of their ways and acknowledge the clear superiority of humans such as the Legend Hunter clan of Cemitério, Brazil. This theory is somewhat undermined by being solely the work of the Legend Hunter clan of Cemitério, Brazil.

Another idea is that the atmosphere between worlds has thickened to such an extent that it can no longer be penetrated. Suggested reasons for this include industrial pollution, global warming, the proliferation of mobile-phone radiation, volcanic eruptions in Iceland and methane released by the, as it were, 'emissions' of cows.

Evidence gleaned through interrogation of the decreasing number of invaders informs us that the Legends' ability to break through the wall between our worlds has diminished in recent years for reasons

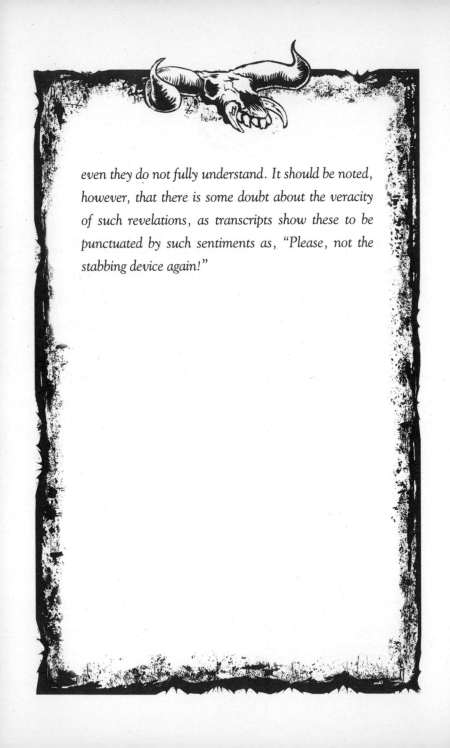

even they do not fully understand. It should be noted, however, that there is some doubt about the veracity of such revelations, as transcripts show these to be punctuated by such sentiments as, "Please, not the stabbing device again!"

Finn woke, blinking against the sunlight that pierced a gap in his bedroom curtains and fell directly on his eyes. From way down in the house, he could hear drilling again. *Skreeeump*. A pulse. Then another. Then quiet.

Sticking his feet into a pair of oversized slippers shaped like grizzly bears, he shuffled downstairs, meeting his mother on her way out to her Saturday morning dental clinic.

"Good morning, Mam," he said, stifling a yawn.

"I wish it was, Finn," she said. "I'm tired, and that racket your dad's making woke me early. Thankfully, a busy morning of staring into people's rotting dental cavities will be just the thing to perk me up."

She grabbed her keys and left. A moment later, the doorbell rang. "What did you forget, Mam?" Finn asked as he opened the door.

"Nice slippers," said Emmie. "Did you kill those in a hunt?"

Finn half hid behind the door, while Emmie waited outside, jumping about to keep warm on the crisp morning. Eventually, she gave him a look that said, "Aren't you going to let me in?"

He let her in. Then he darted upstairs to get some proper clothes on. He reopened his bedroom door to find her standing right outside it.

"What's your bedroom like, Finn?" she asked, walking straight past him to have a look for herself. "Whoa, I thought *my* bedroom was messy."

She spotted the goldfish and gave its glass a tap. "What's his name?"

"Bubbles," Finn answered. "I was younger when I got him," he added in response to Emmie's giggle.

"What are you reading? Is this *The Most Great Lives?*" Needing two hands, she picked up the large book, only for the other smaller book hidden inside to fall from between its pages.

Before Finn could get to it, she had already grabbed it.

"*So You Want to Be a Veterinarian,*" she read. "You want to be a vet?"

"No. Yes. Maybe."

"Aren't you supposed to be, I don't know, *killing* creatures rather than wrapping them in bandages?" She handed the book back to him. "Like, I didn't see too many stethoscopes in those portraits downstairs," she said, now nosily scanning the things on his windowsill.

"Maybe I won't be like all the others on that wall," said Finn.

"Really? Thought you'd no choice. You know, only son of the only Legend Hunter and all that."

"Yeah, well, maybe it's because—" Finn was struggling to find the words to explain himself. He hadn't talked about it before.

"What?" Emmie prompted him.

"Sometimes it feels like maybe I could be a different sort of Legend Hunter. Like, I'm learning all about these incredible creatures, but the only thing I'm supposed to do is fight one when I see it. There could be another way to deal with them that doesn't mean hurting them. Like, my mam does it for people. She helps them with their teeth, I mean. Same sort of thing really, just different animals."

"A Legend Hunter *and* a vet," said Emmie. "What does your dad think about that? From what you've told me about him, I can't imagine he's too happy."

Finn's silence gave her the answer.

"Sorry," she said, then changed the subject by grabbing the eight-limbed cuddly toy off his windowsill. "That looks pretty dangerous. He's got cute little fangs and all."

Finn needed something to rescue his pride, so he blurted out, "I have something better than that." He slid open the drawer, shielding his underpants as best he could, unwrapped the crystal and held it out to her. Low morning sun reflected off it in a dozen directions. Emmie's eyes widened.

"Let me hold it."

He passed it to her and she turned it in her hands, running her finger across its edges and feeling its surprising lightness.

"It came from a Legend," said Finn. "You're holding a part of another world." She gasped just a little at that, and the approval gave Finn a shot of confidence.

"How did it get here?" she asked.

"It was in a Minotaur's nose."

"Gross!" she exclaimed, dropping it on his bed.

From somewhere in the house, Finn heard heavy steps. He grabbed the crystal back and threw it into the drawer.

"Nice underpants," exclaimed Emmie.

And, just like that, Finn's moment of triumph was lost once more.

"Come on," he said, ushering her out again. "I'd better eat. I only just got up."

As they came downstairs, the panels on the narrow door to the Long Hall flashed simultaneously and, with a *clunk*, it opened. Finn's father emerged, carrying what appeared to be half a vacuum cleaner in his arms, exposed wires trailing past his waist.

"Hello," he said, stopping in the doorway, clearly surprised to see a stranger there.

"Dad, this is Emmie, a new girl… a new, er, friend, from school."

"A girlfriend?"

"No," Finn shot back. "A friend."

"Don't mind him," said Finn's dad. "He's very grouchy in the mornings. Nice to meet you, Emmie."

"Hello, Mr…" She seemed to be struggling to think how to address him, as if "Mr The Great" didn't sound quite right. Finally, she settled on: "Hello, Finn's dad."

"Hugo will be cool."

Cool? thought Finn.

"So, what are you kids up to then?" his dad asked.

Kids? Finn would have been happy if the whole world

left him alone this morning, but his dad's disappearance would be a fine start.

"Come on, Emmie, let's go," Finn said, starting for the kitchen in the futile hope he could cut short this conversation.

"What brought your family to Darkmouth, Emmie?" Finn's dad asked, readjusting his hold on the machine part so that he cradled it like a baby.

"Work. My dad's work. It's just me and him."

"What does he do?"

"He's a consultant. Techy things," she said, pulling her fringe forward with one hand. "I don't really understand it."

"Techy things? Like computers?"

"Phone lines, I think."

Finn's dad nodded. "Sounds fascinating. Did Finn tell you what we do?"

Finn's brain was screaming at him to *stop talking right now, this very instant.*

"I'm in what you might call pest control."

Enough, Dad!

"Yeah," said Emmie, energised again. "I know all about it."

"Really?"

"Oh yeah, from books and stuff."

"Books?" asked Finn's father, curious.

"Well, Finn's book. Upstairs. And from Finn too. He's told me so much."

Finn wondered if he looked as embarrassed as he felt.

"Anyway, welcome to Darkmouth, Emmie," said Finn's father. "Don't let the bedbugs bite."

Bedbugs, oh God.

"Finn, I've to go out and get something looked at. You OK on your own?"

To show just how excruciating this was for all of them, Finn rolled his eyes so far he could almost see the inside of his skull.

His dad finally headed outside, and Finn gave an overblown sigh of relief. But, just when he thought it was safe, his dad popped his head back in the house. "Finn, give your fighting suit a wipe, will you? It's beginning to smell like a family of cats lives in it."

Emmie laughed.

Finn's mouth opened in silent frustration. He needed to find something to rescue this situation and quickly.

Suddenly, he knew what it was.

"Do you want to see something?" he asked. "Something really good." Emmie hadn't time to answer before he pressed the panels on the door to the Long Hall. She followed as he quickly dashed down the hall, ignoring the long line of portraits and heading straight for the door at the very end, only hesitating when he reached his destination.

"I'm not really supposed to go in here," he said, pointing to the door marked 'Library'.

"Oh, all right then," she said, then screwed her foot into the floor a bit. "I mean, if you're scared of your dad, I understand..."

That was all it took to persuade Finn. He opened the door.

Beyond it was a space unlike any library anyone could have imagined. The round room was massive, stretching high into the pitch of the roof, crowded shelves covering almost every bit of the walls.

At points along the edges of the floor, full suits of armour stood at attention, complete with spears and swords and shields.

At the centre were a couple of large cluttered desks and near these were two domed cages, one about Emmie's height and another big enough to fit several adults inside, including some on each other's shoulders. Looming over both was a wide object covered with sheets.

Finn stood back, letting her take it all in. She moved towards the desks, one of which had a computer on it with a screensaver scrolling through a selection of images.

A horned skull.

An illustration of an old woman with leather wings.

A photo of Finn as a toddler, grinning and holding an oversized sword while his father, laughing, waved some fierce little creature in his direction.

She moved to the covered object. It was about the height of a grown man and as wide as two. Scattered on the floor around it were various tools, batteries, an electrical fan, the drum of a washing machine, a kettle, what looked like the blade from a food blender and other bits and pieces. As they got closer to it, Finn could feel a low electric hum radiating through the floor and tingling his toes.

"What's this?" Emmie asked.

This, presumably, was the thing Finn's dad had been working on all hours of the night. Finn had no idea what it was, but didn't want to admit that. So he rummaged through his mind for something that would make it sound like he knew what he was talking about. It just came out a bit of a gurgle.

Finn wasn't sure if Emmie was just being polite, but she ignored his meek response and instead began to lift the sheet for a look. Before she got too far, though, her attention was caught by something else on the shelves: a collection of glass jars of various sizes and shapes.

She reached out and lifted one with a hard ball rattling around inside. She read the handwritten label aloud:

"Gargoyle. Adult. Approx. 5ft. Darkmouth. 13.02.1963."

She picked up another. It too contained a hard ball, and its label read *Griffin. Height 4ft, Span 6ft. Darkmouth. 01.05.1946.*

She checked another. A Grendel. Then another. A Gogmagog. She looked up and around. Shelves were lined with jar after jar, of various sizes and shapes, stretching high to the ceiling and halfway round the room. Each contained a hard ball, sometimes leathery, sometimes furry or feathered or hairy, but almost always perfectly spherical.

"They're Legends," said Finn. At last, this was something he knew all about. "Decades, maybe centuries' worth of Legends. They're trapped, collected and stored here." Emmie picked up one jar from a small table beside the shelves, not yet filed away. Finn could see one word on it: *Hogboon.*

"Are they alive?"

"Yes. Well, sort of. Dormant really."

"There must be hundreds here," said Emmie.

"Three thousand and twenty-nine to be accurate," said Finn's father from right behind her. "And we wouldn't want you to be number three thousand and thirty, would we?"

E mmie was so startled by the sudden arrival of Finn's dad that she dropped the jar she was holding. It rolled unbroken to his feet. He picked it up. "You shouldn't be here."

Finn, breathless and a little panicked, blurted, "*Emmie*, the toilet isn't down here."

Hugo and Emmie both shot Finn a look that wilted him.

Finn hadn't seen his father so annoyed in quite some time. At least not so annoyed with anyone other than Finn. "There are things in this room that could kill you," he said, seething. "There are things here that could kill *everybody*. This is *not* a playground."

"Dad—" started Finn.

"It's time your friend went home, Finn."

Finn sighed, but signalled to Emmie to follow him. They were making their way towards the exit when

Emmie stopped and faced Finn's dad. "They're desiccated, aren't they?"

"What?" asked Finn's dad.

"The Desiccators. I heard about them."

"Heard about them?"

"Yeah, Finn told me."

"Did he now?" said his father.

Did I? thought Finn.

"He said the Desiccator net became the weapon of choice for most Legend Hunters centuries ago," continued Emmie, undeterred, "because it trapped Legends but didn't kill them. Is it true?"

"Yes," said Finn's dad, a little calmer now, examining her. "We've used a Desiccator on them."

"All of them?" asked Emmie, gaining a little courage to take a step back into the library.

"Remind me, what did you say your father does?"

"He's a technology consultant," she answered, sounding a little shy again.

"Technology consultant." Finn's father's anger seemed to have ebbed as he became more inquisitive. "And how long are you here for?"

"A short while. Dad's doing stuff with the phone lines. Or something. I didn't pay attention."

"No. Why should you? And you heard all about the Legend Hunters from Finn?"

"Oh yes. I'm fascinated by them now. The life. The battles. What it must be like to come face to face with a Legend. I would love to be one. A Legend Hunter."

"Really?"

"Really."

"But you can't, can you?" said Finn's dad.

"Can't I?" asked Emmie.

"Didn't Finn make that clear? No civilians."

"Oh yeah, of course. But I think about it sometimes all the same."

Finn's father narrowed his eyes and cocked his head. He was holding the jar containing the Hogboon, rolling it deliberately between his palms. "Go on now," he said and shooed them away, shutting the door behind them.

Finn and Emmie walked up the long corridor without a word, entering the house and going straight to the front door. Finn opened it and waited for Emmie to leave.

"I'm sorry, Finn," she said. "I hope I haven't got you into trouble."

Finn felt something unsettling, but he couldn't quite identify the sensation. "Did you mean that? About wanting to be a Legend Hunter?"

"Definitely," Emmie replied, her tone a little regretful. "What you do is amazing. All that excitement, and the Desiccators and other worlds and that huge room at the end of that huge hall. I mean, seriously, who wouldn't want this?"

Finn's face betrayed his deepest feelings about that. Finally, he spoke. "Did I really talk to you about the Desiccator? I don't remember that."

"Oh yeah, you must have. Loads of times, I'm sure. Anyway, I'd better go."

Emmie pulled her hair forward and turned for home. Finn closed the door, not noticing that the bright day had swiftly given way to damp grey, and that Emmie had already disappeared into a veil of gathering mist.

20

"There's one blip." Finn's dad pointed at the computer screen.

Blip.

"And there's the other."

Blip.

Finn stood beside him, not entirely sure what they were both waiting for.

The two spots kept blipping.

Blip.

Blip.

On the screen was a map of the town. Every few seconds, a small green pulse appeared in two distinct spots.

Blip. One at the harbour.

Blip. The other a couple of miles from it, by the short tunnel at the entrance to Darkmouth.

Finn understood what the scanner was telling them:

two gateways had just opened. The alarm had sounded as Finn was making his way back down towards the library, but was silenced quickly. He had arrived in the room expecting his father to be rushing in the other direction. Instead, he was standing over the screen and had motioned for Finn to join him.

"Dad, I didn't know..." Finn started to say.

"Later," came the curt reply.

Blip.

Blip.

"What do you see, Finn?" His dad didn't wait for an answer. "These are two gateways, but they're both small. Only one of them would let through a Legend of any size. Very odd. I'd like you to examine the smaller one while I check out the larger one. You can get changed in the car, before I drop you off."

"Hold on, drop me off?" asked Finn, not liking what he was hearing.

But his dad was already heading for some bookshelves at the back, where he lifted the stopper from a large, empty, triangular jar. To Finn's surprise, a whole section of the wall swung open and Finn's father ran through. Finn stared after him for a moment, irritated.

"A hidden door? When were you going to tell me about that?"

"I just have," said his dad. He stuck his head back into the library. "I didn't want you messing about with it. Now hurry up."

Sighing, Finn followed and found himself in a part of the building he hadn't known existed – a dark, apparently unused remnant of whatever this part of the library used to be before the Legend Hunters moved in, long hidden behind the circular wall, its deep red bricks exposed under crumbled patches of rotting plaster, apparently unchanged since the rest of the street had been colonised by Finn's ancestors.

Ahead of him, his father pulled at a large door, which opened reluctantly until the dull morning light flooded the space and released them on to the street.

"Very odd," his dad repeated as they drove. Finn was in the back, wrestling with his fighting suit, trying to avoid falling against a row of knives lining the interior of the vehicle. "We have two gateways appearing at the same time, but even the bigger one is so small it shouldn't be of too much concern. That must be why this fog has come down instead of rain."

Finn realised he was pulling his suit on backwards, the

armour choking him at the chin. He tried again.

His dad had half an eye on a scanner on the dashboard, which showed the same map and unevenly sized green dots flaring every couple of seconds.

"Here's the thing, Finn," said his dad. "Remember when that second gateway popped up the other day and then disappeared straight away? I looked back at the scanner's records for the previous hunts and what do you think I found?"

Finn really wanted to get this right. "Other gateways?" he guessed, losing his balance again.

"Well done. This has happened four times now. Other tiny gateways opening in Darkmouth while we were off hunting a Legend. The others were so brief they hardly registered." The scanner went blip. "So, this right now is curious. The smaller one might be a failed attempt by a Legend to open a bigger gateway. We need to make sure in any case."

"I really have to check it out on my own?" asked Finn.

"You've got to do it some time," said his dad. "Better when there's probably no great danger."

"Probably?"

The car's lights stabbed an arc in the fog as it turned sharply, causing Finn to flail across the back and crash into a net of canisters.

"If the gateway is still there when we get to it, Finn, all you need to do is mind it until it disappears or I get back, whichever happens first. It'll be too small for any Legends to get through, so there's nothing to worry about. You can reach me on the radio if you need to."

Finn was still fighting with his fighting suit.

"Come on, buster. Hurry up. Seriously."

They arrived near the pier, the car's massive tyres scrunching up along the kerb as it pulled over. Its side doors slid open automatically and Finn half fell out, holding on to his helmet to keep it on his head.

Through the fog, he could see a gently pulsing smudge of golden light hanging in the air. It looked almost like a street lamp, except that it was low down, about eye level with Finn. He was temporarily mesmerised by the thought of this gateway, open, raw. A hole between his world and another.

Despite his recent Legend hunts, Finn had only ever seen gateways in the few blurry videos and photos taken in the days before they closed everywhere but Darkmouth. He had grown up with the idea as commonplace, but his mind now burbled at the sight of an actual portal to a world of Legends. He was a little in awe. He was also very scared.

"Finn?" his dad called out, jolting him. "Forgotten something?"

He dangled Finn's Desiccator from the car window.

"Come on, Finn. I know you can do this, but you've got to use your head sometimes."

Finn tried to crank himself up for a clever response, but his mouth was too dry with fear for him to muster anything useful. He simply took the weapon, wrapped its strap round his wrist and watched his dad drive away until the vehicle was swallowed by the fog.

He continued to assess the gateway from a distance. He had heard many stories of civilians and Hunters getting a little too close to these portals and not having the chance to live to regret it. He had heard tales of Legend Hunter apprentices daring each other to put their heads in a gateway for a look, only for the portal to snap shut and leave them squirming in brief agony before their body was chewed in two, their legs twitching long after their front end had disappeared into the Infested Side.

That was if they were lucky.

There was a popular theory that, once it clamped on to a person, a gateway's energy seeped into the body, becoming one with it. This, went the thinking, would lead the unfortunate individual to live a bodiless existence for all eternity, the monotonous torment relieved only by the special torture of being torn open every so often to let a large creature climb through.

It was only a theory, of course. Writing home to tell everyone about it would be quite difficult under the circumstances.

Still, for horrible ways to die, Finn had a few options on offer to him now. But he tried to push those thoughts away. His dad didn't believe there was any danger. *Probably* no danger anyway. He wouldn't have given Finn this job otherwise. And he expected him to go through with it. Finn had to trust his dad. He knew what he was talking about after all.

Finn really hoped his dad knew what he was talking about.

So he started to creep tentatively towards the gateway, his suit a minor chorus of rattles, his weapon raised and his heartbeat raised even higher.

He could hear the sea to his left, lapping at the stony beach below the pier. The *sqwuaa* of a seagull came from somewhere above the fog. He picked his way carefully over the fishermen's ropes, unused lobster pots and scraps of plastic scattered on the ground.

As he moved closer to the gateway, it became more

defined, emitting a sound like rushing water. Its brilliance was almost inviting, its fringes made up of dazzling, fizzing white light that felt familiar. He quickly recognised them as the same patterns of light he had seen under the microscope in Mr Glad's shop.

But before he had time to dwell on that coincidence, he was startled by a dark silhouette at the gateway. Something. Some *thing*. A tall creature with a broad torso and a horribly misshapen head.

Finn's outfit squeaked. He halted mid-creep. The creature stopped what it was doing at the gateway, turned and looked in his general direction.

Finn hardly dared to breathe as he stood motionless, his foot still half raised.

Apparently seeing nothing, the creature resumed its business at the gateway, bending a little to reach it.

Finn completed his step. Every sound from his suit seemed to him like a minor earthquake in a tin can factory. He crouched, carefully reaching for the button at his neck that activated the radio, and whispered, "Dad? Come in, Dad."

Nothing.

A little louder. "Dad. This is Finn."

Still nothing.

He pressed. Pressed again. Absolute silence. No static, no bleep when he tried to activate it, only the sound of his heart beating a panicked rhythm in his throat. He must have pulled on a wire when wrestling with the suit in the car. Now, even in a fog so thick he could have reached out and carved "Help!" in it, he felt completely exposed.

The figure, a few metres away but still only a smudged silhouette, remained at the gateway. Finn strained his eyes. It looked like it might be *taking* something, some small object, from the portal. But what? Finn took another couple of steps forward to try to see more clearly, his weapon aimed, finger trembling at the trigger, grimacing at every minor creak of his suit.

Seemingly satisfied that its task was done, the creature stood back, with a surprising ruffle through its torso. Finn knew he had to take a shot now or he would never get another chance. He took a deep breath to still his coursing adrenalin, steadied his aim, felt the Desiccator's trigger in the curve of his finger and counted down. *Three. Two. One.*

The creature glanced round. Squinting through the grey, Finn realised he was seeing something stranger than any Legend.

It was a *human*, a man it seemed, wearing a long coat that hung loosely to his knees. Finn couldn't make out the face, which appeared to be almost fully covered by a scarf pulled up over the nose, and what he had thought to be a misshapen head was actually the wide brim of a hat that swept low across the man's brow.

Finn exhaled, released the pressure on the trigger.

Briefly, the gateway's golden light glinted off a pair of eyes, then, with a final pulse and a gulp, the gateway imploded, folding in on itself instantly, leaving behind only a feeble yellow afterglow.

The figure looked round one final time. Finn moved half a step forward to see more clearly.

This turned out to be a very, *very* stupid thing to do.

21

Finn's years of training as a Legend Hunter had been based on the not unreasonable notion that he would have a career hunting Legends.

He may not have been particularly agile, or gifted, or adept, or any other variation on 'useful' at the different types of combat needed to fight these creatures, but he knew all the theory.

He could, in theory, take down a Gorgon. He could, in theory, decapitate a snarling Ophiotaurus. He could, *in theory*, douse the fire of a Chimera's breath.

But he had worked hard to learn all he would need to know in order to become a *Legend* Hunter. Not once had he been warned that, in the course of his career, he might need to take on the role of Human Hunter. If he had known, then things might have turned out a whole lot better.

In that half-step forward, Finn's toe caught the top

of a thick piece of discarded rope that stretched across the pier. He stumbled slightly, gripping the trigger instinctively and sending a Desiccator shot fizzing through the murk.

Its furious blue fire unfurled a net that nicked the edge of the man's hat and travelled on. An almighty crunch of destruction ripped through the grey curtain of fog, echoing round the harbour. Startled, the man turned and charged at him. Finn struggled to right himself quickly enough to aim again and the man was upon him almost immediately, lifting him from the ground so that his feet kicked the air pathetically.

Finn wriggled and forced his feet on to the ground, where he pushed back. His weapon hung loose around his back as they wrestled. Close in, Finn clawed, swung, kicked out, lost his balance as both of them spilled to the ground, his Desiccator digging into his side. He tried to reach around for it, but couldn't free it.

But then he spied a piece of metal beside him, star-shaped, a fishing weight. Finn stretched out a hand, grabbed it and slammed it hard into the man's neck, eliciting a grunt of pain followed by a growl of anger as his attacker lifted Finn again and carried him to the edge of the harbour wall.

Finn felt the man release his hold, then an unnerving plunging sensation.

He hit the water hard.

The freezing water rushed into his suit, his protective armour now an enemy dragging him down below the sea. He fought his way to the surface, the cold and panic shocking his lungs, constricting his breathing, quickly tiring him. He sank again. The seawater flooded his helmet, the rank salt and oil of the harbour lapping at his mouth.

He rose again, swiping his visor open so he could splutter a cry for help, yelling as he scrabbled to stay above water, his head bent back to thrust his mouth and nose into the air.

He slid below the sea again.

The fight seeped from him, exhaustion taking hold, the heavy weight of the suit pulling on him. He tried again, pushing himself up, but his mouth felt the longed-for comfort of the air for only a moment before he dropped down again. His eyes wide but unseeing in the murk. His lungs screaming at him to let go. It was like a foot on his chest, arms wrapped round him, squeezing the life from him. Arms *were* wrapped round him. They let go. He felt someone grabbing at his hands. Then around the head, searching for his shoulders. A fresh surge of panic and adrenalin shot through Finn. The attacker was here, in the sea, ready to finish the job. Finn lashed out. Pushed weak punches through the water.

The hands kept at him, reaching below his shoulders again, grabbing him firmly under the arms and pulling him up. Finn stopped fighting and allowed himself to be dragged to the surface, a hand reaching round his chin and holding it upwards so that all he could see was a weak sun poking through the clearing fog. But he could taste the air, crisp and pure. He gulped greedily, choking momentarily on water pouring off the rim of his helmet and down his throat.

Finn felt himself being hauled on to the stony beach, where he fell forward, coughing, spitting up foul seawater.

"You were almost done for there," said his rescuer. "Thought I wasn't going to be able to get you."

Finn looked up to see Mr Glad sitting beside him, panting with effort, water dripping heavily from his long hair and frayed suit. He spat a gob of seawater on to the stones.

On the road behind them, a car screeched to a halt. Finn's father jumped out and raced down the beach towards them, a canister bouncing around on his belt.

"Look at me, Finn. Look at me!" his dad said, grabbing Finn's head and forcing him to make eye contact. "What happened?"

Finn spluttered. "At the gateway."

"What? A Legend?"

"No... a human. A man."

"What did they want?"

"Give me a chance here, Dad," Finn said, shaking his head free. He looked at Mr Glad. "How did you...?"

"You think you're the only one who can keep track of gateways?" he said, fishing a scanner from inside his jacket and letting water pour from it. "Or I could before our swim. Anyway, I heard a sound like the world was caving in before I even got here. The gateway was gone."

"And the man Finn saw?" asked Finn's dad.

"I didn't see anyone," said Mr Glad, standing up again. "But, in that fog, anyone could have slipped by easily enough."

"Are you absolutely sure you saw someone, Finn? Did you try and stop him? Did you get a shot?"

Finn was slumped where he sat, finally feeling life reassert itself in his body. "I did. But I didn't..."

"He got away then?"

"Yes, he got away," snapped Finn. "After attacking

me and throwing me in the sea. But I'm alive, thanks for asking."

"Is that canister full, Hugo?" asked Mr Glad.

Finn's father lifted it on his belt. "Manticore. Just a small one. He hadn't made it too far from the gateway before I got him. Didn't seem worth his while coming through. But he brought this."

He held up a crystal. It had the rough shape of a claw.

Finn coughed hard, hacking up more foul seawater from his chest. His dad squeezed his shoulders in what was the closest thing to a hug Finn was ever going to get. "Everything is going to be OK."

"I wouldn't be so sure about that," said Mr Glad, nodding at the harbour wall, where a trawler was now visible – or rather the remains of a trawler. It was listing violently, its stern a hard, disfigured lump of wood, steel and rope, clinging tight to the puckered edges of the rest of the vessel.

Finn's shot had hit a target. Just the wrong one.

Further up the road, in the last tendrils of the mist, a dark van pulled away from the pavement. Finn recognised it as the same vehicle that had parked briefly on the street near his house earlier that week.

"Dad, that van—"

But then their attention was diverted by the distant blast of a siren and the flashing lights of an approaching police car.

"We should go," suggested Finn's dad. No one disagreed.

22

Finn sat opposite Mr Glad at the kitchen table. He had dried off and changed, but Mr Glad was still wearing his wet clothes. A smell of rank harbour water filled the room.

Outside, at the front door, Finn could hear muffled voices.

"Have you been on many hunts, Finn?" Mr Glad enquired.

"A few," Finn answered reluctantly. He was still in shock after the events of the morning and his mouth was in solidarity. He hadn't the energy to respond.

Finn stood up and peered through the crack in the door. He could see his father and Sergeant Doyle in heated conversation at the front of the house. The sergeant was simmering with frustration. He caught a glimpse of Finn, who immediately ducked away and sat back down at the table.

"The first time I saw one, I froze," said Mr Glad. "He was a big fella too. A Griffin. Claws that could cut steel. Wings the width of the street. Big dead eyes. Popped down off a roof, right in front of me. And I just stood there. You ever see a Basilisk caught in the headlights?"

He jabbed a thumb at his chest. "That was me. Now I hadn't been trained like you have, but I was a good bit older than you are now, had been in a few scrapes here and there. But that Griffin? It froze me."

From the hallway, the murmur continued, punctuated by Sergeant Doyle's occasionally raised voice. Finn heard him say "that boy" with clear exasperation.

Mr Glad looked through the fruit bowl for something that appealed to him. Finn watched silently, feeling ill. His nostrils still stung from where he'd inhaled the seawater. He tasted diesel in his mouth and failure deep in his stomach.

Mr Glad peeled an orange, his chipped nails digging at the skin while he stared out of the window. "I was always an outsider, deep down. Never really one of them, no matter how much respect they threw my way. I had to be rescued that day, by two generations of Legend Hunters working together. Lived together, trained together, fought together. Tighter than the snakes on a Gorgon's head. I owed them, but resented them at the same time. And you know who those Legend Hunters were?"

He popped a segment of orange in his mouth and bit down on it, wiping juice off his chin with the back of his hand. "Your father and your great-grandfather, Gerald. Disappointed doesn't even halfway cover that man's mood. If you were in debt to him, he never let you forget it."

Finn felt he owed Mr Glad something. His life for starters. But he also felt a discomfort building inside. Whether it was trauma or his secret, or simply the smell of fish and diesel, he couldn't tell, but he almost needed to prick the tension with words. "There is something..."

He was interrupted by his father's return to the kitchen. "Doyle thinks it was another Legend that we were shooting at and we'll let him believe that. But he's not a happy man and says he's not alone. That boat is going to cost us. We'll have to go to the fund again."

Finn knew he was talking about a compensation fund that existed for Legend Hunters who needed to pay for damage to civilian property, or to civilians and property. It was started many centuries before, in Ancient Egypt, when a most unfortunate incident led to the loss of the Sphinx's nose. It was a useful resource, but Finn's father hated using it because it required a lot of paperwork.

"The fund isn't bottomless," he added, propping himself back against the kitchen counter. His face was tight with either concern or disappointment. It hadn't been made clear yet. Finn wasn't sure he wanted to know the answer. "And not a word of this to your mother. No point in worrying her."

"No point in worrying me about what?" she asked, walking into the kitchen.

Mr Glad stood up immediately to welcome her. "Clara, good to see you."

"Ah, Ernest. It's good to see you too," she said. "It seems like a long time since you paid us a visit."

"You remember how it is, Clara. The shop keeps me busy, between one thing and, you know, the other." He seemed a little uncomfortable, concentrated on rubbing orange juice off his hands.

"And your other work?"

"Well, it's not what it used to be, that's true." He looked at Finn's father. "But no complaint in that. It's the way of the, you know..." The sentence trailed off.

"So, what happened to you, Ernest?" asked Finn's mother. "It hasn't been raining heavily as far as I could tell."

They all remained quiet.

"And that smell..."

Silence.

"It's like that, is it? Great secrets of the Legend Hunters. My mother warned me I should have married an accountant."

"Or a Fixer?"

"Ah now, Ernest," she said, seriousness snapping into her voice.

"I didn't mean to..."

"I've had a long day at work. I'm going for a rest," she said, but looked at Hugo before leaving. "When I come back, I'll be hoping for a cup of tea, so don't go dismantling the kettle or anything while I'm gone."

His dad waited until she was out of earshot before saying, in lowered tones, "Glad, I believe we're being watched. A van one night. Just a vague sense another. And—"

"The van was at the harbour again too," said Finn, feeling he ought to contribute something. "I saw it drive off."

"And then this happens – this man at the gateway," said his dad. "Someone has been keeping an eye on us."

"I don't know who it was," said Mr Glad, "but I can

guess what they wanted. I had been on my way to talk to you about this."

From his trouser pocket, he pulled a felt bag tied with string. Water dribbled out as he opened it, releasing the crystal on to the table and a pungent waft of the harbour with it.

Finn's dad threw the latest crystal down beside it.

"Do you know what these are, young man?" asked Mr Glad, leaning forward over the table at Finn, his matted hair slapping at his neck, his palms open. "Well, I'm pretty sure I do. They're magic. Of sorts anyhow. The kind that brings badness into this world."

He picked up one of the crystals, holding it upright between his fingers. He was obviously enjoying this bit of showmanship. "There aren't many records of this sort of thing appearing on our side of the gateways. Official records anyway. But I'm pretty sure that what I'm holding is not just any crystal, but the very substance that allows the Legends to create a hole between their world and ours."

"Coronium," said Finn's dad. "A lifetime dealing with Legends and I've never seen one."

"Very few have," said Mr Glad. "We've known about this substance for years, but it is normally only found on

161

the Infested Side. And now you have a piece all of your own."

Mr Glad placed it in front of Finn and sat back again, with a squelch of wetness.

"And you're sure it's Coronium?" asked Finn's dad.

"I believe so," said Mr Glad.

"We would have touched on it in your training, Finn," said his dad. "From what we know, the Legends attach it to the air, snag it there somehow. And once they've done that..."

"*Boom*," said Mr Glad, spreading his hands. "They open the door and walk on in. They don't usually knock first."

"And they don't usually bring their Coronium with them."

In the quiet of the kitchen, the last drips of seawater fell from Mr Glad's elbows, hitting the floor, *plip-plip-plip*.

Finn thought back to the encounter at the harbour. "Do you think that's what I saw at the gateway? Someone getting one of these crystals passed to them?"

"I doubt it," said his father. "They can't just pass Coronium through the gateways. At least we don't think they can. From what we understand, Coronium can only travel through the gateways when attached to living tissue."

"That's the theory all right," said Glad.

They both looked at Finn, and it dawned on him that they were waiting for him to join the dots. He obliged. "Like a Hogboon's finger."

"Or a Manticore's claw," said his father.

"But why?" asked Finn.

"Maybe that's not the question, boy," said Mr Glad. "Maybe the question is now that we have some, what do we do with them?"

Finn's dad considered this. "Coronium is powerful and volatile. It can rip through the fabric between entirely separate worlds. Way back, at the beginning, it created catastrophic gateways at random."

"Ask the dinosaurs about it," Mr Glad said to Finn.

"Which means it can be naturally explosive. But it seems that the Legends learned long ago how to control it. To use it to create gateways."

Mr Glad rolled a crystal between his fingers. "So the Coronium could be a key. Or a weapon."

"Could it be a power source?" Finn's dad asked him.

"Now there's a thought. Have you told the boy what you've been making in that library of yours, Hugo?"

"Not yet."

"Well, let's go one better," said Mr Glad. "I'm here.

He's here. Neither of us has seen it. Why wait any longer?"

Finn's father kept his chin tucked into his chest for a few seconds. "Yes, maybe it's time I showed you," he said. "It might change your lives after all."

23

They stood before the unveiled device.

Mr Glad gasped with delight.

Finn curled a lip in bafflement.

"Amazing, isn't it, Finn?" said his dad.

Amazing wasn't the word Finn would have picked. Haphazard maybe. Or ramshackle. From what he could see, it was a concoction of sheets of metal, buttons, dials and household appliances ripped out and reused, crowned with a rim of metal dishes running round the device in a rough pattern.

A kitchen timer clung to one side, next to what seemed to be a control panel consisting of a large dial from an old microwave, a keyboard, a particularly chunky light switch and a small screen that Finn realised was from the computer game they'd picked up at Mr Glad's shop. The whole machine was bolted in parts, taped up in others and, through a window, Finn could see a Desiccator

canister at its centre, rigged to a mass of wiring.

"It's beautiful," said Mr Glad, circling it.

"What is it?" asked Finn.

"It's the end of all this," said his father. "Well, it could—"

"It's a doomsday device," interjected Mr Glad. "Your father's been coming to me for parts, a little advice, expertise and such ever since the start, but he has kept this between us because failure would have terrible consequences."

Finn looked at his father, who shrugged. Finn thought he appeared more casual about the terrible consequences than might be expected.

Mr Glad continued, stroking the device like it was a pet. "This takes the basic idea of the Desiccator, but, instead of pointing it at one object, it will be aimed in every direction, and instead of shrinking one target it will shrink every Legend that it comes in contact with."

"So..." said Finn. "It's more like a Desiccator bomb than a gun."

"Basically," said his father.

"The idea is that your dad waits for a gateway to open," said Mr Glad, "then activates the device and a wave of energy desiccates whatever has come through without even needing to leave the house. Hey presto, no more Legends."

"At all?"

"That's right. This device ends the war forever," said his dad.

"What's it called?" asked Finn.

"It doesn't matter," sighed his father. "OK, so I don't have a name for it yet. The Gateway Shutter. The Total Collapser. Whatever. What's important is that this is *the* device."

"Does it work?"

"The future depends on it," Finn's father said quietly.

"All he has to do is find a way to do it without killing everyone in Darkmouth," continued Mr Glad.

"That won't happen," said Finn's father. "Well. It *shouldn't* happen."

"Anyway," said Mr Glad, "your dad's been struggling to identify something strong enough to power it. You can't exactly run it off a car battery. Well, you could, but it would require a grand total of... how many, Hugo?"

"Forty-three thousand."

"Forty-three thousand car batteries. Which would be beyond even me. But these..." He held the two crystals in his hand. "These could be the answer. All that power,

168

in something so small. It's like the atom splitting in a nuclear bomb. You could do some serious damage across a wide area, if you had enough of them."

Finn was hardly listening, instead preoccupied by the low throb of a nagging headache. "But didn't you say the crystals could be volatile? That they could just go off on their own?"

"Maybe," said his father. "Rarely."

"We'd have to be very unlucky," said Mr Glad, trying unsuccessfully to sound reassuring, then abandoning the idea. "But you wouldn't want to be around if one did go off."

And with that, as if Finn's day hadn't been bad enough, he now knew that he'd be going to bed tonight with a potential bomb tucked away in his underwear drawer.

From the publisher's introduction
to the final section of *The Most
Great Lives of the Legend Hunters,
From Ancient Times to the Modern
Day, Vol. 25: 'From Xxogjudqa the
Unpronounceable to Zyta the Last'*

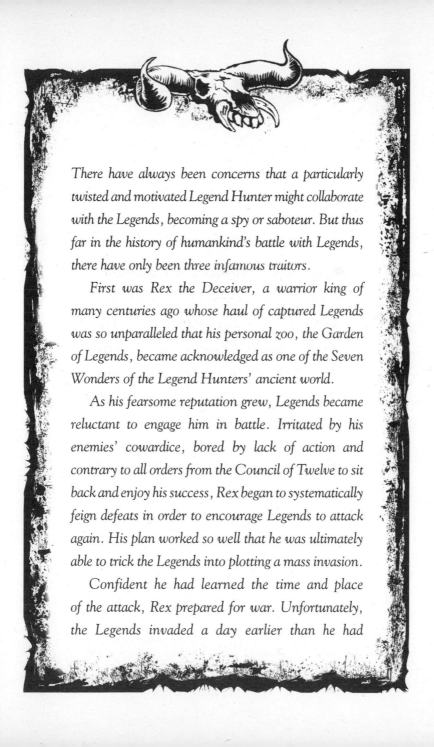

There have always been concerns that a particularly twisted and motivated Legend Hunter might collaborate with the Legends, becoming a spy or saboteur. But thus far in the history of humankind's battle with Legends, there have only been three infamous traitors.

First was Rex the Deceiver, a warrior king of many centuries ago whose haul of captured Legends was so unparalleled that his personal zoo, the Garden of Legends, became acknowledged as one of the Seven Wonders of the Legend Hunters' ancient world.

As his fearsome reputation grew, Legends became reluctant to engage him in battle. Irritated by his enemies' cowardice, bored by lack of action and contrary to all orders from the Council of Twelve to sit back and enjoy his success, Rex began to systematically feign defeats in order to encourage Legends to attack again. His plan worked so well that he was ultimately able to trick the Legends into plotting a mass invasion.

Confident he had learned the time and place of the attack, Rex prepared for war. Unfortunately, the Legends invaded a day earlier than he had

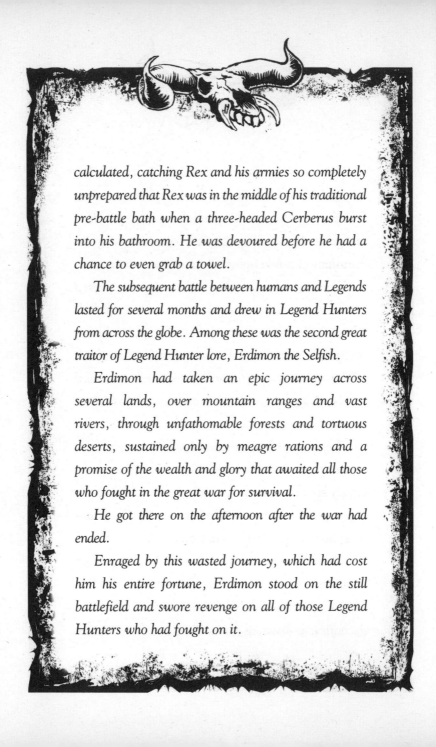

calculated, catching Rex and his armies so completely unprepared that Rex was in the middle of his traditional pre-battle bath when a three-headed Cerberus burst into his bathroom. He was devoured before he had a chance to even grab a towel.

The subsequent battle between humans and Legends lasted for several months and drew in Legend Hunters from across the globe. Among these was the second great traitor of Legend Hunter lore, Erdimon the Selfish.

Erdimon had taken an epic journey across several lands, over mountain ranges and vast rivers, through unfathomable forests and tortuous deserts, sustained only by meagre rations and a promise of the wealth and glory that awaited all those who fought in the great war for survival.

He got there on the afternoon after the war had ended.

Enraged by this wasted journey, which had cost him his entire fortune, Erdimon stood on the still battlefield and swore revenge on all of those Legend Hunters who had fought on it.

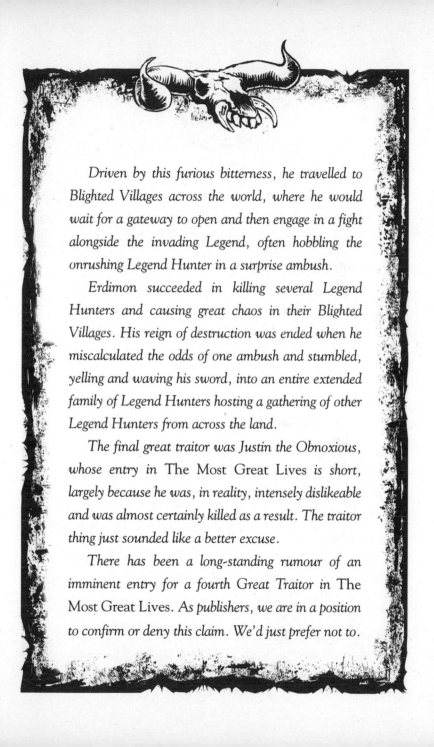

Driven by this furious bitterness, he travelled to Blighted Villages across the world, where he would wait for a gateway to open and then engage in a fight alongside the invading Legend, often hobbling the onrushing Legend Hunter in a surprise ambush.

Erdimon succeeded in killing several Legend Hunters and causing great chaos in their Blighted Villages. His reign of destruction was ended when he miscalculated the odds of one ambush and stumbled, yelling and waving his sword, into an entire extended family of Legend Hunters hosting a gathering of other Legend Hunters from across the land.

The final great traitor was Justin the Obnoxious, whose entry in The Most Great Lives is short, largely because he was, in reality, intensely dislikeable and was almost certainly killed as a result. The traitor thing just sounded like a better excuse.

There has been a long-standing rumour of an imminent entry for a fourth Great Traitor in The Most Great Lives. As publishers, we are in a position to confirm or deny this claim. We'd just prefer not to.

On the Infested Side, a small Wolpertinger hurried through bleak corridors with a metal tube clamped between his jaws. This creature looked like someone had tipped a bucket full of creature parts on to a floor and fashioned something from whatever fell out. Antlers. Fangs. Fur. A few feathers. Tiny leather wings stretched across armpits. At a push, you might describe it as rabbitesque, with a hint of reindeer and a sprinkling of vampire. In another time, Wolpertingers had been dispatched to scare the Blighted Villages of Germany. It always required something particularly crazy

Wolpertinger

to scare the Germans.

The Wolpertinger moved as quickly as he could, breaking stride only once, when he tripped on an object that, on quick inspection, turned out to be a skull. He redoubled his intention not to be late, while hoping that the metal tube he was holding did not contain bad news – for bringing bad news to Gantrua was like handing him your own death warrant and asking him to sign on the dotted line.

He did not know what he held, only that it had been deposited through the gateway at the expected place and time. The human fingertips that poked through the hole in the air and pushed the tube across had looked delicious and the Wolpertinger had fought hard to resist the temptation to have a little nibble on them.

He had grabbed the object and pelted through the bare forest, across the fields of sharp scrub, knowing he would not be disturbed en route. No one would dare interrupt the journey of one of Gantrua's messengers.

He finally reached the hall of fires where the two brutish Fomorian guards stood in his way. He waved the object at them. One of the giants leaned down to him, a crescent-shaped scar raised on his forehead and a string of drool dancing at the side of his mouth. "No funny business, little Wolpertinger. Or I will rip your eyes from your head and make you watch as I snap every bone in your body one by one."

"Trom is very creative when it comes to pain," said the other guard, slowly but sincerely. "He's very good at his job."

"It's more a hobby than a job really," said Trom, the drool snapping at his chin. "When you love what you do, it makes getting off the floor every morning that much easier. Doesn't it, Cryf?"

"It does, Trom."

The Wolpertinger waited, shuffling a little in his eagerness to deliver the message. When their act of intimidation seemed to have satisfied them, the guards stepped slowly aside so that the messenger could finally move forward into the great room where the heat of the cauldrons lining the walls almost blistered his skin.

He scampered towards the plinth, the ends of the soft hair on his back crackling.

"Give it to me," ordered Gantrua from where he sat, a great sword attached to his waist. One of the guards snatched the tube from the Wolpertinger's mouth and handed it over.

Opening the canister, Gantrua removed a roll of

paper. The messenger looked for a reaction in the deep valleys of Gantrua's brow as he read the message, but saw only concentration. He could make out no movement in his mouth which was just barely visible behind the arc of shattered teeth rising from the metal wrapped round his jaw.

Gantrua crushed the canister. "Our spy has reported back. The Minotaur failed to deliver the crystal."

The Wolpertinger's eyes were becoming used to the flickering light and he could now make out the outline of a hooded figure, a good deal smaller than Gantrua, stooped at a column behind the plinth.

The figure spoke, his voice thin and brittle. "But the boy?"

"He is there."

"Then we must send another crystal so that we can wake the sleeping army before it is too late. The invasion from within must commence."

Gantrua inhaled deeply, his chest swelling so much that his armour moaned as if it was about to split into a thousand fragments. The Wolpertinger waited. He began to worry that he might actually be cooking. A bead of sweat ran down his face and dropped to the ground, making an almost imperceptible *splat* picked up immediately by Gantrua's enormous ear and reminding him of the messenger's presence.

Gantrua lifted the piece of paper in his hand and let the hot air waft it towards the ceiling, where it curled and burst into flames. "Wolpertinger, what do they say out there? What do you hear about the prophecy?"

The Wolpertinger stared, perplexed.

"I am fully aware that your kind are mute. I do not expect an answer. But your eyes tell me what I need to know. The Legends believe it. They fear it. The rumour has spread and they think a mere child will be responsible for closing off the Promised World for the rest of eternity. That our banishment, already insufferable for millennia, will be complete."

Gantrua stood and walked forward, the sword in its scabbard dragging across the stone floor, its tip screeching and sparking. "But you will also have heard rumours of the great work in the Coronium mines."

The Wolpertinger's knees buckled a little at the mention.

"There is truth in that too." Gantrua grabbed his sword and eased it from its scabbard, causing the messenger to recoil. But, instead of slashing at him, Gantrua struck down hard on the floor, summoning Trom and Cryf. "The

Coronium crystals grow rarer and more precious. What is found comes here. Show him."

The Fomorians lumbered over to levers that jutted from the wall at the end of each row of flaming cauldrons. Grasping them, they gave each other a nod to synchronise the next move, before pulling down hard. It seemed they needed every ounce of their formidable strength to do so.

Throughout the great hall, there was a sound of cogs turning and pulleys creaking. Then the cauldrons pitched forward, dribbling fire over their lips. There was a stutter, followed by a crash, as a single cauldron finally and abruptly tipped over, sending molten splashes to the floor. The Wolpertinger jumped back, grabbing his tail to avoid it doubling as a candle wick.

After a few seconds of awful intensity, the fire burned out. Beneath the gaping mouth of the cauldron lay two crystals.

Gantrua towered over the Wolpertinger. "These crystals are our path. One of them will be a weapon delivered to the Promised World so that we can gut it from the inside out."

The small messenger felt his hair prickle with anxiety, his feathers stiffen with fear, his skin crawl with anxiety.

"You like the crystals, don't you?" Gantrua asked. "So choose one."

Nerves twitching through his freakish clash of body parts, the Wolpertinger selected a crystal, biting on it with his fangs and returning to drop it on the floor in front of Gantrua.

The Fomorian guards moved in. Later, at the expense of more blood than he ever cared to spill again, and sporting a crystal where a beautiful, precious fang had once been, the unfortunate Legend realised he'd never really had any choice at all.

"Here, monster boy, I want a word with you!" Finn had been on the school grounds for four seconds and already the Savage twins were moving towards him with fists and jaws clenched. Behind them trailed a posse of three others, hovering about in a manner that suggested they were up for a fight as long as everyone else was.

Finn kept walking towards the car park between him and the school doors, keeping the five boys in view on his right. If he had looked left, he would have seen a sixth lurking and ducked *before* this boy swung his bag hard at the base of Finn's neck.

But he didn't look left.

"Ow!" said Finn as the bag slammed into him.

Dropping into a defensive crouch, he tried to shake off the sting of the blow. The twins stood over him. "That was James that hit you," said Conn. "His dad has a boat.

Or rather he *had* a boat. It's mangled now."

Finn raised himself gingerly, slowly stretching to his full height, but confirming that this only brought him up to their chins. Conn's gnarled ear looked like a discarded crisp packet.

Another boy aimed a kick in his direction, which Finn managed to dodge awkwardly.

"*His* granny was out doing her shopping," said Manus, "and saw the Cookie Monster or whatever it was that you were supposed to be protecting us from. She got a huge shock. Dropped all her shopping."

"We had to bring her our leftover dinner," said the boy who had kicked at him.

"What was it?" asked Finn.

"One of your creatures, a big one, that's what."

"No, the leftover dinner. What was it? Was it nice?" When nothing he said was going to be right, Finn had quickly decided that a reckless response was as good as any. Besides, he felt surprisingly calm under the circumstances.

James swung his bag again. Finn dodged it, but the gang had surrounded him now, and a crowd of onlookers was gathering in anticipation of a scrap.

"Our da says your family keeps those monsters at home,

like pets," said Conn.

"He says your da holds on to them because he'd be nothing without them and that he releases them so as to frighten people," added Manus. "Just to give himself something to do."

"Did your da hear that down the pub?" Finn asked. "He spends enough time there."

Finn didn't know why, but he was enjoying this. Time seemed to be running a little slower. He felt relaxed, in control. He noted each of their positions, calculated their moves. Registered it all almost subconsciously. It was as if the near-death experience in the water had drained him of fear. He felt good. He felt confident.

He felt a clout on the back of his head.

With a high-pitched shout, almost admonishing the boy behind him for not playing fair, Finn spun round. As he did so, he got a whack on the legs from another bag. Time was still running a little slow, but his confidence was unravelling slowly too.

Yet, when the bag swung again, Finn reacted quickly enough to grab and yank its holder forward into the boy beside him. They both went down in a heap. There was a pause while everyone tried to figure out what was going on, then a cheer went up from the crowd. This was turning out more exciting than any of them had dared hope.

Finn automatically assumed a martial-arts position: hands out, right toe pointed up. It was one of the first moves he had learned in his training because it was considered useful for simultaneous defence (with the hands) and attack (kicking whatever bit of Legend was closest). He'd forgotten he knew it.

The crowd laughed.

Conn took a run at him. Finn stood to one side and, keeping his foot outstretched, tripped him up while grabbing the back of his jacket to help him land with some dignity.

The crowd *aahed*.

They were on his side, thought Finn with a tingle of triumph. Manus took advantage of Finn's momentary imbalance to take a swipe at him, a slap connecting with the side of his head and sending him spinning.

The crowd *oohed*.

Finn realised they were just on the side of whoever was entertaining them most at any moment.

The boys crowded in. Finn wrapped his arms round a torso and pushed. Their grunting scrum lurched forward a few metres, forcing the crowd to jump out of the way. Finn was buried in there, wrestling amid the press of

coats, soft bodies and hard breathing. It was going well.

Then it wasn't going so well. Someone had him in a headlock and someone else was pulling at his leg. Through the crush of bodies, Finn felt something wooden and long being pushed into his hand. He grabbed it and dug it into the stomach of whoever had him in a headlock, then heaved Manus Savage off him. Finally seeing it was a hockey stick he was holding, he swung low and wide, hooking Conn's legs away, then swiped hard again, upending another boy and then another, flipping them over on to their backs until he was clear.

Jumping from the scrap, he saw a starburst of red hair and knew where the hockey stick had come from.

"Anyone else want a go?" he said, brandishing the stick as menacingly as he could manage.

The mob, trouser knees scraped, picked themselves up and scrambled away. "Say thank you to your girlfriend," sneered Conn as he left.

Finn did nothing of the sort, instead straightening out his clothes, picking up his bag and heading away through the dissipating crowd. He handed Emmie her hockey stick on the way through. She followed. "Finn! Hey, Finn. You're bleeding."

He searched, eventually finding blood on his temple.

He hadn't noticed it in the scrap, but now he knew a cut was there it began to throb.

"I just took out six guys on my own," he said, still walking. "Well, pretty much on my own."

"That was brilliant!" said Emmie. "I saw it, and saw it was you, and I thought, what can I do? So I gave you the hockey stick and you hooked them, and then... wow. Just brilliant."

They stopped walking. "I was doing fine on my own," said Finn, a quiver in his voice as the adrenalin began to drain from his body.

"I just thought I could help."

"You did," he admitted. "Thanks."

"Wait until you see how everyone treats you today, Finn. You'll get so much respect."

She was wrong.

The day was one of sniggers, pointing and wolf whistles, and a steady erosion of whatever respect his display of courage might have earned.

In class, Mrs McDaid eyed him suspiciously all through their morning maths class, and kept glancing at the cut on his head even as she droned on about angles and triangles. "Isosceles," she said, a beady eye scanning him.

Meanwhile, the glares of the Savage twins drilled a hole in the back of his head.

"Equilateral," Mrs McDaid continued.

Finn could feel the whole class watching him. Could sense them watching the Savages watching him.

He was the Legend Hunter who had needed a civilian to dig him out of a scrap with enemies who had a standard four limbs, just one head each and bodies that weren't a crazy mix of several dangerous animals.

But he had beaten them nonetheless. It hadn't been pretty. It hadn't been smooth. But it had been a victory.

He looked round at Emmie and gave her a smile. She grinned back.

One of the Savages wolf-whistled.

26

"*Uuurghle. Aaargglle. Ckeuck.*"

"What's that, Mr Laird?" asked Finn's mother, her mask billowing as she spoke. She was hovering over the patient, who was tilted back in the chair with his mouth wedged open.

"*Ight sssss llling horgh.*"

"I'm sure it is feeling sore, Mr Laird. But we'll soon have it sorted, don't you worry." She gave Finn a mischievous glance. He was sitting on a chair in the corner, a mask over his mouth too. He had a woollen hat pulled hard over his head, covering the angry graze on his temple.

He had always liked watching his mother work. He was awed by her expertise, her manner and the grace with which she could pull a tooth. He wondered if he could be the same with animals, so gentle and perceptive, and imagined himself in her position, only with a large Alsatian in place of Mr Laird.

Mr Laird gurgled in pain.

"Ah, I see the problem," Finn's mother said.

"*Eegghhh*," Mr Laird responded.

"Don't worry, I haven't touched anything yet, Mr Laird. Just looking."

Still in her chair, Finn's mum wheeled backwards across the floor to a cupboard. She searched through her keys for the right one, unlocked the little door and removed a bottle. Plunging a needle into it, she carefully withdrew a measure of clear liquid.

"This may sting a little, Mr Laird, but only for a few seconds."

Finn watched intently, trying not to wince too much as the needle was brought close to the patient.

"All done now."

She gave Mr Laird a few moments to settle.

"That stuff's powerful, Finn," she whispered. "It would calm a rhino."

"Not really," mumbled Finn.

"What's that, love?"

"You'd need a lot more for a rhino," Finn said, a little more boldly. "The larger the animal, the more anaesthetic you'd need."

He felt somewhat exposed all of a sudden, wanting

to share his knowledge with her, yet forcing down the impulse. He pulled the brim of his hat a little lower.

Finn's mother stopped and watched him, momentarily intrigued by this sudden flowering of knowledge. "Well, maybe a small rhino then," she said and resumed her work. "Now how about you? I'm guessing you're not here to see Mr Laird's molar cavity."

"I just needed to get out," answered Finn.

"Was there another gateway this morning? I didn't notice any rain. Or does this have to do with the other day? There's a reason why that kitchen smelled of rotting prawns, isn't there?"

Finn thought out what he wanted to say and what he should say. He decided on an edited, mam-friendly version. "I sort of shot a boat."

"A boat?"

"A trawler."

"Oh, Finn."

From the chair came a gurgle. "*Arrm cagh hrrr chlllluths.*"

"What's that, Mr Laird?" asked Finn's mother, removing the tool propping his mouth open.

"I can hear the clouds," Mr Laird said dreamily.

"It's great stuff, isn't it? Now let's get that tooth out."

A few minutes later, the tooth had been uprooted and

the patient was burbling away happily in the chair. "We'll give you a little while to come around, Mr Laird," Finn's mother told him, pulling the mask below her chin.

"Mam?" asked Finn.

"Yep?" she said.

"Do you ever regret it? Marrying Dad, I mean. A Legend Hunter. And staying in Darkmouth."

"Ah now, Finn, that's a heavy question. Two questions, I suppose, but with completely different answers." She began to clean up. Mr Laird was snoring gently. "I fancied your dad from the moment I met him."

Finn squirmed at that sort of talk, already half sorry he'd asked.

"Everyone did, Finn," she laughed warmly. "As for Darkmouth, well, I didn't fancy it so much. I grew up here, but, like so many others, I always thought I'd leave. Even when I married your father, neither of us imagined the Legends would last. They were stopping everywhere else, so why not here?"

She began to gather up her tools, carrying them over to a sink as she talked. "Even when you came along, I convinced myself you'd get some training, and some fun, some good times with your dad, but that you'd never have to use all those skills. But the Legends didn't stop. And your dad, well, he hasn't stopped either. Maybe I shouldn't be surprised he's so driven, what with his family, and especially how everything changed after your granddad Niall, but still..."

"Mam, what did happen to Granddad? Dad's never talked about it."

"I'm sure he'll tell you when he's ready, Finn."

"Has he told you?" Finn asked.

"No."

Finn watched his mother carefully place her tools along a roll of paper, lining them up expertly, counting them out, making sure she had what she needed. She washed her hands methodically. Finn admired the precision, the care, imagined himself preparing for work that way, readying himself to heal instead of harm.

"It'll be strange when he's away so much," said Finn. "Dad, I mean. He's always been around."

"It mightn't be so bad," his mother said, drying her hands. "I might get a holiday out of it at last. A chance to finally be able to get out of Darkmouth every now and again. To be normal. At least as close to normal as being married to a Legend Hunter gets."

Worry crept across Finn's face. His mam registered it.

"Don't worry, we won't abandon you. I won't abandon

you. And you'll never be alone. I'm sure your dad will make sure that Ernest – Mr Glad – will be there to keep an eye on you, help you out when you need it."

"How long have you known Mr Glad?" Finn asked.

"Why?" she said, somewhat defensively. "What's your father been saying?"

"Nothing." Finn kicked the floor with the tips of his shoes.

His mother eyed him for a moment before speaking. "Ernest and I grew up on the same street and went to school together. We were close once."

"How close?" asked Finn, not sure he wanted an answer.

"We went out with each other for a while, before I got together with your father."

"Was it serious?"

"No!" his mother said emphatically. "Not for me anyway. Still, that was a long time ago now. Your father came along and, well, that was that. Ernest became a Fixer for your dad, travelled a bit, but always returned home to that shop of his. I haven't seen too much of him over the years. It was a bit of a surprise to see him sitting in the kitchen the other day, especially in that sodden state."

Mr Laird snorted awake.

"Now, Mr Laird. Feeling better?" asked Finn's mam.

He was looking at his hands, wiggling his thumbs. "Did you ever notice the colour of fingertips before? It's sort of... musical."

"I think we'd better call you a lift, Mr Laird."

"My fingers are pushing the sky."

Finn looked at him, wrinkled his nose. "What did he say?"

"Mr Laird?" said his mam.

"Yes."

"My fingers," said Mr Laird again dreamily. "The sky."

"There you go," said Finn's mother.

"Pushing the sky," Finn murmured.

"That stuff really does make your mind go a bit la-la," she said.

But Finn had stopped listening. All he heard were Mr Laird's words repeating in his head, prodding at his brain until a realisation burst out. *Pushing the sky.* He leaped up and dashed for the door.

"I'd better go. Thanks, Mam, see you later."

"Finn...?"

But he was gone.

Finn ran straight to the library, following the now
familiar thuds and whirrs of activity.

"Dad, I've just thought of something!"

Finn's father was at the machine, trying to work
something out of a crevice. Mr Glad emerged from around
the other side of the device, the sleeves of his shirt rolled
up to the elbows. He lifted his chin by way of a greeting.

The smaller of the room's empty cages had been pulled
forward. Between it and the device stood a small round
table holding two things: an apple and Finn's goldfish
tank. Bubbles the fish bumped lazily against the glass.

On the floor in front of the device was a ring of bonsai
trees.

"Dad, I just figured something out about the man at
the gateway."

"Go on," said his father, not looking up.

"I thought the man was taking something from it.

That's what it looked like to me anyway."

"Yuh?" With a grunt, his dad snapped out whatever he'd been working at. It sparked, singeing his fingers.

"Only... what if he wasn't taking something *from* the gateway, but *putting something into it?*"

"Like what?" said his dad, distracted.

"I don't know." Finn hadn't thought that far. "How about an object? Or a message maybe?"

Shaking his stinging fingers, his father stood up to ponder that idea. His face slowly broke into an aspect Finn wasn't entirely familiar with, but guessed might be something approaching respect.

"That's not bad," he said. "I suppose it would make sense if someone over here was working with... Hold on, what happened to your head?"

Finn had absent-mindedly flung off his hat as he'd run into the house, exposing the cut at his temple. "Nothing," he said.

"Nothing?" said his dad. "That's a lot of blood for 'nothing'."

Mr Glad, who had been busying himself around the machine, interrupted. "I think we're ready to go, Hugo."

Finn looked at the machine, then at his goldfish bowl. "Um, why is Bubbles here?"

The two men ignored him, engaging in a flurry of checks and cross-checks while Finn hovered, feeling somewhat deflated. Mr Glad carefully stepped over the bonsai perimeter and walked to the adjacent shelves and began rifling roughly through the jars. "What'll we use? A Hippalektryon? Too unpredictable. The Hippogriff? Too dangerous."

"I nearly lost a kidney to that," said Finn's dad.

"That was a tough day all right. How about the Hogboon?"

"Yes, use him. He brought the crystal here so he can have the privilege of seeing how we're putting it to good use."

Mr Glad lifted the stopper from the jar and placed the hard ball of desiccated Hogboon in the cage.

Finn's father darted over to a wall and grabbed a Desiccator. Expertly, he pulled its barrel free, twisting its handle away. Removing the gun's canister, he peered inside, sloshed it about a little and then screwed the canister and barrel together so it was more like a rod with a fat end to it.

"I've never shown you a Reanimation before, Finn," said his father. "Never needed to. You're going to love this."

Finn had read about Reanimations, and understood the process as well as he understood the science behind a Desiccation – which was not very much at all.

"As long as it's organic," explained his father, "what can be shrunk can also be brought back to its proper size and shape. Most of the time. The plan is to bring this fella back so that we can test the device. Mr Glad offered to lend a hand."

"I shall be the beautiful assistant in this magic trick," grinned Mr Glad.

Finn's father unclicked the trigger unit from the Desiccator's handle and, as he walked back, slotted it into a groove at the base of the canister. "The Desiccator and Reanimator do the same thing in a way, Finn, only backwards. One shrinks, the other expands. Same principle, same chemicals, only reversed. Legend Hunters used to carry two weapons, one for each job, on the off chance they wanted to reanimate a Legend to interrogate them or experiment on them or, as would happen, just to annoy them. But I thought one would do, so I adapted a Desiccator to do both."

"He made his first when he was just fifteen," remarked Mr Glad, still pottering about the device. "He called it the De-desiccator."

"It sounded right at the time," said his dad as he held the reconstituted weapon to his right eye and peered down its length, then felt the solidity of the trigger sitting beneath the canister.

"But why do you need my fish?" asked Finn.

"For years we've been dealing with the Legends one by one," his father said. "Shoot one, put it in a jar, wait for another, shoot it, put it in a jar, and on and on, attack by attack. The machine I've been working on will put a stop to them once and for all. The trick was to do it without turning the whole of Darkmouth into a giant lump. And that's where having a few live Legends on the shelves comes in useful."

He approached the cage, barrel outstretched. With his thumb, he pushed the brass switch upwards and a low whine built from within, getting higher and higher in pitch before becoming impossible to hear. Then came a steady *tick, tick, tick*.

The Reanimator was ready.

In his bowl, Bubbles was nibbling the stone at the bottom of his bowl.

"We're going to give this a go," said Finn's dad, "but, when I say run, you run out that door, you understand? And don't come in until I say so."

Finn nodded. His temple throbbed. "What about Bubbles?"

"If all goes according to plan, he'll be grazing on his own poo as normal tonight."

Through the bars of the cage, his father tapped the hard ball of Hogboon with the rod. The desiccated Legend was briefly engulfed in a deep, even green glow that died down quickly.

The ball hopped. Like a jumping bean, it lurched forward, sideways, forward again.

There was an almighty scream.

28

Broonie screamed.

And screamed.

And continued screaming.

If the scream had been broken down into its constituent parts, it would have been discovered to contain approximately forty-three vowels, twenty-eight consonants and several sounds that could fit in either category, or neither, or both.

He couldn't quite decide which was worse: being desiccated or being reanimated. He knew a bit about Desiccation. They taught them about it on the Infested Side, how the net smothered the Legend, slowing its metabolism remarkably so that, from the victim's point of view, time stretched on for much longer than the half-second or so it actually took to be desiccated. How long depended on size. For a creature about as big as an adult human – or, indeed, an actual human – it could feel as long as a day, depending on what he or she had for lunch.

But for, say, a Hydra, about the size of three elephants, give or take its seven dragon heads, the experience of desiccation would stretch a horribly long time. To the only Hydra ever to have been hit by a Desiccator, it would have felt like he had been frozen for exactly 243 years. Given that it happened 150 years ago, presumably from his perspective he's still there and really quite furious about it.

Hydra

Broonie's experience had involved feeling stuck for a great many hours, while the world around him appeared frozen. There was nothing to do but wait as the stream penetrated every part of his body – every fibre, every cell, every molecule. One of the great mercies of the Desiccator net, Broonie discovered, was that, during this phase, its victim felt nothing at all. Except, of course, great boredom.

Finally, as the process neared its end, there was a mildly peculiar sensation, a bit like a butterfly snoozing on Broonie's neck. He even allowed himself to think, *You know what? This isn't so bad after all.*

Then nothing.

Until...

The final phase of Reanimation felt as follows:

1) Like having his body pulled by his nose through a tea strainer.
2) Like being a balloon a millisecond before it bursts.
3) Like waking up to find all his insides on the outside. (The outside of the house that is.)

When Broonie finally stopped screaming, he lay panting on the floor for a moment before he assessed exactly where he was. Which was in a cage. In a large room. In a world of pain.

The chief mercy of Reanimation was that it lasted for a relatively short space of time and there was a small part of the middle toe of his right foot which didn't feel any pain. At least not much pain when compared to the rest of his body.

But the air was revitalising. Clean. Cool. The air of the Promised World. And, as he came to, it became clear that there were three humans staring at him. He didn't recognise the oldest one, but the other two were familiar. One was the Legend Hunter. The other was the boy.

Broonie pushed himself up, slowly, painfully, trying to put as much weight as he could on the one toe on his right foot that didn't feel so bad. Eventually, he raised himself enough to reach out a hand towards the boy.

He pointed a finger at him.

"What's he doing?" asked the boy.

"Charge the device, Hugo," said the older man.

"Wait!" shouted the boy.

Broonie extended the finger towards the child and willed himself to be articulate now that he had another chance to deliver his message. "The..." he managed to say.

Finn's dad turned a large dial about a third of the way along its clock.

"Now, Hugo!"

"...boy..." stuttered Broonie.

The Legend Hunter struck hard on a fat red button.

"...will..."

In the window on the side of the device, the crystals sparked, then flared a yellow that momentarily filled the room.

Broonie gurgled a final word, but it was drowned by a great sound from the device, as if it was taking a breath deep enough to suck all the oxygen from the room.

"Run!" shouted the Legend Hunter, but the boy stayed where he was, mouth open, until the Legend Hunter grabbed him by the elbow and pulled him away.

An explosion ripped through the room, followed by a shockwave of crackling atoms. Broonie raised his arms in defence, but it was useless.

With a stifled *whooop*, he was once again sucked into a hard ball small enough to fit inside the average pocket.

It was a bit more pleasant than being reanimated.

But only a very, very small bit.

Finn, his dad and Mr Glad burst back in through the door. Finn was confused and desperate to know just who, and why, and when, and *what* that Hogboon had been talking about.

His father ran straight to the cage, which he picked up and rattled until its door swung open and the desiccated Hogboon rolled out across the floor.

Mr Glad picked up the apple. "Shall I?" he asked.

"By all means," said Finn's father.

Mr Glad took a deep bite from the apple's pink skin, chewed on it and pulled a face like it was the greatest tasting apple any human being had ever had the pleasure of sinking their teeth into.

Finn's father dropped to his hands and knees and inspected the bonsai trees. "Not so much as a twig out of place. Not a leaf. Nothing!" He hopped to his feet again.

Finn walked over to his fish, tapping the glass to see if

Bubbles was OK.

"I think it worked," declared Finn's father.

"You did it, Hugo," said Mr Glad, taking another bite of the apple. "Great stuff."

"Dad..." Finn uttered quietly.

"I wasn't sure, Glad, to be honest. I mean, I had oscillated the frequency, and narrowed the range, and all of that, but still I couldn't be sure."

"Dad, the fish..." Finn prompted a little louder.

"You'd have done Gerald proud, Hugo."

Finn's father's delight fell away a little at that.

"Sorry, Hugo, I didn't mean to remind you of... It wasn't my intention."

"Dad?"

"What is it, Finn?"

He walked over to where Finn was inspecting the glass.

"Dad, where's Bubbles?"

The goldfish was gone. The only signs he had ever been there were shaken pebbles, drifting slowly downwards, and a few scales floating free on the surface. Finn looked on the floor, but Bubbles had not jumped or fallen out. He was simply gone.

A frown had planted itself on Finn's father's face. It wasn't going to be leaving any time soon. "I'll get you another goldfish. You won't know the difference."

Finn thought of all the things that could have happened to Bubbles. Maybe he'd been desiccated into something smaller than dust. Maybe he'd been zapped, exploded, disintegrated, made invisible. Anything. He felt loss well inside him. His only pet. The only animal he was allowed to keep in a bowl in his room rather than in a jar in the library.

"Poor Bubbles," Finn muttered. Then he remembered the Hogboon's words. "He said it again, Dad. The Hogboon said something to me. It was definitely me."

"Finn, you have to ignore that," said his father. "He was disorientated. His head was all over the place."

"But he was talking to me."

"Finn, we're trying to create the greatest weapon any Legend Hunter could hope for. OK, so it still needs tweaking. There's obviously some kind of problem here that we need to look into, but we scattered a wave that shrunk a small Legend, and not the apple or the plants. I don't know what happened to your fish, but we'll figure that out eventually. I don't know if this will work on bigger Legends, but we'll figure that out too. This will change everything. For us. For you."

"But the Hogboon," pleaded Finn.

"*Enough* about the Hogboon!" his father snapped. "Can't you let me have one moment of pleasure?"

The atmosphere spoiled, Mr Glad put his apple down and began picking up some of the parts scattered around the device. Finn went to the table and lifted the fish bowl, careful not to let the water spill. Just in case Bubbles was still in there. Invisible. Or just really tiny.

"Finn, it's training time," said his dad.

"What?" Finn protested, a small wave of water sloshing out of the bowl and splashing on his hand.

"I'll give you fifteen minutes."

Finn left the library and didn't return for a full nineteen minutes. It was as brave a protest as he could muster under the circumstances.

30

"Come on, Finn, this could save your life."

"What life? I don't have a life. I'm here doing this with you."

Finn was wearing his fighting suit, which his father had handed to him as soon as he had arrived at the training room. Finn took it as an ominous sign, and that sat almost as heavily on him as the loose-fitting armour.

He tried again to perform the move his father was teaching him. He failed again.

Finn was frustrated: he *knew* these moves. He knew how they should go. He could play them out in his head. He could even imagine his own body performing them.

He just couldn't, well, actually *do* them.

But he did the slide, then a bit more of a slide, grimaced and stumbled to his feet, a wooden training sword outstretched and wobbling. As he rose, he was distracted by a Desiccator lying in a corner. Finn had a nagging concern that it was there for a reason as yet unrevealed.

Mr Glad wandered into the room and watched. "Drop your hips and slide," he suggested. "Don't force it. Use your momentum. Let me show you."

"We've got this covered, Glad, thanks," said Finn's father tetchily. "I think there was a problem with the core fluctuator on the device. Would you mind checking that out? It might need a spring or something."

"The core fluctuator?" asked Mr Glad.

"It's the thing that looks like the old vacuum cleaner. *Is* the old vacuum cleaner."

Mr Glad waited a moment, his eyebrow betraying a ripple of irritation, before slowly shuffling out.

"Now, Finn," said his dad. "Drop your hips. Feel the patterns."

"*Feel* the patterns? I don't even know what that means," said Finn.

"Of movement. In yourself. Your opponents. It's all in your mind."

Finn's dad threw himself at the ground, slid deftly and sprang to his feet facing Finn again, his wooden sword held steady at the tip of his son's nose.

"Then you clobber them. Got that, Finn?"

"No."

"Great," said his dad. "Now try it again."

Finn was horribly conscious of how clumsy he was. Rather than the move ending with him springing to his feet with liquid agility, he hauled himself up like an old man trying to get out of bed while wearing a concrete hat.

"That was good," said his father.

"If you're going to lie, at least put some effort into it," responded Finn, panting.

His dad ignored him. "Let's do it again."

Finn gave it another go, this time stumbling backwards as he tried to get to his feet, and ending up on his back before rolling over to haul himself up once more.

Closing his eyes to retain some composure, his dad said, "OK, one more. Slowly. I'll go first."

"I don't want to," said Finn.

"You have to."

"Why?" asked Finn, holding his sword limply by his side. "You're building a machine in there that'll do my job for me. Just press a button and they'll be gone. I don't need to do this now."

"Wrong," said his father, the steel now evident in his attitude. "You went to school today and came back with a wound."

"It was a tree!"

"You got hit by something by the looks of it. Too wide for a stone. Definitely not a branch." Finn's face betrayed him. His father switched to a more soothing tone. "Finn, twice in a few days you've struggled with people instead of Legends. The truth is that if you can't handle one you can't handle the other. I know this isn't always easy, but I believe in you. I have faith in you. You're my boy. It will click for you."

"I need to know what—" started Finn.

"I'll teach you exactly what you *need* to know," interrupted his father.

"No, I need to know what the Hogboon meant." His father broke away, but Finn pressed on. "You know something, don't you, Dad? There's something you won't tell me."

His dad's jaw was tense. A small vein pulsed in his neck. "Maybe a challenge will help sharpen you up," he announced, before striding out of the room.

He returned, carrying something in his arms covered in a blue blanket. He placed it on the ground between Finn and the Desiccator. "Sometimes the quickest way is just to jump in the deep end." He yanked the blanket away. "I reanimated a Legend for you."

There, snoring gently, was a Manticore. The poisonous

darts on his tail were each plugged with a wine cork and his mouth was muzzled, but his paws were free.

Finn's dad began backing out of the room.

"Where are you going?" Finn asked, battling the panic in his voice.

"Just remember your training," said Finn's dad. As he left, he pulled a rope from the belt round his waist and whipped the Manticore's behind. It shrieked into life.

"Dad!"

A grate opened in the door and Finn saw his dad's eyes peering through, then, briefly, his mouth. "You'll be fine. Good lad."

The Manticore was groggy and disorientated, like it was waking from a mid-afternoon nap, but, upon seeing Finn, its instincts kicked in immediately and it shot a dart at him. The dart bounced off Finn's forehead and rolled away, still wedged in the cork.

The Manticore flapped to the ceiling, dug its claws in and clung there for a moment, trying to regain its senses. Finn guessed it was also trying to think of a fiendish riddle to shock him with.

Finn's dad reached in through the door and pressed a switch that sent sparks dancing through the ceiling. The Legend howled and dropped to the floor, the nasty aroma of frazzled fur filling the room.

Finn dashed for the door, but too late. It shut again.

Picking itself up, the Manticore focused on Finn.

"*Mmmpf mmpf mmmmmmpf,*" the Manticore riddled, only to realise that its jaw was wired shut.

That was clearly the final indignity. Muscles pulsed through its forelegs, ligaments rippling downwards until its claws sprang into view. They were ivory daggers, bright white in the dull light. The Legend went for Finn, who raised an arm instinctively, deflecting the Manticore into the wall with a thump. But the Legend quickly recovered and came at Finn again, who backed away and raised his wooden sword, pressing it into the creature's belly and vaulting it over his head.

"Good boy," shouted his dad from where he watched through the door's wide grate.

"Stop it, Dad, this is unfair!"

"You're doing great. Watch out!"

The Manticore landed directly on Finn's chest, claws scrabbling at the boy's armour plate and winding Finn as it forced him to the floor. Finn gripped the sword at each end, using it to hold off the creature as it scratched furiously at his face, until he instinctively used its handle to jab the Legend in the eye.

As the Manticore howled and dropped off him, Finn quickly pushed himself to his feet. "Doing great!" he heard his dad say, but time had slowed, his vision had narrowed. All he saw was the Manticore, squaring off at the opposite end of the room and then leaping towards him.

Finn felt attuned to each moment as the Legend arced through the air. He slid under it, sword by his side, towards the Desiccator and, with a deftness that surprised him, returned to his feet in a single move.

He just happened, like Wrigley the Headless before him, to do it a moment too soon.

Finn collided with the Manticore's ribcage, sending both of them collapsing to the ground and groaning in pain.

His dad came back in. "That was much better, Finn," he said. "Best you've done."

Finn's ears were ringing. The Manticore gurgled in protest on the floor.

"That wasn't fair!" yelled Finn, slapping at his ears in the hope that the ringing would clear.

"But it worked, Finn," his dad said, gripping him by the shoulders. "More or less anyway. You'll be a great Legend Hunter some day. You just need a push, that's all."

"All you do is push," spat Finn. "Maybe everybody is right. Maybe the Legends only come here because of us. Because of *you*."

His dad let go of him, took a step back.

"Why is it, Dad, that you've spent every year fighting these things, that everyone in those paintings spent their lives fighting, but they're still coming? Yet you never change. I'm the one who's supposed to be learning, but you never learn anything at all."

Finn threw the wooden sword to the floor and began tearing off his fighting suit.

"Look, Finn," said his father, "ours is not an easy life—"

"Maybe it's not supposed to be *my* life!" shouted Finn, tugging the fighting suit over his head. "There's something you won't let me hear, something you're not telling me. That Hogboon keeps trying to say it and you keep shutting him up."

"I'm doing my best for you, Finn."

"You keep telling me what I'm going to be. You've never asked me what I *want* to be," said Finn, on the floor now, kicking off the fighting suit's leg armour. "I won't be this. I won't be you."

His fighting suit finally flung off, Finn stood up and ran out of the door, leaving his father alone in the training room.

From the floor, the Manticore gave a muzzled gurgle of protest. Remembering it was there, Finn's dad reached for the Desiccator and casually blasted it. The Legend's brief and stunted mumble was a parting reminder to itself to just shut up in future.

32

Finn ran straight to Emmie's house. He knocked on her door loudly. There was no answer. Standing back, he searched for signs of life, but there was nothing. He banged on the door again, just in case, and this time it gave way. He pushed it open and, with just a moment's hesitation, went inside.

"Emmie?"

Still no response. He looked around the kitchen, gazed into the small garden out the back and snooped about the living room, where the only sign of life was the TV left on with the sound low.

Each part of the house was sparse. There were no pictures on the walls, little furnishing, no ornaments or lamps. Other than some food in the kitchen, it hardly looked like anyone lived there.

On the TV, an audience burst into laughter and applause. From above, Finn heard a noise. A scrape of shoes perhaps.

"Emmie?"

Cautiously, he climbed the narrow stairs. A creak above stopped him briefly, but he urged himself to go on. He chose a door and opened it slowly. Something fell out at him. Startled, he kicked back, before realising it was just a pile of towels and that he'd opened the door to the airing cupboard.

He composed himself, picked another door and opened it.

This room was dim, the blinds half pulled so that the light edged through the slats. But he could clearly see the row of cameras, all set up on tripods and facing a window.

Sure there was no one in the room, Finn walked over to the equipment. There was one video camera and the rest had long lenses that Finn knew were used for taking pictures from a distance. But of what? Finn stood on his toes to examine one. What he saw made his head spin.

The lens was focused on a house. Finn's house.

Finn moved to the other camera. This one was also trained on his house, as was the video camera. Finn looked for a play button, pressed it and watched footage of himself running through his front door a couple of hours before, woollen hat pulled over his head.

He rewound. There was Mr Glad entering the house.

He rewound further and watched the footage of his dad going in and out from the car with parts, his mother giving Finn a peck on the cheek as she headed to work.

Finn felt nausea rise through him.

Emmie and her dad were *spying* on him.

A toilet flushed. Footsteps. A door to Finn's left opened and standing there was a man with a newspaper under his arm and his eyes wide with surprise. He moved towards Finn. "Oh hello. You're not supposed to be in here."

Finn bolted before the man could grab him, jumping down the stairs four at a time and almost collapsing out of the front door in the panic to get home. Emmie arrived at the same time, a shopping bag in her hand. He stared at her. His friend was suddenly a stranger to him.

"Finn?" she asked.

He kept running.

33

As soon as Finn ran into his house, blurting out a stream of hurried information, his father grabbed the Desiccator and sprinted out on to the street. Mr Glad followed, frowning.

The man from Emmie's house was running round the corner towards them. Instead of coming to a sudden halt at the sight of the weapon, he slowed to a jog before walking casually forward as if it was a totally normal thing to have a Desiccator pointed at him.

Finn saw Emmie standing a little distance behind the man. She gave him a pleading look. He didn't hold eye contact, instead letting the hurt burn through him.

"Who are you?" demanded Finn's father, with an authority that removed any need to shout.

"I'm Emmie's father."

"Interesting." Finn's dad kept the weapon steady. "I'd guess that 'stay-at-home dad' is not what's on your business card. So what is?"

"I wouldn't wave that Desiccator about. If it goes off, you won't get many answers from me."

"If I have to ask again, it'll be after I've desiccated you and then reanimated you inside the belly of a diseased Cerberus. So, for the last time..."

Emmie's father inflated his chest. "I am the son of Eric the Invincible. Grandson of James the Everlasting. Great-grandson of..."

"Did I ask you to list your great-aunts or did I ask for your name?"

"It's Steve," said Emmie, stepping forward. Her father shot an angry glare at her.

"Steve?" Hugo spluttered a mocking laugh. "Really? Steve? Did you hear that, Glad? Not much of a name for a traitor. Steve. If you're going to pick a cover name, pick something just a little more evil, like..."

"Herman," suggested Mr Glad.

"Or Attila," added Finn's father. "Something more, I don't know, traitorous." He looked at Mr Glad. "Is traitorous a word?"

Mr Glad shrugged.

Emmie's father looked riled. "I am no traitor."

"We only came to help," said Emmie. She was speaking

directly to Finn, quietly imploring him for a response.

"I let you in my house," said Finn, stepping back. He felt the world dissolving beneath his feet, the deep gorge of disappointment eating into his chest. "I told you stuff."

"Leave this to me, Emmie," her dad said.

"Yes, listen to Steve, young lady," said Finn's father. "So, what really brings you to Darkmouth, Steve? Are you a fan? If you just wanted an autograph, all you had to do was ask. Finn, grab a pen."

"You really don't know, do you, Hugo?"

"Of course I do." Finn's father strode forward, weapon still raised. "You're a Legend Hunter, as your little family history lesson suggested, but you have the soft skin of a Legend Hunter who doesn't actually hunt Legends, and the giddiness of a puppy. I know your type. You became Complete long ago, but haven't seen a real Legend in what, years? Decades? The question is, why am I being spied on by you and Santa's little helper?"

Steve stepped up to his stare. "You're going to be on the Council of Twelve, Hugo. You think they just drop an invitation in the post and wait for you to turn up?"

"I don't expect them to stick a camera lens through my window."

"Checks, Hugo. Procedures. They would have told you that."

"And *you're* what they sent? They running short on minions these days?" said Finn's father.

"They have to know they can trust you to join them, Hugo," Steve continued, working hard to maintain a sense of control, that he had the upper hand. "And that they could trust your boy to stay behind and look after Darkmouth when you're not here."

Finn's mouth dropped open. But there was nothing he could say as humiliation bedded into his mind once more.

"So, I was sent here to check on you. And what did I find?" said Steve. "Legends causing havoc. You leaving your boy alone at a gateway so that he almost drowns."

"This is a Blighted Village, *Steve*."

"The only one still actually blighted by Legends."

"What did you expect? A funfair? Maybe a petting zoo," retorted Finn's father.

"I didn't expect *this* mess, that's for sure," said Steve.

"So," said Finn's father. "The Council of Twelve sent you to make things worse."

"To observe," said Steve. "To report back. To step in if necessary. Did you expect them to just sit back and hope for the best? That's not how the Council operates. Wars are not won that way."

"Nice speech. Did you practise that in front of the mirror last night?" sneered Finn's father.

"And for your information I *have* been fighting Legends," said Steve, lifting his chin. "Many of them."

"Where?" asked Hugo. "Last time I checked, they weren't making guest appearances anywhere else."

"In training. The Twelve have a store of them they reanimate when required."

"Ah, in *training*. Lovely. Did you get special badges for that? Or maybe they gave you a good Hunter name. What is it again?"

Steve didn't reply. Finn's dad lifted the Desiccator again. "Let's guess, shall we? Any ideas, Glad?"

"Steve the Nameless," suggested Mr Glad, hanging back beside Finn.

"Finn, want a guess?"

He didn't. He just wanted to go inside, collapse in bed and not come out again for a while, say until the world ended.

"OK, I'll try," continued his dad. "Steve the Sixty Words a Minute Typist. You know, something really epic like that."

"You accuse me of being soft," said Steve, squaring up

to Hugo. "But look at you. You wouldn't get far without that weapon in your hand. It's just point and click. No art to it at all."

Hugo raised an eyebrow. "No *art* to it?"

"No craft. No real skill."

"No *skill*?" Hugo stepped back, opening out his arms in invitation. "I tell you what, Steve, why don't I give you a head start, then I'll put a blindfold on and we'll see if there's any skill to what I still manage to do to you."

"Where's the purity?" asked Steve.

"Purity?"

"Hand-to-hand fighting. Up-close weapons. Subduing a Legend using cunning, not technology. If I was the Legend Hunter in this town—"

"If you weren't busy sharpening your pencils, you mean." A satisfied smile hovered on Finn's father's lips. "But do go on."

"If I was the Legend Hunter in this town, I would do things differently." Steve paused for a moment. "And I wouldn't have raised such a soft boy either."

"Hey!" protested Finn.

"Hey!" protested Emmie.

Finally forced to meet her stare, Finn gritted his teeth, silently willing her to realise he did not want her help.

"Be careful now, Steve," warned Finn's father.

"How long until he's supposed to be Complete? A year? Less now? Has he even managed the three basic hunts yet?" Emmie's father looked at Finn. "No offence, son."

That kicked Finn into a response. "Don't call me that. I'm not your son."

"He's supposed to be the first true Legend Hunter in a long time, Hugo," continued Emmie's father, still looking at Finn. "There are big plans for the ceremony. Dignitaries. A choir. Live Legends for some mysterious reason, but it's bound to be a good one. But he knows all that, right?"

Live Legends? thought Finn, alarmed. *What?*

"Last chance," said his dad, stepping forward.

"Then again," Steve continued, "when you marry a civilian, your children are half-civilian. You know he wants to be a vet, don't you?"

In the moment it took him to say those last three words, Finn's dad had closed the gap between the two and had pulled the barrel of the Desiccator round Steve's neck. Steve grabbed at it, choking. "Let's see how softly your neck snaps," snarled Hugo. "Let's see if I can put some art into *that*."

He twisted the barrel. Steve gurgled in protest. "How

does that feel, Steve?" Hugo whispered into his ear. "Does it feel like it needs a little craft? Just tell me if I'm going wrong at any point."

Steve was turning purple, gurgling for breath, fighting to dislodge Hugo's grip.

Finn danced a little on the spot, feeling trapped, growing less sure by the second that his father wouldn't actually go through with it.

"Leave him alone!" Emmie ran at Hugo, jumping on his back, pulling at his hair until he released the hold and brushed her off. Steve coughed for air.

"Here's the thing, Steve," Finn's dad said, leaning down into his ear. "I actually believe you. I can believe you were sent here by the Twelve to keep an eye on me, because no Legend I have ever fought has been so meek. Your little girl here has more fight in her."

Steve spluttered. "That's rich coming from someone who's still chasing Legends while the rest of the world have defeated theirs."

"Here's what really bothers me, though, Steve. If you're a Legend Hunter, what were you taking from that gateway?"

"What are you talking about?"

Finn's father stepped forward aggressively. "Someone

used the harbour gateway as a postbox and then attacked my son. I'd say the prime candidate is the man who's been secretly filming my family and who used his daughter to infiltrate my house."

He trained the Desiccator between Emmie's father's eyes. "You have until the count of three to tell me what you were doing there or from now on your daughter will know you only as a paperweight on my desk."

"It wasn't me."

"One."

"You really sure I'm a traitor?" Steve shouted with growing fretfulness.

"Two!" shouted Finn's father.

"You think the Twelve would send someone they couldn't trust?"

"Three! Enjoy the snooze, *Steve*."

A small black box on Hugo's belt buzzed. Then bleeped. A red light winked. In the house, an alarm began to wail. From darkened skies, rain began to fall.

34

Finn's father remained poised, breathing angrily through flared nostrils, Desiccator held firm at Steve's forehead. Finn's heart was pounding like it was trying to escape and, for the first time since he met her, Emmie appeared vulnerable and lost.

From the house, the alarm continued its urgent shriek.

"You have no choice, Hugo," said Steve as calmly as he could muster. "Press that trigger and the Twelve will have you locked up by sunset. The boy too."

The alarm rose in pitch, as if desperate for attention.

Hugo lowered the Desiccator and leaned in to Steve's ear. "Saved by the bell." He dropped the weapon and moved away. Steve slumped to his knees, breathing hard.

Mr Glad blocked Hugo's path. "Do you really want to let him go? After what Finn found?"

"I can deal with him later," said Hugo, pushing him aside. "We have to sort this out first."

Mr Glad nodded and started to follow. Hugo paused and turned to him. "Not you, Glad," he said. "This is for Legend Hunters only, you know that."

Finn and Mr Glad stood side by side for a moment. "It's not in my job description, is it, boy?" muttered Mr Glad. "We mustn't get above ourselves." Pulling his coat collar up round his neck, he trudged away in the direction of his shop.

Reaching the car, Hugo stopped and motioned to Finn to follow. "What are you still standing there for? Come on."

Finn followed dutifully.

"She seemed all right, Dad," he said as he sat in his seat. They watched Emmie approach her father, who waved away her offer of help and gingerly jogged back in the direction of his house.

"You couldn't have known," Finn's father said, starting the engine.

"I let her into our house."

"You did," his dad answered, then looked at him, "but you also blew their cover. Take the credit when you can get it."

Finn considered that and allowed it to lift his gloom just a little. "I suppose I did..." he started, but didn't get to finish that thought because he was pressed back in his seat by the sudden acceleration of the vehicle.

A black van had screeched round the corner. It was the same vehicle that had shadowed them at the harbour and had been in their street. Emmie and her father sat in the front. Finn's father put his foot down and gave chase.

As they sped through Darkmouth, something else occurred to Finn.

"Dad?"

"Yes, Finn."

"Are there really going to be live Legends at my Completion?"

His dad didn't answer, instead speeding up, engine noise filling the car, until he eventually glanced Finn's way.

"A vet, Finn? Seriously?"

35

The growl of the vehicles carried across the town, causing dogs to look up and cats to stop licking themselves. The people of Darkmouth were already busy ducking into doorways and off the streets. The weather forecast that morning had said it would be dry. It wasn't, so it was time to get out of the way.

In shops and cafes, the townspeople exchanged glances and tuts. In a hairdresser's on the main street, one woman, with her hair in curls pulled tighter than leather trousers on a sumo wrestler, dropped her magazine and looked out at the damp street. She watched the two black vehicles race by the window in a blast of spray and engine noise.

Drawing a sigh from deep within her lungs, she announced to the rest of the room: "This can't go on."

There was a low chorus of approval from her fellow customers.

On the main street a gateway had appeared. The car

and van screamed to a halt on either side of it, just in time to see a Wolpertinger slide out. The Legend shook the fur on its head and the feathers on its back, as the gateway gulped into oblivion.

Finn's mind was drowned in hurt and confusion and a new-found revulsion as Emmie sidestepped closer to him.

"I'm sorry," she said.

Finn moved away. He just wanted to go home. On his own again. It had been easier that way, when there was no one to let him down.

"Emmie, stay back," said Steve. "I'll deal with this."

"You too, Finn," ordered his father. "The lesson isn't for you this time."

The Wolpertinger appeared to hesitate for a moment, then settled itself, deciding to turn and fight and enjoy the chance to snack on some human flesh.

But which human to fight? Finn saw it size up the Legend Hunters' near-identical armour, both shimmering against the background, the impenetrable black of their helmets giving no hint of what emotion lay beneath. Yet one fighting suit looked battleworn, scratched, gouged, bitten.

The other might well have been freshly made that morning.

The Wolpertinger took a final look at each of them and appeared to make up its mind. It ran for a man cowering behind a lamp-post.

Finn's father raised his Desiccator, but Steve stepped forward just as he squeezed the trigger, pushing the gun downwards so that a chunk of tarmac was gouged from the road and left to roll in the bottom of a new crater.

"This one is mine," said Steve, reaching behind his waist to yank forward a long chain topped with a small spiked ball. He swung the mace in an arc above his head and released it. The chain straightened and the weapon cut a graceful swathe towards its target. Glancing over its shoulder, the Wolpertinger changed direction at the last moment, pouncing into the air, pushing off a wall and somersaulting away from danger.

The mace wrapped tightly round the lamp-post, its spikes embedding into the wood a few centimetres above the head of the shrieking man hiding behind it.

Finn's father lifted his Desiccator again, sighing. "This is ridiculous."

Steve stepped in front of the weapon's barrel. "I've waited my whole life for this chance."

"And you still missed."

Finn watched, only half aware of what was happening

right in front of him.

"I didn't mean to hurt you really," Emmie said. "I hated lying to you."

"You did a good job of looking like you were enjoying it," Finn responded flatly, only to get a jolt as Emmie pushed past him.

"Dad!" she shouted.

The Wolpertinger had taken its chance to dart at Steve's back. Instead of jumping away, though, Steve reacted immediately, lifting his sword as he turned and charged directly at the oncoming Legend. The Wolpertinger held a collision course, leaping to attack at the precise moment that Steve lurched forward, smashing down visor-first on the road, his sword spilling to the ground ahead of him.

From his bound feet trailed a rope. Finn's father held the other end. Using his free hand, he pulled the trigger on the Desiccator. With a stifled *whooop*, the Wolpertinger became a furry, feathery and bony husk of its former self, bouncing off Steve's helmet on the way to the ground.

"Is that the sort of purity you were looking for, Steve?"

Finn dragged his feet back towards the car, the heat of his humiliation refusing to let in even a glimmer of joy from watching Emmie and her father humiliated in return. She had run forward to help her father, but hesitated when it was clear he really didn't want her to.

Hugo came close and pulled out a knife. Steve flinched.

"Stay still, for crying out loud. You're worse than one of them," said Hugo. From the armour at the base of Steve's neck, he prised a crystal fang. "Look what the nice bunny brought us."

Hugo walked away, halting briefly to pick up the desiccated Wolpertinger and toss it into Steve's gloved hands. "Make sure to put all this in your report."

He reached the car. Wearily, Finn pushed himself off the bonnet to follow his father.

"What about the second gateway, Hugo?" shouted Steve from the ground, where he was using his sword to free his legs. "Ask yourself what you're not seeing."

Finn's father had already started the engine, drowning him out as he bounced the vehicle through the street's new crater.

Above Darkmouth, the drizzle eased and light began to push again into the day. The townspeople emerged on to the streets, catching a glimpse of this stranger in armour picking himself off the street, a young girl by his side, the bent lamp-post creaking above them and the pothole in the street.

*

A short distance away, Sergeant Doyle sat in his small station with a half-drunk cup of coffee and took call after call asking what he was going to do about this ongoing problem.

"It's getting worse," they complained.

"Why is Darkmouth the only place left where this is happening?" they moaned. "Isn't that family supposed to be solving the problem, not making it worse?"

"That useless boy..." they said.

"Hugo the Not So Great..." they said.

"I tell you," they said. "That family needs those Legends or they're nothing. They *let* them attack us. Maybe it's time we attacked *them* to show them we won't take it any more." Sergeant Doyle tried to calm them, talk them down, assure them that he was on the case and would treat the matter with the greatest urgency. Then he took out a pen and writing paper and began to draft yet another letter requesting a transfer.

There must, he suggested, be a high-security prison for the most dangerous criminals that could do with his help.

From *A Concise Guide to the*
Legend Hunter World, Vol. 5,
Chapter 23: 'The Council of Twelve'

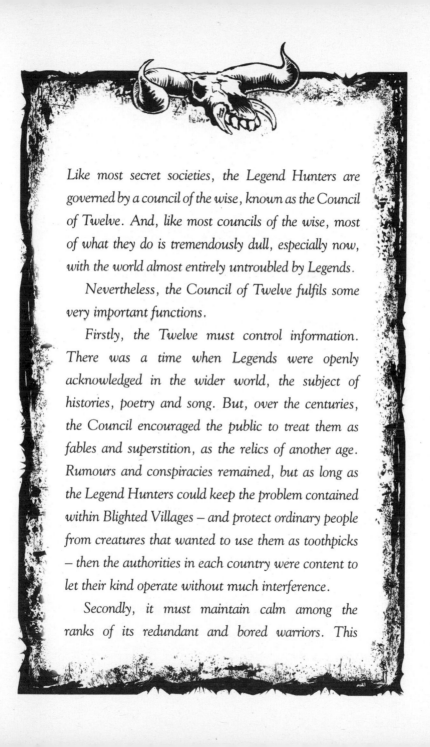

Like most secret societies, the Legend Hunters are governed by a council of the wise, known as the Council of Twelve. And, like most councils of the wise, most of what they do is tremendously dull, especially now, with the world almost entirely untroubled by Legends.

Nevertheless, the Council of Twelve fulfils some very important functions.

Firstly, the Twelve must control information. There was a time when Legends were openly acknowledged in the wider world, the subject of histories, poetry and song. But, over the centuries, the Council encouraged the public to treat them as fables and superstition, as the relics of another age. Rumours and conspiracies remained, but as long as the Legend Hunters could keep the problem contained within Blighted Villages – and protect ordinary people from creatures that wanted to use them as toothpicks – then the authorities in each country were content to let their kind operate without much interference.

Secondly, it must maintain calm among the ranks of its redundant and bored warriors. This

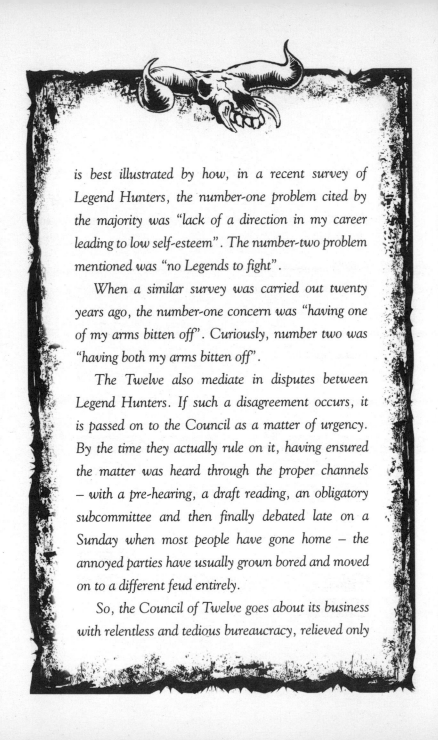

is best illustrated by how, in a recent survey of Legend Hunters, the number-one problem cited by the majority was "lack of a direction in my career leading to low self-esteem". The number-two problem mentioned was "no Legends to fight".

When a similar survey was carried out twenty years ago, the number-one concern was "having one of my arms bitten off". Curiously, number two was "having both my arms bitten off".

The Twelve also mediate in disputes between Legend Hunters. If such a disagreement occurs, it is passed on to the Council as a matter of urgency. By the time they actually rule on it, having ensured the matter was heard through the proper channels – with a pre-hearing, a draft reading, an obligatory subcommittee and then finally debated late on a Sunday when most people have gone home – the annoyed parties have usually grown bored and moved on to a different feud entirely.

So, the Council of Twelve goes about its business with relentless and tedious bureaucracy, relieved only

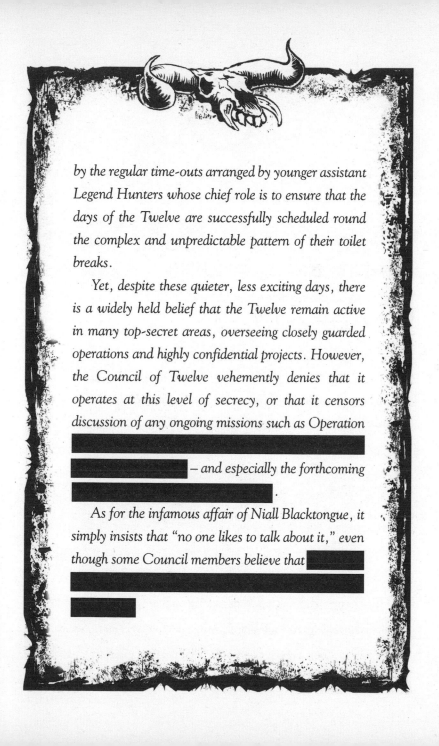

by the regular time-outs arranged by younger assistant Legend Hunters whose chief role is to ensure that the days of the Twelve are successfully scheduled round the complex and unpredictable pattern of their toilet breaks.

Yet, despite these quieter, less exciting days, there is a widely held belief that the Twelve remain active in many top-secret areas, overseeing closely guarded operations and highly confidential projects. However, the Council of Twelve vehemently denies that it operates at this level of secrecy, or that it censors discussion of any ongoing missions such as Operation ███████████████████████████████████ ████████████████████ – and especially the forthcoming ███████████████████████.

As for the infamous affair of Niall Blacktongue, it simply insists that "no one likes to talk about it," even though some Council members believe that ████████ ████████████████████████████████ ████████.

36

From his perch on the hill, Gantrua observed the movement in the valley below, as a convoy of Hogboons carried rock and soil from the chasm in the mountain that led to the vast network of Coronium mines. The only reward for their labour was the promise that they would not be burned out of their hovels. Not a great reward perhaps, but an effective motivation nonetheless.

The harvested rocks were being taken to great sorting fields, where every crumb would be picked over in search of crystals. Findings were meagre. These were the remnants of the last-known deposits of Coronium, buried in the last place in this world where they could still be hooked on to the air to tear it open.

Gantrua had dispatched teams across the land to find more deposits, all without success. Only here did they find what they needed. Here, where the gateways led to

a single village in the Promised World. And one target.

Under Gantrua's command, the Legends would eventually shred the fabric between worlds and tunnel their way through, boring a pathway between this place and the other side. An army would be waiting, woken from their slumber for this great moment.

Gantrua could smell victory. Or he would have if the overpowering stench of his Fomorian guards wasn't wafting up towards him.

Below him, Trom was taking some pleasure in hurling rocks into the cavalcades of Hogboons, sending them ducking and scattering. Cryf was rating his efforts.

"I still don't understand," said Trom to Gantrua while heaving another stone at the lines as casually as if he was skimming pebbles on a lake. Hogboons shrieked and dived out of the way.

"Seven out of ten," said Cryf.

"What do you not understand, fool?" asked Gantrua, indulging him.

"Why we're invading without an army." Trom hauled up and threw another large rock.

Cryf grimaced. "Only a five out of ten there, my lumpen friend."

Gantrua surveyed the scene as the light faded on

another day – hardly a dramatic fall in light, more a deepening of the usual darkness that pervaded even at the brightest of hours. He longed to be gone from this place.

"We have an army, you idiot." Gantrua sighed. "It is as invisible to you as wisdom. As out of reach as intelligence. As hidden from you as…"

Trom flung another rock. Half a dozen Hogboons danced out of the way.

"Oh, an eight there, I would say," observed Cryf.

Gantrua lifted a foot and pushed hard on Trom's shoulder, sending him into a violent tumble down the hill and straight into a line of Hogboons, who scattered and fell in all directions. Rock and dirt spilled among the hard stubble sprouting from the poisoned ground.

Cryf practically doubled over in laughter at the sight. Gantrua kicked him too.

He then retreated down the far side of the hill to his tent that lay away from the hubbub of the convoys and the roaring of the Fomorian guards. Gantrua pulled aside the canvas and squeezed his mighty bulk inside, pulling his sword in behind him.

His eyes struggled in the glare of the low fires set up inside. He could feel the hatred rotting his heart; could sense its beating becoming slower and slower as if his body was rebelling against being here. The end could not come soon enough.

"You must be patient, my friend," said a weak voice from a far corner of the tent. "Try some meditation. Communicate with the ether rather than your anger. It will do you good."

Gantrua's shoulders heaved with the depth of his breathing. He squinted at the hooded figure sitting cross-legged on the floor. "That may be your way," he snarled. "It is not mine."

The figure lifted his head a little, dim light catching the thin lips and the wrinkled skin of his chin. "And yet here we are. Still trapped in this world. And they still in theirs."

Gantrua did not answer. The only sound was the drawing of the stale air into his lungs, like the low drone of a great organ.

"What's happening out there?" asked the hooded figure.

"The crystals are being gathered. We have almost exhausted the Coronium mines entirely, for only a handful of stones."

"But is it enough to keep the gateways open?"

"Yes."

The hooded figure shifted a little in his place, then settled back. "It is not about what we do here, Gantrua. It is about what happens in the Promised World. A great army sleeps there and we have delivered the power our agent needs to wake them. You will have your final push to victory."

"And the child?" asked Gantrua.

"The child is only a threat to you if he survives. And he will not."

Gantrua placed a hand on the hooded figure's shoulder and squeezed gently with just enough force that it could be taken either as affection or a threat. "You had better be right."

37

A heavy silence had fallen. On Finn's house. On his family. There had been little sight of his father in days, no sound from the library, no squeal of tools, no clatter of parts. And no gateways either.

For days, worry had been written on his mother's face. What little Finn had learned of the aftermath of the revelations about Emmie and her father, he had heard from her, when he visited the surgery on Broken Road. She told him that contact had been made with the Twelve, informing them of Hugo's complaint against Steve, but that verification and instruction would only come after the message had been dealt with in the proper manner, "according to paragraph 52, subsection 3.1 of the Legend Hunters' constitution, and following due process, etc., etc.".

"That could be tomorrow," said Finn's mother. "It

could be next month. When he asked them for permission to leave Darkmouth so we could go on honeymoon, the response came two days before our first wedding anniversary. And the answer was still no."

Finn sat in her examining room, knees pulled up on to the seat, face mask billowed by his breath. He whirred a dentist's drill until his mother grabbed it back from him.

"Listen, Mam, there's something he's not telling me."

"Who?" asked Finn's mother absent-mindedly. She was preparing for her next patient, but without the lightness that Finn normally saw in her when she worked.

"Dad. We captured that Hogboon and it said something to me. It seemed to recognise me."

"I don't know, Finn," she said wearily.

"It did. And it had some sort of message. It said, 'the boy shall fall,' and it was talking directly to me, but Dad says it's nothing."

"Then maybe it is nothing," said his mother.

"Do you think I might ever get an answer?" Finn asked.

"From who?"

"From Dad. From the Twelve. From anyone!"

"Look, Finn," she said, seeming a little irked now. "He doesn't tell me everything. God knows I wish he would, but he doesn't. And the Council obviously doesn't tell him everything either. And that's what they all do. They lie or hold on to secrets or just avoid things in the hope that they go away."

His mother took a breath, then kept talking, as if releasing something she'd been holding in for too long. "I've spent years going along with that because that's just how they are. And what's worse is you'll end up doing the same. It's what happens. Until it all goes wrong some day."

"Do you think he knows what the Hogboon meant?" said Finn.

"Who knows what he knows."

"But couldn't you ask him? Was the Hogboon saying that I'm different? That I'm, I don't know, special?"

His mother wheeled her chair up close to his, kindness returning to her tone. "Finn, before you were even born we knew you'd be special. When you were born, we knew you'd be special. You have to understand that you *are* special. And your father knows that too."

The door opened and a woman came in. Finn's mother stood and beckoned her over to the chair. "OK, Mrs Stack, let's see how that abscess is coming along."

Finn loitered a little until his mother ushered him out. As he stood in the doorway and pulled the hood over his head, he sensed movement to his right. But there was nothing unusual when he looked, except the stares of passers-by, their eyes dark with anger.

That evening, Finn turned up for training as usual, back to room T2, with its long mirror running along one wall and soft mats on the floor. He waited for his dad to arrive. No one came.

Eventually, Finn sat with his back pressed against the mirror, his fighting suit on his lap, and, with a needle, thread and some rivets, worked at tightening up the armour.

Then he walked the Long Hall, where the dead watched from the walls, disapproval burning into him from each set of eyes. It seemed even they were aware of the sullen hush that seeped through the house and poisoned every room.

On Monday morning, Emmie was waiting at the junction of their streets when Finn left for school. He picked up his pace as he passed silently, fuelled by anger, shame and a surge of adrenalin that put an uncontrollable wobble in his legs.

On Monday afternoon, she was at the school gates. So he hopped a wall, snagging his trousers on broken glass as he hauled himself over it. She followed him home, from a distance, her unshakeable presence giving him an itch in his shoulders.

On Tuesday morning, she was at the corner again. "Finn!" Emmie half shouted. He crossed the road, took a turn in the wrong direction, dodged through a laneway, across another and emerged on an unfamiliar route to school. Thirty seconds later, she was trailing him again.

On Tuesday afternoon, Finn did the same thing, in reverse. So did Emmie.

On Wednesday, he took a lift with his mother. It was the only way. And in school he sat at the back of the classroom so she couldn't burn a hole in his head with her stare. Instead, he tried very hard not to stare at the back of *her* head. He failed, but convinced himself that she didn't know that.

On Thursday, Emmie wasn't there. She wasn't on the road or at school. Mrs McDaid called her name a couple of times during roll-call, but where she should have been, sitting under an explosion of red hair, there was only an empty chair. Finn looked at the vacant seat and wondered where she could be until his thoughts were interrupted by a wet pea-sized ball of paper stinging the side of his head. The Savage twins pulled matching sad faces at him.

On Friday morning, Emmie was missing again and Finn could feel a surprising sensation creeping up inside him. He almost didn't recognise it at first. She was gone. She had left Darkmouth, returned to the city, to her old life. And Finn... *missed* her. Just a little bit. But enough that he had to recall his anger from where it had briefly retreated.

He walked home slowly that afternoon, half wishing to turn round and find her shadowing him from afar. There was no sign.

He passed the corner, but she wasn't there. Finn took the short route to her house, then hesitated for a few seconds, caught between approaching the front door and going home. No, he decided, he should just leave Emmie and her father behind as nothing more than a painful lesson in trust. It was time to get on with whatever the rest of his life was to bring.

He turned round and headed home.

"Finn?"

The fright pretty much sent him leaping into the air.

"Sorry. I didn't mean to scare you," said Emmie. She stood on the path to Finn's house.

His anger came bubbling back to the surface as he brushed past her.

"I'm sorry," she said.

"Just leave me alone."

"I didn't tell my dad about the crystal you took."

Finn stopped. "So?"

"I could have told him," said Emmie. "I was supposed to tell him. But I didn't."

"Great, you're trying to blackmail me now," said Finn. "Brilliant way of showing how sorry you are."

"I didn't tell him because I realised I didn't *want* to. I was supposed to pass back all the information, and I thought I could do that. But the crystal, that was your secret. And you shared it with me. That's when I knew I couldn't do what they wanted. Because you were my friend."

"You're right. I *was* your friend. Past tense," said Finn.

"I'm sorry for everything. I didn't mean to—"

"You meant it all. Every bit of it. You used me to get to my dad. It's the only reason you came to Darkmouth." Finn started to march away.

"No, it's not," said Emmie.

"Liar!" said Finn.

"No, Finn. I mean we weren't here to watch your father."

"More lies," said Finn, still walking away.

"We were here to watch *you*," Emmie shouted after him.

Finn stopped again, anger and confusion swirling inside him while he tried to figure this all out. "So, even they don't think I'll ever be Complete—"

"It's more than that," said Emmie. "Something else. I don't know exactly what, and my dad doesn't tell me much, but I've picked up bits and pieces. About the Twelve. They talk about you a lot. They're worried about you. About some kind of..." She hesitated, as if afraid to

259

speak the word. "…prophecy."

He felt the world tumble, like the day he fell chasing the Minotaur and lay stranded, rain dropping from the flat grey far above him.

They stood on the empty street. Finn thought she looked different and it took a moment to realise why. Her hair was pulled back, revealing her face from ear to ear. Now that he noticed it, she didn't just look different, she was almost unrecognisable.

"Don't believe you," he said and left.

Emmie's arms were rigid by her side, her fists clenched. She shouted after him. "It's true. That's why they asked me to become your friend."

"Still don't believe you," he shouted, not breaking stride. But he wasn't so sure. The Hogboon had tried to give *him* a message. Emmie and Steve had come here to watch *him*. He felt like he was being sucked into the centre of something.

Something big.

He kept walking, but the anger and the confusion were swiftly being overwhelmed by another emotion he was all too familiar with. By the time he reached his house, he felt very scared indeed.

39

Finn waited for training again that night, fighting suit on, helmet in his hand, but no father there to punch. Down the Long Hall, the rim of light at the door to the library told him that his father was inside. Finn knew what he had to do to break the silence, knew it was time to offer one secret for another, even if the result might bring things crashing down on his head.

Before entering the library, Finn stopped at the portrait of Gerald the Disappointed. There was no doubt about it: if there was ever a man who looked as if life had glued a coin to the floor and kicked him in the backside when he tried to pick it up, it was Finn's great-grandfather.

What would it be like to be brought up by a man who was so openly unhappy with how things had turned out? What would it be like to try and please a man who looked as if every ounce of pleasure had been squeezed from his life?

And what would it be like to lose your father, the man whose portrait on the wall was a constant reminder of his absence?

It would harden a person, Finn guessed. It would turn them into his dad.

He took a deep breath and entered the library.

His father was sitting with his back to the door, staring at the computer screen with his shoulders drooping. Finn walked towards him, the silence amplifying every step, but his dad seemed oblivious to his presence, simply rubbing his forehead as if trying to work a thought out from deep within.

On the computer, photographs scrolled across the screen, including a favourite of Finn's that showed him when he was four years old sitting with his mam and dad on Darkmouth's stony beach. He was holding a bucket and spade, for all the use it would be.

They looked like a normal family, on a normal day out, in a normal town.

Finn put his hands inside the breast of his fighting suit and, from a pocket under the armour, pulled out the Minotaur's crystal. He held it close by his side.

"That was a good day," his father announced, his back still to Finn. "We took you for a swim, but you wouldn't wear any inflatable rings. You just wanted to run straight in there and swim. So, I let you have a go. I stood there and watched you splash and kick and do everything to stay afloat. Your mother was shouting and screaming at me to pick you up, but I told her you'd be fine."

"Did I swim?"

"No, I had to rescue you. But that's not the point. The point is that you tried. You showed courage and a stubbornness that I knew would make you a great Legend Hunter. That I *know* will make you great."

The picture scrolled over to another. It was the portrait of Gerald the Disappointed that hung in the Long Hall. His father turned off the monitor. "But it hasn't been great so far, let's be honest. And I have tried. *We* have tried."

Finn frowned, thinking of the Hogboon and the message it had tried to give him. "Dad, what was the Hogboon saying about me? Am I different in some way? I know there's something you're not telling me."

"Finn, you need to get that nonsense out of your head and quick."

Finn pushed the crystal back inside his fighting suit as his father spun round on the chair.

"But Mam admitted it."

"Admitted what?" asked his dad.

"She said I was special," said Finn.

"She did?"

"That you knew I'd be special even before I was born."

His father grabbed Finn by the shoulders, took a breath and gave him a laser-beam stare. "Of course she told you you were special, Finn. *Every* mammy thinks their child is special. That's what mammies are supposed to say."

The crush Finn felt was the closest he might ever get to knowing what it was like to be desiccated.

"Am I interrupting a touching moment between father and son?" Mr Glad stood at the door of the library, his hands thrust in the pockets of his stained coat. Sensing his joke had fallen flat, he laughed awkwardly. "Sorry, I didn't mean to. Anyway, Hugo, it's time you got back to work. Actually, it's time you got out of those sweatpants before they need to be cut off you. And open a window in here. I've smelled Griffins sweeter than this room."

He marched in, heading straight for the device, and started to clear up tools, coffee cups and odds and ends.

Finn had turned away to hide the upset tensing his face. His father glanced at Mr Glad, but didn't stand up. "It doesn't feel like a priority right now, Glad."

"Look, Hugo," said Mr Glad, "so the Twelve sent Coco

the Clown or whatever his name is to check up on you and your boy. That's the Twelve. It's their way. Those guys wouldn't order chicken soup before first finding out what colour feathers the chicken had."

A mildly perplexed look briefly interrupted Hugo's self-pity. "They looked for reasons to stop me joining the Twelve," he said. "They have plenty now."

Finn sidled away, beginning to head towards the door.

"Did you ever think you'd see your father give up so easily, young man?" said Mr Glad as he passed. Finn paused. "He didn't give up during the Christmas Day invasion all those years ago," continued Mr Glad. "He didn't give up despite that whole business with your grandfather Niall. But now, here he is, giving up on all that. And even giving up on you."

Anger flashed in Hugo's eyes. "Don't bring Finn into this."

"It's the only way it can be, Hugo."

Finn's father swivelled round to the desk and placed his head between his large hands. "I've given a lifetime to Darkmouth," he said.

"Then a few more days won't do any harm," said Mr Glad.

"They've already started the process of taking all this

away from me," said Hugo. "That rookie spy they sent will probably convince them he can take over."

"Then you need to give them a reason why that shouldn't happen. Finishing the device will do that." There was something close to pleading in Mr Glad's voice. "I've never seen you as the type to give up. And I'm sure your son hasn't either."

Finn stayed where he was, head down, caught between the need for truth, the need to escape and the need for everything to go back to normal. He remembered what the device offered for his future. "My dad never gives up on anyone," he said, hardly audible.

"What's that, Finn?" asked Mr Glad.

"It's OK, Finn," said Hugo. "You don't need to say anything."

Finn spoke, louder, and stared at his father. "I said that Dad never gives up."

Finn closed his eyes, unable to hold his father's gaze any longer. He tried to wish away the tightness creeping through his throat, and noticed the musky smell of Mr Glad's clothes, heard the creak of a chair.

He opened his eyes again to see his father walking slowly towards the device, dragging himself to it, and, with laboured effort, reaching down to the floor to pick up a hammer. Approaching the contraption, he held the hammer so tightly in his fists Finn could see his knuckles whiten. His father's breath was quick, deep. His great shoulders rose and fell. He lifted the hammer above his shoulder, as if preparing to strike the machine down.

Finn held his breath. Mr Glad's eyes widened.

Hugo hesitantly lowered his arm, bringing the hammer's head into the palm of his free hand. He sighed, and the tension and intent seemed to be released from him. "Get me that blade," he said.

Mr Glad realised he was addressing him. "Ah yes, the blade. Which one?"

"The one that looks like it's from a desk fan. It *is* the desk fan." Hugo went to work on some wiring within the device.

Mr Glad looked at Finn, a smile crossing his face. Finn couldn't identify what type. Satisfied maybe. Relieved. Triumphant. But, whatever kind, it troubled Finn.

"This is going to change everything, young man," Mr Glad said. "I know you're not too keen on harming any more animals, but sometimes sacrifices are necessary, right?"

Finn caught sight of something and flinched, but quickly composed himself. "I've got homework to do," he announced and left as speedily as he could manage without looking like he was running away. Which he was.

He could sense Mr Glad watching him go, felt his pinhole eyes following him all the way to the door. What Finn couldn't tell was if Glad was following him with curiosity or suspicion. Did he know that, as his hair hung forward, it had revealed a dark bruise on his neck? Its edges were yellow and fading, but pressed into his flesh was the unmistakable imprint of a star.

Just the kind of bruise someone might have if they had been hit with a star-shaped fishing weight.

It had been Mr Glad at the harbour.

Mr Glad at the gateway.

Mr Glad who was communicating with the Legends.

40

"Say that again, just so we can be clear about how wrong you are."

Finn's father had emerged for dinner that evening a little less gloomy than he had been over the past few days. The lighter mood had lasted all of the two minutes it took him to ask Finn if he was OK, and for Finn to reply with a series of tentative questions about Mr Glad, how long his dad had known him, how close they were and if he had any suspicions that, you know, maybe he could be, if you want to call him that, a traitor.

"Go on, Finn. Run it by me again."

"Don't wave the fork at him, Hugo," said Finn's mother.

Finn wrapped his arms tightly across his chest. "I know I rammed something into the neck of whoever attacked me at the harbour. I'm just saying what I saw."

"No, you're saying what you *think* you saw. Glad has been through enough scrapes to earn a few bruises and scars. When I was your age…"

"Great, here we go again."

Finn's dad glared at him and continued. "When I was your age, Mr Glad practically lived in this house. He comes from a family of Fixers. Loyal. Always there when we wanted them."

"Finn obviously believes he saw something," said Finn's mother. "You should have told me about this fight in the first place anyway."

"Don't start, Clara. I'm the one out there with him, training him, trying to get him ready to become a Legend Hunter. It's hard going, trust me. This sort of stuff is going on in his head all the time."

"I'm right here, you know," said Finn. "Say it to me directly."

"My place on the Council of Twelve is probably gone because of everything that happened at the harbour."

"Why do you even want to join them, Dad? I don't get it. It sounds totally boring, just rules and regulations and sitting at desks all day and—"

His father cut him off. "There are countless Legend Hunters across the world sitting around doing nothing but polishing their spears. I refuse to be one of those when Darkmouth is finally rid of Legends for good.

Besides, despite *everything* that's happened in this family, they're giving me a chance to rescue its reputation. *Our* reputation. I won't have you ruin that for me."

"Calm down, Hugo," said Finn's mother. "Show some sympathy."

"I'm trying. Every day I'm trying, but there's always something else to test me."

"Did it ever occur to you, Dad, that this mightn't be my path?" asked Finn.

"Your path?" he said, a fleck of meat shooting across the table. "Your *path*?"

"I'm trying to tell you something, but you won't believe me," said Finn, knife and fork gripped upright. "I've been trying to talk to you about lots of things, but you won't ever listen. About Mr Glad, and that Hogboon and what he said. And now Emmie has told me they came here to watch me."

"When are you going to learn not to believe anything they say to you?" said his father.

"So, maybe there is something going on. Maybe I'm not even supposed to be a Legend Hunter," said Finn. "Maybe I *am* meant to be different?"

His father released his cutlery halfway across the table. "You're different all right. Don't think I haven't

271

noticed how you hardly touch your meat, Finn. You push it around the plate, trying to hide it, but it doesn't go near your mouth. He's a vegetarian, Clara. Where did he pick that up from? Not from my side."

"Something is happening, Dad. It doesn't matter how much you try and distract me from it, I know there's something you're not saying."

"Hugo, you need to listen to him," said Finn's mother. "And it's time you told him a few truths too."

"Right, Finn," his dad continued. "Here's a truth. Just before I become the first member of this family to join the Twelve, you want me to go to the Council and tell them that my Fixer – a man they gave their highest honour to – is conspiring with the Infested Side."

"I'm only telling you what I saw, Dad."

"Maybe I'll make some jokes about their personal hygiene while I'm at it."

"It was Mr Glad who attacked me," said Finn. "I know it."

"When you know something, it's because I tell you. And here's today's lesson: the Infested Side will freeze over before I accept that my oldest friend is a traitor."

Finn's father was breathing angrily through his nostrils, his chest rising and falling. His phone buzzed, sliding a few centimetres across the table, and he picked it up and read a message. As he did, his left eye twitched.

He looked at Clara.

"What does it say?" she asked.

He handed her the phone, got up and left the room.

Finn stood up to lean over his mother's shoulder and read the message. There was only one line.

PRIORITY EXECUTE ORDER 23b PARAGRAPH 5.
SUBJECT: GLAD.

"What does that mean, Mam?"

"I'm not positive," said Finn's mum slowly, "but I have an idea it means your dad needs to start listening to someone other than himself."

41

Finn's father poked his head round the kitchen door again, a stony expression on his face. "Follow me."

Finn dragged himself away from the table and trailed his father through the Long Hall, figuring they were heading to the library. But his dad stopped short in front of the portrait of Gerald the Disappointed.

"That wasn't his original Hunter name," said his father. "Do you know what it was?"

Finn shook his head.

"Gerald the Fierce. And do you know why they changed it?"

"No."

"Because of me. When he sat for this portrait, he was supposed to be finished as a Legend Hunter. He was supposed to be tending to those bonsai trees, whittling axes and generally enjoying his hobbies. He was supposed to be free from the day-after-day, hour-after-hour, minute-by-minute responsibility of keeping Darkmouth safe."

His father angrily opened the door to a narrow room opposite and from within it grabbed a fighting suit. Sliding into it, he snapped shut clasps round his legs and shoulders. "Instead, while that portrait was being painted, he had a child running around his office. Me. And he wasn't free because of the man next to him. His son. My father. Niall Blacktongue."

Finn peered at Niall Blacktongue's portrait. The Legend Hunter looked nervous, as if he was afraid to meet the eye of the viewer. He seemed more interested in the bits and pieces scattered around him.

"If you want to do things differently, Finn, then go ahead," snapped his father. "Try it. But you'll end up like my father, abandoning everything you're supposed to protect. And I'll end up like Gerald, picking up the pieces."

Finn examined his grandfather's face. He thought he saw something new in those eyes. A clarity of purpose suggesting itself through the meekness Finn had always seen.

"If you don't tell me what he did, how can I avoid whatever mistakes he made?"

His father sighed deeply before lifting his helmet and pushing through the door into the library and grabbing a Desiccator. Then he made straight for the hidden way through the shelves. Finn followed him, emerging on to the street to find Steve, in a fighting suit, leaning casually against his van.

"You got the order from the Twelve then?" asked Emmie's father.

"I guessed that was your doing," said Hugo.

"I saw what happened at the harbour. I tracked that gateway and watched from the van. I had to report to the Twelve."

"The fog there was thicker than your skull. You can't have seen much."

"Mr Glad was first on the scene, but I didn't see him approach, only leave. He must have got there before any of us. When you said there had been a human at the gateway, I didn't add it up at first. But then I figured it out: it had to be him. And we have to arrest him."

Finn finally realised what was going on, understood that he was right in his suspicions.

"Maybe. But did you tell the Twelve that we saw *you*

leave that scene too?" asked his father.

"The problem here, Hugo, is that you can only see what you want to," responded Steve.

"I already told you, this is my town."

"And this is your mess."

"The Twelve gave me this order – I don't need an apprentice getting in my way," said Hugo.

"But you do need that place on the Twelve. You can leave me behind, but I don't think you'll abandon that chance."

"Wait here, Finn," said his father. Then he jumped in his car and pulled out quickly. When Steve ran to his van and tore away in pursuit, Finn saw Emmie standing on the road in the twilight.

"Oh great," groaned Finn.

"My dad told me to stay here while he gets Mr Glad." she said contritely. "He even brought a Desiccator this time, so it must be serious."

This surprised Finn. His dad had left with a Desiccator too, but he hadn't expected it to be used on a human. Emmie and Finn listened to the distant grunt of the vehicles on their way to Mr Glad's. A question burned in Finn's mind.

"Emmie, why do you think the Council wanted you to watch me?"

"I told you," said Emmie. "I don't know. They're

concerned about you."

"Why?"

"I don't know."

Finn rubbed his face, tried to wipe the frustration away. "You said there was a prophecy."

"Yeah, but I don't know what it is."

"You won't tell me, you mean," said Finn.

"No, honestly, I don't know," insisted Emmie. "I was just asked to hang around with you, to get inside your house, to tell Dad what was going on with you."

"You're just another person who won't tell me what I have a right to know. Even the Legends seem to know something about me that no one else will talk about."

"Then why don't you ask one of them?" said Emmie.

"One of who?"

"The Legends."

"Yeah, sure, just wait for a portal to open and—"

"You don't need to wait for that," said Emmie.

It took him a few seconds to cotton on to what she was getting at.

"Er, the library?" she said slowly, as if he was an idiot.

Which, he realised, he was.

42

Finn stood in the centre of the library knowing two things: he shouldn't be doing this; and Emmie certainly shouldn't be anywhere near him while he was doing it.

It was a simple matter really. The reconstructed parts of the weapon that made up the Reanimator were still propped up against the library wall. The Hogboon was in his jar, at the front of a low shelf.

"I wanted to tell you we were here to spy on you," Emmie was saying now. "I just couldn't. I wasn't allowed. I would have got into awful trouble."

Finn grabbed what he needed while she blabbered.

"But I really enjoyed hanging out with you," she continued. "Really. I hated lying to you. Although I didn't lie, I just never told you the truth."

"I'm fine on my own," said Finn.

"I thought you might want my help here, with

the Re—"

"I don't just mean right now."

"Oh."

Even as he fought to keep his distance from Emmie, he felt an infectious creep of bravado. What he was doing went against everything his father would want him to do, but it felt like the only thing he could do.

"I think I can remember enough about how my dad reanimated the Legend," he said, still refusing to make eye contact with Emmie. "You grab that Desiccator and shoot if there are any problems."

"Yeah, about that..."

"Just do whatever you've done in training." He started to move about, grabbing what he needed.

"I..." said Emmie hesitantly. "I haven't trained that way."

"Really?"

"My dad's quite protective. I mean, I train, but he won't let me use a Desiccator yet. He did let me hold one once, but that was it. He said it might take my eye out."

Finn allowed a sense of superiority to warm his mood. This night was getting a little better already.

A weak light came from Mr Glad's shop, leaking in through a darkening laneway, throwing Hugo and Steve's shadows against the wall they crouched by.

"We'll go round the back," whispered Steve, visor raised, Desiccator propped on his shoulder.

"We'll go in the front," said Hugo, standing up and moving on ahead.

They stood either side of the doorway. Baskets of electrical bric-a-brac were piled at the shopfront, ready for another day of waiting for customers who would never come.

"You still don't believe he would betray us, do you, Hugo?"

"He has nothing to gain."

"Looking at the state of this place, it looks to me like he has nothing much to lose," said Steve.

Hugo raised his Desiccator to his shoulder. "There will be no need to shoot, so don't do anything stupid. Now let's get this over with."

From his belt, Hugo fished out a small cigar-shaped object, jammed it into the keyhole and pressed the top. There was the muffled crack of a splintering lock. The door eased open.

"Drag that cage over here," Finn told Emmie.

She had finally stopped talking and, as Finn placed the

sphere of desiccated Hogboon on the floor of the cage, he caught her watching him, knowing she wasn't just curious but impressed by his apparent expertise. He put on his most convincing look of confidence, all the while willing himself not to screw it up.

Finn took hold of the Reanimator and repeated the moves he had seen his father make, pushing up the switch with his thumb and waiting as its high whine gave way to a tick of readiness. Then he placed its tip on the shrivelled Hogboon. "You might want to stand back," he told Emmie.

The desiccated ball glowed, then cooled, hopped and twitched, until the return of the Legend was announced with a scream that might have been heard in every Blighted Village on the continent.

The low, soft light in the shop threw shadows against the wall, the silhouettes of old brass kettles and plastic pipes hanging from the ceiling in bunches, clanging a little as the two men crept by. Hugo stopped to find a switch on his helmet that turned on the built-in night vision, sending his world flaring into shades of granulated green. Steve walked into the back of him.

"Why don't you just ring the doorbell?" hissed Hugo.

"And why don't you give him a call if you believe he's no reason to hide?" was Steve's whispered reply.

They moved on through the shop, stepping over boxes and barrels, picking their way through the gap in the countertop and towards the rear room, hidden behind the gentle sway of hanging beads. They waited either side of the door. Squinting through the quarter-light, Steve thought he could see a figure on a chair by the far wall. Through his night vision, Hugo could see the definite silhouette of a person, unmoving, slumped forward a little under a wide-brimmed hat.

Steve placed a hand in the beads to move inside. Hugo gripped his wrist, holding him back, then slid ahead through the curtain. He crept towards the figure in the chair silently. Reaching it, he slowly bent down and peered into its face for a second until he was sure of what he was seeing.

He turned off his night vision and lifted his visor. "It's just a mannequin," he said.

"A decoy?"

Hugo listened, but heard nothing in the building save for the thoughts whirring through his head and the crumbling of his certainty. He walked to the bed and prodded it, knowing that Mr Glad wasn't there. He turned on a lamp, bringing soft light to the room.

"Not exactly penthouse luxury, although he's got some nice gear here," said Steve. "Does he have any other hideouts?"

Hugo shook his head, thinking it through, staring at one of Mr Glad's Fingerless Grenades that was sitting on the floor.

"I'll have to grab a few things from here," Steve said, moving slowly across the room towards the mannequin. "Once we've found him and desiccated him, of course. Maybe our plastic friend here will tell us something."

Hugo saw the line of wire running from one grenade that was nuzzled close to another, and on to another, until the wire ended, tied to the mannequin's big toe.

"Don't move that!"

But Steve had already spun the mannequin round, yanking on the wire. Blades sprang from the closest grenade, pushing out a pin and triggering the blades on the next grenade, and the next, in a cascade running halfway round the room.

Tick, went the grenades. *Tick*.

43

"Stop doing that!" screamed Broonie, before collapsing to the floor.

Fifty-three seemingly endless seconds later, Broonie's intolerable tsunami of pain had receded into an almost bearable buzz of pins and needles through his small gnarled body. Some energy had seeped back into him, from the knotted knuckles of his toes to the drooping ends of his ears, and he had returned to a healthier, greener pallor.

Nevertheless, he steeled himself for disaster at any moment. This trip to the Promised World had not exactly gone well so far. Any journey that begins with having your finger cut off is never bound to be much of a holiday. But the way these humans kept destroying and remaking his body over and over made even the Fomorians look softer than the mud that pooled outside his hovel back home.

He really missed his hovel right now.

When he looked up again, the boy was pointing a weapon at him nervously.

"That was *brilliant!*" squealed the girl. "Let's shrink him and do it again."

"No, please," Broonie begged. "It feels like someone's pulled my brain out through my backside and then stuffed it in again."

Then Broonie's eyes narrowed with suspicion. "Where are the others? The adults?"

"Where does it hurt exactly?" asked the boy. "I've read a bit about animals, you know, medical stuff. I might be able to help."

"Animals!" Broonie said, horribly insulted. "I am not an animal. You're the animals. If you think I look strange, you should know you don't look too good yourselves, with your tiny ears, square teeth, strange-coloured skin and those pathetic little nostrils. You'd never find a mate with a nose that small."

"He's so cute," said the girl. "I wonder if he's met any Gorgons."

"Excuse me?" said Broonie.

"Or a Cyclops. Or any giants really. I'd love to meet one of those."

"I'm sure one could find space in its stomach if you really want to meet one that badly," said Broonie.

"Sorry about the whole shrivelling you and blowing you up again thing," said the boy, with a politeness that surprised Broonie. He'd been expecting to be hanging by his guts from a hook by now. That's the kind of thing he'd been told humans did. Apologising wasn't supposed to be in their character.

The boy continued talking. "My name is Finn. I live here. Her name is Emmie and you're better off ignoring her. Do you have a name?"

"*Do I have a name?* Honestly. What do you take me for?" The young humans kept staring at him until he gave in. "Brooniathon Elgin Astrophor Fleriphus." He registered their blank faces. "Broonie."

"I don't want to hurt you, Broonie," said Finn. "I just need to know what you meant, when you spoke to me."

"What I... what I meant?"

"You said something, to me. The other day. Just before..."

The other *day*? How long had it been since they had last conducted their magic on him? Evidently even longer than it had felt. Still, Broonie had to think back to that moment, to recall just what it was he had uttered. Then it all came back to him.

"I'm not sure," he lied. "Maybe it was important. Maybe it wasn't. I'm finding it hard to remember."

"Oh, he's adorable," squealed Emmie. "A real Legend! You should keep him as a pet, Finn."

Broonie's eyes widened in disgust.

"But you said something to me," Finn pleaded. "I heard you."

"Did I? I don't know. It's hard to think clearly in this cage. So claustrophobic." He crouched, hands over his head. "Maybe I could breathe a little better if you let me out of here."

"No," said the boy.

"Then send me back into that half-death. If you cannot let me out, then I am of no use to you."

Finn hesitated, then moved forward, pulling a key from his pocket. "If you promise you won't do anything dangerous, then I will let you out. But *only* if you tell me what I need to know."

Broonie peeked out from behind his remaining fingers. He pitied these ugly humans with their ridiculous hairless ears.

"I promise," he said.

44

Finn opened the cage. The Legend that called itself Broonie stepped out and stood to its full height, which was still well short of Finn's.

"So?" enquired Finn.

"I'm thirsty," said the Hogboon.

There was a bottle of water on the desk and Finn motioned for Emmie to grab it. She handed it to Broonie.

He guzzled so that it ran down his cheeks and chin. "Extraordinary. I've never tasted anything like it," he gasped. "How did you get the taste of carcasses out of this water?"

"So?" Finn repeated, ignoring Broonie's question.

"So?"

"What did you mean earlier?"

"Oh yes, I'm having difficulty recalling it," said Broonie. "That shrinking device must have scrambled me a bit."

Emmie jerked forward. "You promised him! He let you out and you said you'd talk."

"But he hasn't let me out, has he?" said Broonie, looking towards the door, a gleam in his eye.

Finn's face fell in defeat.

"OK," he said, after a pause.

Emmie looked surprised. "If you want my advice, Finn..."

"I don't." Finn put his Desiccator down and stood over Broonie. "I need you to tell me what you know. If you do that, I'll help you leave. I'll help you escape."

Broonie licked the edge of his hand, savouring the last clinging drops of his water. "Then I will tell you what I know, which is that he is coming. It may already be too late."

"Who's coming?" asked Finn.

"Gantrua." He registered Finn's blank look. "Gantrua? Big violent type? Scars on top of scars. Rules over many Legends? Collects teeth? Owes me a finger?" Broonie held up his mutilated hand. "You haven't heard of Gantrua? Well, him. And his army. To be honest, I don't think I've got across just how terrible Gantrua is. He once used his bare hands to pull the head from—"

"Don't," interrupted Finn.

"Pulled the head off what?" asked Emmie.

Finn lifted a hand for silence. "Just tell me, what has that got to do with me?"

"I was getting to that," said Broonie. "There's a prophecy, a warning. I was sent here to give it to you."

"A prophecy about me?" asked Finn, his mind clogged as he tried to process the information.

"A child of the last Legend Hunter. They say he will be key to the closing of worlds."

"What does the prophecy say exactly?"

Broonie drew a breath in through his nose, his nostrils flaring like tiny green parachutes catching the wind. Then he recited what he knew. *"The Legends are rising, the boy shall fall."*

"What?" asked Emmie. "Like, he'll fall over? That doesn't sound—"

"No," said Broonie testily. "The boy shall *fall*. Die."

45

The word sat there between them for a few moments, foreboding and horrible.

Die.

"That's probably just a threat," Emmie insisted.

"No," said Broonie. "The prophecy is quite clear really. *The boy shall fall.*"

"I..." started Finn, but he didn't really know what to say.

"But maybe it's not even about Finn," Emmie said. "It's a bit vague."

"No, it's quite detailed actually," said Broonie. "There's more, you see:

Out of the dark mouth shall come the last child of the last Legend Hunter.

He shall end the war and open up the Promised Land.

His death on the Infested Side will be greater than any other."

"Oh," said Emmie.

"It's quite specific in fact," added Broonie.

Finn was breaking it down in his head, trying to put it back together in a way that might reassure him it was about something else or nothing at all. "I'm not even Complete yet," he said. "How do I know I'm even the last? It could mean someone else entirely."

He looked at Emmie, who realised she was supposed to be reassuring him. "Yeah, Finn. Could be anyone."

"Except," said Finn, "you said the Twelve sent you here to watch me, Emmie. Do you think they know something? I'm pretty sure my dad does."

"Could be," said Emmie.

There was a long pause.

"You going to be OK about it?" asked Emmie.

"About which bit? The whole finding out I'm going to die thing? Or the Legends rising up part?"

Emmie dropped her head. "Oh."

Finn looked at the Hogboon standing beside him and recalled something. A little giddiness skipped through him. "It can't happen yet, though, can it?"

"What can't happen?" replied Broonie.

"You said my death will be the greatest, but *'on the*

294

Infested Side'. Unless I travel there, I'm not going to die."

"Well, if that makes you feel better, then why not?"

"As long as I'm here," said Finn, "I'm safe."

"Maybe you'll be fine," said Broonie. "I mean, to start with you have to end the war, that's the first part of the prophecy. And how hard can it be to close off the gateways between two worlds and end thousands of years of war between humans and our kind?"

The Hogboon coughed up a forced laugh. Finn and Emmie stared at him.

"Ahem," said Broonie. "Anyway, I've told you what I know. Now it's your turn to hold up your end of the bargain."

"What a load of rubbish," said Emmie. "Give me the Desiccator. I'll shoot him."

"No!" shouted Broonie. "You're not blasting me with that thing again. I gave you what you needed, now give me what I was promised."

Finn grabbed Broonie by the arm and dragged him towards the back of the room.

"If you work that evil shrinking trick on me again," said Broonie, "I swear by my mother's feet I'll haunt you until the day your skin turns to soil."

Finn pulled Broonie through the dusty space, on to the

street, and released him.

"Run," said Finn.

Broonie looked around. "Run where?"

"Anywhere," said Finn. "Just don't come back."

But before the Hogboon could move, orange flashed against the night sky, a splash of fire from somewhere deep in Darkmouth. It was quickly followed by the crack of an explosion.

"What was that?" asked Emmie.

Finn's eyes told him one thing, but his heart confirmed it. He knew immediately the blast could only have come from one building.

46

Broonie ran from the house, dashing as fast as he could up the street and away. But Finn and Emmie didn't move, didn't speak, didn't flinch, even as a flash of lightning threw their silhouettes against the wall and thunder cracked hard against the sky. For a few moments, they felt their world burn in that fire, saw their worst fears engulfed in the smoke now pouring upwards into the black sky. When they finally spoke, they said the same word, at the same time.

"Dad."

Then, from the library, they heard a radio crackle into life and Finn's father coughing out an inaudible message.

Finn ran to the radio, picked up the receiver and shouted, "Dad? You're alive!"

"Just about. Booby trap. Shop destroyed." He coughed again through waves of static. The radio cut out briefly. "... only just made it out in time. Bad news about Steve, though."

Emmie looked at the radio, her dread clear.

"He's alive too," said Hugo, followed by an audible and angry protest from Steve. Emmie slumped in relief.

A crackle of interference bit through the radio static. A second later, a peal of thunder rumbled across Darkmouth. Rain began to hammer down.

"Finn!" shouted Hugo. "That sky. Get your suit on. Something big is…"

The rest was lost in white noise.

The alarm began to wail.

Lightning tore through the sky, shocking a realisation into Finn. "When my dad finds out about all of this, about me letting a Hogboon go, it won't matter whether I'm on this side or the Infested Side. He's going to kill me first."

From *A Concise Guide to the*
Legend Hunter World, Vol. 6,
Chapter 13: 'Prophecies – Past,
Present and Future'

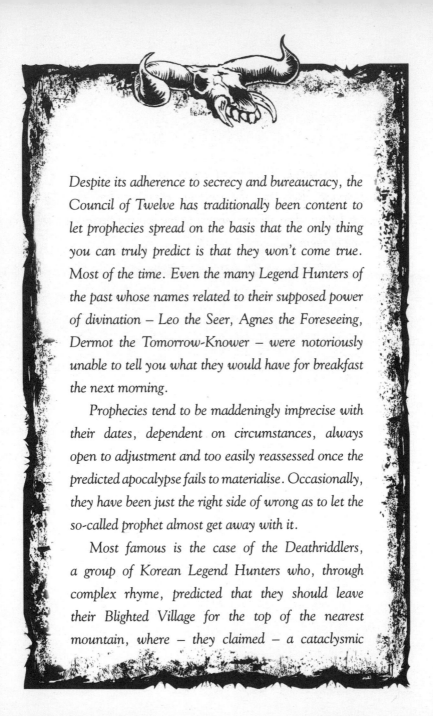

Despite its adherence to secrecy and bureaucracy, the Council of Twelve has traditionally been content to let prophecies spread on the basis that the only thing you can truly predict is that they won't come true. Most of the time. Even the many Legend Hunters of the past whose names related to their supposed power of divination – Leo the Seer, Agnes the Foreseeing, Dermot the Tomorrow-Knower – were notoriously unable to tell you what they would have for breakfast the next morning.

Prophecies tend to be maddeningly imprecise with their dates, dependent on circumstances, always open to adjustment and too easily reassessed once the predicted apocalypse fails to materialise. Occasionally, they have been just the right side of wrong as to let the so-called prophet almost get away with it.

Most famous is the case of the Deathriddlers, a group of Korean Legend Hunters who, through complex rhyme, predicted that they should leave their Blighted Village for the top of the nearest mountain, where – they claimed – a cataclysmic

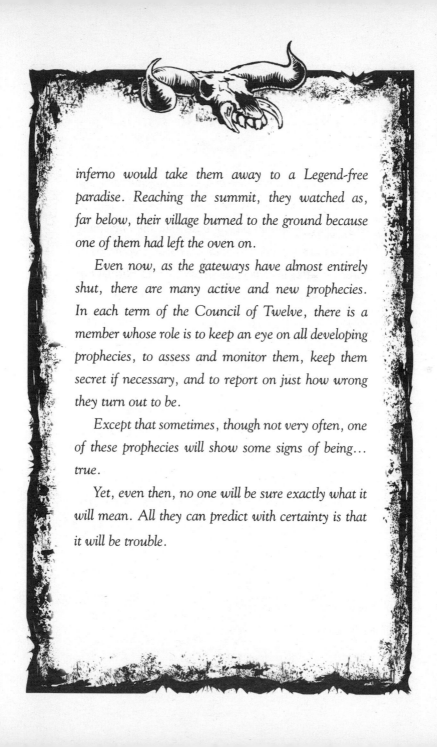

inferno would take them away to a Legend-free
paradise. Reaching the summit, they watched as,
far below, their village burned to the ground because
one of them had left the oven on.

Even now, as the gateways have almost entirely
shut, there are many active and new prophecies.
In each term of the Council of Twelve, there is a
member whose role is to keep an eye on all developing
prophecies, to assess and monitor them, keep them
secret if necessary, and to report on just how wrong
they turn out to be.

Except that sometimes, though not very often, one
of these prophecies will show some signs of being...
true.

Yet, even then, no one will be sure exactly what it
will mean. All they can predict with certainty is that
it will be trouble.

47

Finn ran down his street, his fighting suit clattering like cymbals alongside the unpredictable beat of the thunder crashing down on Darkmouth. He reached the end of his road just in time to be met by his father screeching to a stop, throwing open the door of the car and telling him to jump in.

Finn's father looked scorched, his face bloodied and blackened, his fighting suit splattered with the dust of pulverised brick, but he seemed to be otherwise OK.

"Dad, I'm so glad you're—"

"Look at that," Hugo said, gesturing at the scanner.

It was riddled with green pulses. Finn counted five, maybe six. Some flashed in and out and didn't reappear. Others seemed to be fixed and ominous.

"An attack?" asked Finn.

"An invasion," said his father.

"Are we going to use that device in your library?" asked

Finn. "Just blast them all?"

"No," his father said firmly. "It didn't work properly last time, and I still don't know why. It might destroy them, it might not. It might do worse. A few vaporised goldfish I can live with. A few vaporised townspeople would be a different matter. I can't risk that. Not yet. We'll take the old-fashioned route for now."

"Are we going to be able to hold them all off?"

"There's only one way to find out," said his father, pulling away again so fast the wheels threw up a spray of gravel. Steve's van screeched into view, skidding in front of them and forcing him to swerve to a stop.

Emmie's father ran out from the van, his fighting suit and helmet on, visor pulled open as he squinted through the driving rain. He rapped on the window. "There are too many gateways opening for just the two of you."

"Cover the strand," said Hugo. "There are two gateways there. Keep your radio on my frequency. No medieval weapons. Don't be an idiot. And, if I tell you to do something, do it. Think you can manage to handle that?"

Steve sighed and sprinted back to the van. As he opened the door, Finn could see Emmie in the passenger seat. She was wearing her fighting suit. Even from a distance, both it and the helmet she held in her lap gleamed in their newness. He couldn't be sure, but Finn thought she flashed him a smile, perhaps an effort to be reassuring when she was clearly looking for reassurance herself.

He gave her a thumbs up.

Both vehicles headed off, turning in different directions at the end of the street.

"Finn," said his father, "this is probably going to get rough. You're going to have to cover a gateway by yourself. You can take the one near the school and I'll handle the couple that are popping up near the bridge." He pulled the small screen from the dashboard and handed it to Finn. "Keep an eye on the scanner. If your gateway closes, run to the nearest alternative. Is your radio working this time?"

Finn pressed its button, wincing at the feedback that pained his eardrum.

"Dad, what happened at Mr Glad's?"

"You were right about that man," said his father. "That's what happened."

Finn felt a mixture of relief and embarrassment at this strange moment in which he had been right and his father wrong, rather than the other way round. Even as they sped through familiar streets, it felt as if the world had turned upside down.

The car splashed down a narrow road, bumping through a mini lake in the crater gouged from the main street by a Desiccator where the Wolpertinger had come through.

"There's something else on your mind, though," his father said. "I can practically hear your brain working."

Finn thought about saying more and decided against it. "I'm feeling OK, I think."

The car pulled up at the school. Carrying his Desiccator and hooking the scanner to his belt, Finn pushed open the car door and jumped straight into a deep puddle. His boots immediately filled with water.

"Sorry I can't stay, Finn."

"You'd only get in my way, Dad."

Smiling, his father drove off.

Finn ran towards the school, diving through the narrow gap in its high front walls. On the other side of the empty car park, up a rise by the entrance to the school, he saw the gateway. There was no sign of anything else. No Legend scrabbling for a way out. No thick dust settling even in the wet. No man in a hat primed to strangle him. Nothing.

The gateway cast a golden glow on the water running down the brick and into a stream that snaked through the street. There was nothing for Finn to do but crouch down in his sodden boots and wait.

The radio hissed into action. He heard Steve's voice. "We're here. Lock and load," he announced.

Finn winced, wondering how Emmie was reacting to her father's obvious giddiness. He imagined her out there in Darkmouth, at a gateway with her father, hair pushed back inside the helmet, mouth open at the sight of that window into the Infested Side. Untrained. Vulnerable.

"I'm at a gateway at the top end of Deadhill Lane," said his father over the radio. "No sign of life here. Anybody?"

"Not here," said Steve.

"Nothing, Dad," confirmed Finn.

"There's another one a bit further west," said Hugo. "I'll check that. Stay alert, everyone."

After a minute, Emmie's voice came over the radio. "Finn? Can you hear me? How are you doing?"

"Essential communication only, you two," his father interrupted. "I'm at the other gateway now. It's about the same size, but nothing has come through it. I'm going to sit tight here. I'd suggest everyone do the same."

Rain fired at the ground like shrapnel; a crescendo in

the alley where Finn huddled and waited. The gateway remained where it was, fixed in place, effervescent light gently pulsing at its edges. For something that had brought such terror into this world, Finn found it strangely inviting.

He edged closer, until the light lapped at his visor. Pulling a glove from his right hand with his teeth, he touched it.

The gateway's surface was warm, almost ticklish. He pushed his hand in a little further and watched the light pool about it like liquid. His hand almost entirely disappeared until his fingertips registered a shock of cold air. Then he remembered the stories of Legend Hunters who'd got too close to these things and pulled back quickly, examining the dark dust forming over his fingers, thickening under his nails, stubborn even in the heavy rain.

He put the glove back on and resumed his wait.

Steve's voice came on the radio again. "They've got us on a wild Legend chase."

Nothing followed but the hiss of the radio and the rumble of thunder.

Concentration wavering, Finn lifted his visor a little and, using his forearm to wipe the rain off the scanner

screen, looked at the blinking green lights. They seemed to have become fixed in place, five in all, spaced irregularly. But there was something about the arrangement of the gateways that bothered him, something he thought he should be seeing.

But he didn't get a chance to think about it.

The gateway dimmed a little, then brightened again. Finn raised his Desiccator and took a step back as a Manticore appeared in the air, claws drawn and teeth bared. Finn pulled the trigger.

Nothing happened.

48

Leaping from the gateway, the Manticore hit the ground awkwardly, collapsing on to its shoulder and skidding.

Finn pulled the trigger again. Still nothing. No blue fire. No glowing net. Only a pathetic, sickly wheeze from its malfunctioning barrel.

The radio clicked into action. It was Steve. "Hold on, Hugo, something is... Here they come!" It was followed by the violent *phzzzzt* of a Desiccator firing, then the hiss of static.

"What is it?" demanded Finn's father over the radio. "What type?"

Steve's response was drowned by the sound of shooting. Finn was sure he heard Emmie scream.

Then the radio cut out again.

The Manticore quickly righted itself and pounced at him. Finn yelped and threw his Desiccator at the airborne Legend. With pure luck, it struck the creature right between the eyes and the Manticore crashed to the ground and lay there, unmoving.

Finn breathed heavy gulps of relief, the steam rising and fading on his visor, and tried to figure out if he'd been unlucky that his Desiccator didn't work or lucky with his throw. Either way, the Manticore was out cold because of him, and he allowed a small smile to force its way on to his face.

He remembered the radio and hesitated before pressing the button. "Dad..." he began.

His father came back on, shouting, "Contact! Contact!"

Over the radio, Finn heard a sound that was suddenly sickeningly familiar: the wheeze of a malfunctioning Desiccator.

Steve's voice returned, struggling to be heard above the sound of a fierce battle. "Manticores!" A *phzzzzt*. Silence again.

Hold on, thought Finn. *Manticores?*

Then his father's voice. "More coming through here too. Desiccator not firing. Switching to close-quarter weapons."

"Time to get medieval, Hugo!" Steve yelled in glee

over the din at his end.

"Finn?" asked his father. "What's your status?"

At that moment, Finn's head was busy with three competing thoughts.

First was how unlikely the odds were that both his and his father's Desiccators would seize up, in the same way, at exactly the same time.

The second was that there was still something about the pattern of these gateways that seemed a little too neat.

And third, gradually elbowing its way to the front of his mind, was the realisation that in the gateway he faced, a dark blob was getting closer.

Another Manticore spilled on to the tarmac. A second emerged almost immediately behind, landing on top of the first, scratching and biting.

When the Manticores finally stopped attacking each other, Finn was gone.

49

For half a second, lightning showed Finn the way down the empty school corridor, illuminating a thousand forced grins on the faded class photos scattered along the wall.

Then blackness again. No sound but for Finn's slow creak past classrooms. Through his radio, he could hear the sounds of a town under attack, his father occasionally shouting the latest from his hand-to-claw fight with invading Manticores, Steve responding with yells of delight and the spit of a Desiccator. He heard Emmie too, saying something. "I'll go to the car," or maybe, "I'll throw the bar," he wasn't sure. But she sounded OK, and he felt relief at that.

From inside or outside the school – he couldn't be sure which – Finn heard the distant sound of a bin being knocked over and a crash of cans tipping out. He froze and lifted his visor a little to hear better. All he could make out was the rain outside.

Finn kept moving through the corridors, looking for the right place to hide, perhaps to ambush. But ambush with what? He had his Desiccator, but it felt lifeless in his hand.

He crept onwards through the building. Lightning briefly revealed a stuffed fox mid-prowl, mid-snarl, in a glass box. A rumble of thunder followed.

He wondered what his father would do in these circumstances, but quickly remembered that his father *was* in these circumstances and wasn't creeping round a school, looking for somewhere to hide.

Maybe it was better to ask himself what his father would *want* Finn to do in these circumstances. But he knew it definitely wouldn't involve creeping round a school, looking for somewhere to hide.

Yet here he was.

It seemed as if the storm had abated a little. The gaps between flashes of lightning were longer, meaning greater stretches of the pitch-blackness as Finn moved through the corridors. He checked his scanner and saw that the gateway outside the school had closed.

Finn reassured himself that he knew these halls, strolled through them almost every day, knew their angles and turns, could have navigated them blindfolded. Then he walked smack into a wall he didn't expect to be there.

His grunt, and the sound of a small shockwave rippling through the suit, seemed to echo round the entire building. He held his breath, stood absolutely still, his eyes wide.

Lightning lit the hall. No Manticores. Darkness again.

He lifted his visor a little, but couldn't see any better. In the blackness, he searched for the button on the side of his helmet that activated the night-vision function and switched it on. Instantly, the world shifted: becoming a basic rendering of green blobs and dark patches.

Especially green was the Manticore-shaped blob only a couple of metres away.

Maybe it would go away if he turned the night vision off. So he did that.

An otherworldly voice, low and malevolent, floated across the blackness: "What is in the dark and not too bright?"

He turned the night vision back on. The green blob jumped at him, snarling.

Finn fell on to the floor and began scrabbling away backwards, but the Manticore reached him quickly and sank its teeth into the armour at Finn's knee.

He belted the Legend with the butt of his Desiccator until it let go, a couple of its teeth following after it. As the Manticore jumped again at him, Finn launched his Desiccator at it, striking it square in the jaw. Another tooth popped free.

Undeterred, the Manticore swung its tail towards him and fired off a poisonous dart. Finn felt the missile lodge in the small gap he had opened in his visor, its razor tip almost scratching at his chin.

In shock, Finn yanked the dart out. The Manticore came at him again, claws and broken teeth bared, and, just as its front paws reached his shoulder, Finn stabbed the creature in the belly with its own dart. The Manticore howled and, with its claws dug into Finn's suit, began to flail horribly until Finn threw the Legend free. The Manticore dropped to the ground, jabbering crazily. Despite its aggression, Finn felt a welling sympathy for it. This close up, it was actually a beautiful creature, its coat a golden sheen, the skin beneath it taut against its muscles. He half reached out, wondering if he should perhaps help it.

It tried to bite him. Finn jumped back, suitably chastened, feeling a crunch beneath his feet. The Manticore's jabbering calmed and it slumped suddenly into complete stillness.

As Finn's nerves settled again, he felt a growing delight bubble through. *Does this count?* he wondered. He had stopped two Manticores after all. He had felled them, immobilised them, finally beaten Legends. *Is this a successful hunt? And that crunchy stuff I stepped on: that was its teeth!*

He stepped away and tried not to think about that.

His radio came to life again, but all he could hear was his father's steady, controlled grunts as he fought. It clicked off, then on once more, replaced by Steve's Desiccator firing furiously. Finn again thought of Emmie out there, and wondered if she was involved in that battle or stuck in the van, safely removed from the action.

His vision went white with lightning, except for the long dark shadow of the final Manticore, which loomed along the wall of a bisecting corridor.

Finn's radio crackled in his earpiece. Flustered, he grabbed at it to muffle its tinny sound. But it was too late.

Out there in the dark corridors, the remaining Manticore had heard the tiny disturbance. The Legend turned and stalked in his direction.

50

The human was close. The Manticore could feel it. It could smell it too, although the scent was almost overpowered by the appalling odour of generations of juvenile humans that had soaked into every pore of the building.

The Legend moved stealthily forward while trying to concoct a particularly impressive riddle for its moment of triumph. Something original, perhaps witty. Something to tell its friends about when it returned home.

Briefly distracted by that thought, it rounded a corner on to another corridor, registered nothing and moved on.

Then a radio crackled again, louder this time. The Manticore paused, listened, its ears upright and swivelling like antennae.

It turned back towards the corner it had just passed and made its way up the hall.

In the darkness, the Legend could just about make

out the line of closed doors on either side of the corridor. Except for one. From behind that open door, a radio fizzled, throwing out distorted voices. The creature licked its lips, smiled at its fortune and at the particularly brilliant riddle it had decided upon.

The Manticore charged through the open door, pouncing into the room with a blood-burbling snarl. It smashed straight into brush handles and a stack of paint tins.

Lying on the floor was the radio. It crackled again.

Finn slammed shut the door to the janitor's cupboard before the Manticore could escape. He dragged a table across the door to wedge it tight. Then he grabbed another table and pushed it across too. He also rammed a chair against that table. Better to be safe than sorry.

Trapped, the Manticore scratched frantically at the door in an angry, loud, futile attempt to get out.

Relieved, Finn half fell backwards through the door of a classroom. It was his own. Feeling his way into it, he backed against a wall and slid down on to the floor. The night vision was becoming a strain on his eyes, so he turned it off.

As his eyes became used to the dark, he peered up at the window. Outside, the night grunted with thunder.

The scanner glowed weakly. There was nothing now where his gateway had been, but another had opened further east. He would be expected to handle it.

The position of these gateways prodded at his brain again. Something about them seemed to matter. He just couldn't figure out what.

From across the corridor, the Manticore continued its attempts to dig its way out of the cupboard, its vicious curses echoing across the halls.

Lightning lit the classroom, flashing bright across the whiteboard, which was decorated with the triangles and angles from Finn's maths class. As thunder rumbled across the sky, a realisation crossed Finn's brain.

He hauled himself up and used the dim light of the scanner to illuminate the whiteboard. Then he looked at the screen of his scanner again. It wasn't obvious. It wasn't neat. But the gateways formed a rough pattern over the town. It looked like a crystal.

Across the screen, he pulled his fingers from each point inwards. His eyes widened. His mouth fell open. The lines he had drawn led to one definite point at the centre of Darkmouth.

One particular street.

One single building.

Finn narrowed his eyes. It was almost as if the gateways had been designed to draw attention *away* from that building, to distract from something happening there.

He hesitated for a moment, pushed down his fear. He knew what he needed to do. He knew where he needed to be.

He turned and sprinted for home.

51

Across Darkmouth, the rain flowed along the streets, windows shook with thunder and street lights flickered in the storm. Not for the first time, bizarre hybrid creatures were attempting to run riot through the town.

But the people of Darkmouth didn't do what they usually did. They didn't cower in doorways. They didn't hide indoors. The murmurings of discontent had grown in the stores and cafes, in the beauty salons and butchers, at the school gates where parents gathered and in the schoolyards where children played. The people of Darkmouth had been passive for too long. A storm had broken and their patience with it.

They emerged from houses and shops and restaurants. One by one. Then two by two. Small groups merging to march through the damp streets. All heading in one direction. To the source of this misery in their town.

*

Finn ran hard. As he got closer to his house, and further from any open gateway, it occurred to him that he had better be right about this – because he was supposed to be heading for another gateway, not away from them.

At the same time, he felt the familiar wobble in his legs as fear urged him out of any notions of being a hero. He ran through it, tried to leave it behind him on the drenched streets. The pattern of recent gateways had seemed unmistakable to him: they formed a jagged perimeter, spread wide away from the centre. That centre was his house.

If someone wanted to drag Finn and his father away from their base, this would be an effective way of doing it. And, if someone wanted to drag a Legend Hunter away from his base, it was never going to be for the most kind-hearted of reasons.

But, more than that, his mam was there.

It took him a while to notice the steady trickle of townspeople, despite the storm, moving in a direction that was suspiciously similar to the one he was headed in. He pushed on through Darkmouth's maze of streets, every step announced by the splash of boots in water and the clatter of his uniform. Rain obscured his vision and he almost missed the mob gathered in a small gap of a laneway.

He slowed and doubled back to see the crowd massed at a wall, screaming demands, calling for blood. Through their legs, Finn could make out a figure cowering against the brickwork and batting away the occasional kick and punch.

It was Broonie.

"Stand back," Finn said in the deepest, most authoritative voice he could muster, which wasn't particularly deep. Or authoritative. "I've got this Legend."

The crowd paused in their attack to watch Finn stride towards them, as tall as he could, visor down, waving them aside.

One man resumed his attempt to kick Broonie.

"I wouldn't do that if I were you," Finn said. "Kick that creature in the wrong spot and it will explode."

Everyone took a step back, although they didn't look entirely convinced.

Broonie jumped from the wet ground.

"Why should we trust you?" asked a man.

"Our mobile Legend Hunting unit is round the corner,"

said Finn. "We'll deal with this creature there."

"Don't let him take me," pleaded Broonie theatrically. "They do such awful things there."

"Go and get one of your weapons then," the man said to Finn. "We'll hold on to him until you come back and shoot him here."

"I could do that," said Finn. "But only if you want to all run the risk of being sucked into the, erm, Vortex of Tears."

"The Vortex of Tears?"

"It happened to my uncle once. He was there a thousand years before he was found again."

He pushed through the people, grabbed Broonie by the arm and dragged him away from the crowd. "That actually hurts," Broonie muttered.

"Silence, Legend," Finn commanded. He pulled Broonie round the corner, out of sight, and said, "Run."

"That's what you told me last time," said Broonie. "A direction would be good."

"Anywhere."

Broonie shook his head, sighed and pelted away, allowing Finn to resume his race back home, followed by a small angry mob that had quickly realised that there was no mobile Legend Hunting unit round the corner, no intention to kill the Legend and probably no Vortex of Tears, although no one was prepared to take the risk on that one.

52

Finn turned on to his street. There were a few dozen people there already, their anger crackling with the thunder.

"I stood in the salon and watched these people tear dangerously through our streets," he heard a woman say, her hair high and stiff, protected under a large orange umbrella. "This cannot go on any longer. We need to take matters into our own hands!"

"Should we ring the doorbell?" asked a man.

"I don't see Hugo's car here," said another. "Maybe they're not at home. We can call back later."

"No!" insisted the first woman. "We will not be kept out."

"Excuse me," said Finn, pushing his way to the front. He struggled to fish a keyring from a pocket tucked within his armour, and finally, under the uncomfortable gaze of a mob temporarily disconcerted by his arrival, managed to unlock the front door and go inside.

"Well, of all the..." harrumphed the ringleader before she was silenced by Finn closing the door on her.

Inside, the house was dark save for the occasional flicker of lightning; quiet except for the rain on the windows and the creak of Finn's fighting suit. He lifted his visor and crept on.

"Mam?" he croaked as loudly as he could. "You here?"

In a flash of light, Finn saw that the door to the Long Hall was open. He was startled by a bang behind him. Then the urgent rapping of a palm on the door. He spun back round towards the front door and saw a familiar silhouette hammering on its glass.

He let go of his weapon and opened the door for Emmie.

"Now listen, young man—" said the increasingly irritated woman at the head of the growing protest, but the rest of her speech was cut off by Finn slamming the door shut on her again.

"What are you doing here?" he asked Emmie.

"We've been calling you on the radio," she said, trying to catch her breath, "and it was silent until there was just some snarling from what sounded like a really angry Legend. I was worried something had happened to you, but my dad was having too much fun to care. It's like Christmas morning for him, all this shooting. Only he wouldn't let me do anything but watch from the van. So I said I'd run over to see if you were here. Which you are. So is everyone in the town. They're not happy out there. These fighting suits are itchy, aren't they?"

She finally took a deep breath.

Finn checked the scanner on his belt. Three gateways remained open.

"What are we actually doing here, Finn?" asked Emmie.

"I don't know exactly, but I suspect it's because someone doesn't want us here."

"Brilliant," said Emmie, then cocked her head in a quizzical manner. "Hold on. What?"

Finn showed her the scanner. "The gateways opened around the town, bringing us *away* from the house."

"So, we needed to come to your house because there are no gateways here."

"Yes, but that means there must be something else," he said eagerly, before calming down. "I think."

Emmie thought about that for a second. "Do you think that something could be a *someone*? Or a some*thing*?"

A sudden, distant thud echoed up the Long Hall.

Emmie looked at Finn. "You don't have to do this."

"No, *you're* the one who doesn't have to do this," said Finn. He moved towards the open door to the Long Hall, fighting the urge to stall and failing. "I'm supposed to be the Legend Hunter here. You don't have to come with me."

"Are you kidding?" she said, smiling. "We're in this together. I owe you that. Besides, you're the one with a Desiccator. Hold on, where's your Desiccator?"

"Oh yeah, about that. I threw it at a Manticore. It was a great shot actually..." But Emmie was already through the door. Finn followed, telling himself that whatever lay at the end of this hall would be nothing he couldn't deal with. He was a Legend Hunter. Almost. Some day soon. Maybe.

But then he reminded himself of all he had done so far tonight. Defeating Manticores. Outwitting them. Figuring out whatever it was he'd figured out, even if he hadn't quite figured out what that was yet.

And he'd done that despite wanting to run away at every turn. Even if he *had* actually run away at the school. But still. He had won. He had survived. So far.

They crept down the Long Hall, towards the thin

rim of light they could make out round the library door. The light cast a weak glow on the portraits – face after face – of Finn's ancestors, observing him and Emmie as they passed.

"It's the first time I've ever thought I might get a portrait one day," he whispered.

"You will, Finn. I know you will. You'll be Complete. You'll have a great ceremony."

"What do you mean?" asked Finn.

"My dad told me about the cannons."

"*Cannons?*"

His fighting suit clanked once and he paused for a moment, embarrassed. Emmie kept moving on.

"But that's not really what scares me right now," he said, catching up to her.

"What does?"

"That I might be the last portrait. That what the Hogboon said is true and that, when it all ends, I end with it too."

They had reached the library door and Finn's legs felt weak.

A stifled bang from within grabbed their attention. Finn looked again at Emmie for confirmation that she'd heard it too. She stared back. Neither of them said anything. It was only when she screwed up her face a little that Finn realised she was waiting for him to go first. He took a deep breath and opened the door.

He quickly wished he hadn't.

53

Mr Glad was scampering about the device that Finn's father had built. Punching buttons. Running a finger over the computer screen. Checking wires. Giving it a tap here and there with the back of a screwdriver.

"What are you doing?" asked Finn.

Mr Glad jumped as if startled, held a hand over his heart. "Well, boy, you took me by surprise there. So, you did make it after all. Maybe there's more to you than I thought. And I see you have your wee friend with you. Nice tailoring on that fighting suit, young lady."

He resumed tinkering.

On a desk, beside the computer, a radio clicked. Finn's father's voice emerged into the room briefly, almost incomprehensible against the noise of an ongoing fight. Mr Glad paused to listen, until the radio settled into silence again.

Something that sounded like scratching came from behind his father's invention.

"Mr Glad, what are you doing?" asked Finn again.

"I'd imagine it's quite chaotic out there," Mr Glad replied. "A little problem with the Desiccators, was there? Whoever could have known?"

There was more scratching from behind the device. Insistent. Maybe frenzied.

Mr Glad took his watch from the inside of his coat, examined it, then returned it to his pocket. "You know, boy, there are some advantages to earning the trust of a Legend Hunter. They let you inside their world. Not all the way in. Not to the centre. No. Only as far as they want to. But that can be enough to creep through their arrogance and condescension and into the blind spot. There's a lesson for you. Not that you'll get to use it."

He gestured at the centre of the floor. A mass of wires ran from the large device, coalescing at a glass of blue liquid that sat inside a metal cylinder smothered in electrical tape. Attached to it was a kitchen timer, its face grinding round with a fast *tick-tick-tick*.

"Is that a bomb?" Finn asked.

"Of course it's a bomb. Of a sort anyhow."

Finn peered at it. There were five minutes left on the timer.

The scratching continued from behind the device. Finn couldn't see what was causing it. He edged a little closer. "I don't get it," he said.

"You really are such a child, aren't you?" said Mr Glad, resuming his task.

"Why did you try to drown me?"

"You're forgetting that I rescued you, boy."

"I almost died," said Finn.

"I was angry. You provoked me, hit me. Anyway, the whole thing was a mistake. You and your father were both supposed to be busy at the other gateway as you had been the previous times. I did not intend to kill you. Not then anyway."

"Um… what kind of bomb is this?" Emmie asked nervously.

"Finally, someone with a whit of curiosity." Seeming invigorated, Mr Glad picked up the bomb and examined it. "It's more like the opposite of a bomb, to be accurate. Bombs destroy life. When the timer counts down and the liquid heats up, Hugo's device, as I have reconfigured it with the aid of this bomb, will…"

He gestured at the shelves lined with jars of desiccated Legends. "...*reanimate* life."

Finn turned slowly, dread creeping down his spine. He and Emmie scanned the dormant husks of Legends, gathered over many years, stored one on top of the other from floor to ceiling. Thousands of them.

An unimaginable army, about to be awoken.

The Legends are rising. Finn felt his legs weaken further.

Mr Glad returned to Finn's father's invention and gave it a tap with the end of the screwdriver. "Just as a Desiccator can be used to reanimate, this can do the same. Same principle, just on a grander scale. It was meant to shrink the entire Infested Side. Instead, it's going to wake them. All the ones here in our world."

"You're working for the Legends," said Finn.

"I am working for *myself* for once," said Mr Glad, losing his composure for a moment before regaining it, jiggling the screwdriver in his hand. "They just helped me make sure that, when your father built this device, he also brought into this room the only thing that could power it."

He opened his coat to reveal the three crystals – the Hogboon's finger, the Manticore's claw and the

Wolpertinger's fang. He pulled out two, opened the battery compartment and began attaching wires.

"It didn't work properly last time," said Finn.

"Of course it didn't. I made sure of that."

The scratching resumed. There was what sounded like a moan.

The timer counted down.

On the desk, the radio clicked. Emmie's father spoke, breathless. "They've slowed," he said. A burst of Desiccator fire followed. "I think the gateway's dimming."

Silence again.

"Now, boy, you've never struck me as the heroic type, but I won't take any risks. Step back."

"Why should I do that?" asked Finn.

"Because of this." Mr Glad reached down behind the device and pulled Finn's mother into view. Her arms were bound and her mouth was taped shut. Her eyes were wide with distress. Finn instinctively took a couple of steps towards her.

"I wouldn't go any further," said Mr Glad, pulling a fat-barrelled pistol from inside his coat and pressing it against Clara's temple. "I made this one myself. It turns the bones inside out. It's quite impressive actually,

338

although it's hell to clean up afterwards."

Finn stepped back. He couldn't take his eyes off his mother and fought every impulse to run towards her.

"Do you know how long it took me to tie your mother up, boy?" Mr Glad said. "She has some strength for a mere dentist. It's pulling all those teeth, I suppose. Now step back or her head will be messier than your room."

"But why are you doing this?" asked Finn.

"That's not for you to know," said Mr Glad, waving away the question with his pistol. But he reconsidered. "What I will say is that I'm doing this in part because of you. Enjoy that thought, young man."

Finn did not enjoy that thought. Nor did he understand what it meant.

"It's almost time!" exclaimed Mr Glad excitedly. He pushed Finn's mother down to the floor, then rooted in his breast pockets once again.

"Time for what?" asked Emmie.

"You're some girl for the questions, aren't you? You must drive your father quite mad."

Mr Glad removed the remaining crystal from his coat, juggled it until his palm held it in a firm grip, then raised it to just above shoulder level. "I have enjoyed our little chat. I really have. But I don't want to leave this any longer."

It was as if Mr Glad was trying to snag the crystal on the air beside him. He held it flat against his palm and pressed it outwards. Frustrated, he stood back, looked round the room while making some silent calculation, then shifted his position a couple of steps to the right.

This time, when he pulled his palm back, the crystal stayed where it was, fixed somehow on the air. Mr Glad stood away, before remembering to grab Finn's mother, who protested as he pulled her back with him.

A gust of wind whipped through the room, carrying a low, unnatural roar.

Mr Glad pulled Finn's bound mother further back as she struggled to push against the ground to keep pace with him. "You might want to get out of the way!" he shouted.

The air ripped open and a gateway exploded into the room.

Finn fell back, shielding his eyes from the momentary glare.

Mr Glad's mouth broke into a deep grin that stretched from one side of his greasy fringe to the other. "Isn't it beautiful?" he shouted.

And, at that moment, Emmie released her hand from the radio switch on the side of her helmet through which she been transmitting the last couple of minutes of Mr Glad's confession.

54

The day had begun for Sergeant Doyle as it always did. The toast popped. The kettle boiled. The police radio crackled on standby. And his letterbox jiggled with new mail that was never the mail he wanted.

This morning, his post had consisted of: an electricity bill; a flyer from the local supermarket that put the idea in his head that he'd have rashers for his dinner; and precisely no letters from headquarters confirming that he had been granted a transfer to Anywhere But Darkmouth.

Still, as he did most mornings, he ate his breakfast while fantasising about the arrival of such news. He pictured the envelope. The address: 'Sergeant Alphonsus Doyle, Darkmouth'. The official watermark stamped on the corner. He imagined unfolding the crisp white paper to steal a glance at the first line.

"Dear Sergeant Doyle," it would read, "We are

delighted to accept..." And there he would stop, savour the moment, sip on his cup of tea, compose himself before moving on. "We are delighted to accept your request for a transfer from Darkmouth. We are further pleased to inform you that you are to immediately report to your new posting on the tropical island paradise of Tahiti."

Maybe the Tahiti bit was overdoing it, but it was his fantasy, so he was allowed to dream as big as he wanted.

Today had kicked off with the customary absence of any such letter, only the realisation that it would inevitably be a day like every other. Or, given the frequency of Legend incursions in recent weeks, a day like every second day. He couldn't be sure if his patrol would be dull or disheartening. Either way, they weren't great options.

The complaint calls had been coming more regularly than ever. There were those with a specific grievance against Hugo's family: the McAnallys who had lost half a car to that clumsy child Finn; Mrs Lacey who had dropped her shopping when menaced by a monster; half of Jim Lacey's trawler being turned to metal mush in an instant by that boy again.

Then there were those who were just fed up.

"Why does this still happen?" they would ask him over the phone.

"What can be done about it?" they would enquire as he bought his lunchtime sandwich.

"What are you doing to end it?" they would nag when he stopped to tie his bootlaces.

This, he had decided, was way above his pay grade. Sergeant Doyle drove to town, making house calls to older townspeople, checking up on the businesses. He did some paperwork in the afternoon, although things were a little quieter than normal. For twenty minutes after 3pm, he locked the station door and took a nap at his desk.

When he was young and fresh to the force, Sergeant Doyle had nurtured ambitions of becoming a detective, of taking on a case, cracking the clues, identifying the guilty party after a moment of great logic, of the bad guy confessing all under the weight of Doyle's astonishing powers of deduction. "How did you ever guess it was me, Doyle?" they would ask as they were being led away in handcuffs.

"You almost got away with it, but for one fatal error..." he would explain in noble triumph.

None of which happened. Sergeant Doyle was a good policeman, but not a great one. Except good was useful. Good was acceptable. And good was considered enough for Darkmouth. There was no point in sending someone totally incompetent. They had done that once before and they were still finding bits of him a month later.

But neither was there any point in sending someone brilliant, because what was happening in Darkmouth was not a crime that needed solving.

So, good would do just fine. And Sergeant Doyle was a good man, in every sense of the word.

As the day had started like any other, so the evening repeated the pattern of the many that had gone before. He took the car out on a final patrol of the town, except that this one was greeted by a crack of thunder and rain falling fat and hard. Was that the forecast? He should have checked. Time would tell what kind of storm it really was.

He stopped off in the shop to grab a few rashers and threw in half a dozen sausages, some eggs, a handful of mushrooms and a tin of beans. Plus a couple of spicy wedges for good measure. He dashed back through the downpour and tossed it all on the passenger seat of his car, unclipped his tie and was about to turn the key in the ignition when he heard a sound that might generally be described as a commotion. Sergeant Doyle wondered if starting his car would mean he couldn't hear it and allow him the excuse of ignorance. But there it was again, this time all too clearly identifiable as a kerfuffle. The sergeant was a good man. He knew his duty. He pointed the car in the direction of the trouble and drove towards it, knowing the likely destination.

Even in the storm, people were streaming towards the street with no name. There were a couple of hundred at least. Maybe more.

They were shouting from under their hoods, waving their umbrellas as if they were spears. It was the cacophony of a town that had, finally, had enough. Sergeant Doyle stepped out of the car, zipped up his bright yellow jacket and dipped into his deep reserves of authority as he strode over to the front of the house. He pushed his way between the mob and the front door.

"Get out of the way, Doyle!" yelled a man.

"Now, folks..." he began.

"Stop protecting them and start protecting *us*," screamed a woman.

He raised his hands to calm them.

At the front of the crowd was a woman holding an orange umbrella over her sculpted hair. "Something must be done about those monsters in there," she announced, to the approval of the crowd around her. "They're destroying this town. They're destroying our livelihoods.

If you're not going to do it, then we will."

"Ah now, Mary, let's not be rash," said Sergeant Doyle in as soothing a voice as he could muster through his irritation. "It's a delicate situation for all of us."

A melon smashed against a window to his right, sending mush and seeds dripping down the arm of his uniform. That stain would take an age to get out. "Right," he said angrily. "That's enough."

There was another surge from the crowd, which seemed to have doubled already. They pushed forward, climbing the small stone wall, trampling through the small garden, crushing flowers. They jostled Sergeant Doyle aside and began pounding on the door.

"Get out of the way," said one particularly large man as he stepped back and took a shoulder charge at the door. With an alarming grunt, he bounced off it and on to his back.

"Here, give me a go," said another man. The door bowed just a little under his charge, with the sound of wood splintering around the locks inside. The man rushed at it again and the door buckled a little more. Then a final charge and it burst open, sending him crashing through on to the floor.

The crowd cheered. Sergeant Doyle sighed.

Behind them, someone screamed.

At the far end of the street, strange, cat-like creatures stalked under the street lights, spreading out to block the avenues of escape. One lifted itself and spread leathery, stunted wings. Then, much to the surprise of those people nearest, one of the creatures spoke.

"What becomes easier to kill the bigger it is?"

Somewhat alarmed and bemused by this turn of events, the crowd remained still. Finally, one man stepped from the pack and asked, "I'm sorry, but could you give us another clue?"

The Manticores attacked.

55

In the library, the timer on the bomb wound down. Three minutes left.

The gateway pulsed briefly. It sent a tiny shockwave through the room, which travelled across the floor, pushing up eddies of dust.

From the space behind the bookshelves came a cough: an audible splutter that echoed round the abandoned room.

They all turned sharply towards the sound. Finn recognised it. He saw his mother's eyes widen and knew she recognised it as well. Mr Glad grabbed her, lifted her to her feet and placed his weapon at her temple.

"Hugo?" he called.

No answer.

"Hugo, I know you're behind the trick bookshelf," Mr Glad said. Keeping an eye on the shelf, he addressed Finn. "I was here the day your father built that thing, young man. He has seen a lot of movies." Finn felt the breath leave him for a moment, then caught it again. There was a violence building in Mr Glad, his tightly clasped fists giving away the anger beginning to boil within him.

The only sound was the low rushing of the gateway and the rapid *tick-tick-tick* of the timer. Mr Glad pulled Finn's mam closer.

Finn's heart felt knotted. He was trapped, cornered. He looked to Emmie, whose face told him she was way out of her depth here. This was not the adventure she had expected. So, Finn did what he always wanted to do when trapped. He called out for his father.

"He has Mam, Dad!" he shouted. "He's going to hurt her."

"He can see that, you idiot," scolded Mr Glad, then focused again on the unseen figure behind the shelves. "Can't you, Hugo? You *are* there, I know it, like you're always there to remind me of my place. Like all the Legend Hunters. Countless numbers of them are alive thanks to people like me, yet it's always the Fixer who has to make the sacrifice. I've given my whole life to being an odd-job man."

Mr Glad pulled Finn's mother closer to the gateway.

"But you got a whole building, a whole street, a whole

town to call your own. You got Clara and, for all that he's worth, this idiot boy. What did I get? A certificate. *A piece of paper.*"

Spittle ran down the side of Mr Glad's mouth; the gun now trembled under his fevered grip. He glanced over at the timer as it ticked down. Two minutes.

Keeping his eye on his mother, Finn took a step forward, a small one, careful not to rattle his suit.

"Right, I'm sick of talking to a wall. Come out, Hugo, and show me some respect. *They* show me respect," Mr Glad shouted, pointing his weapon at the gateway.

The bookshelf swung open. Hugo emerged from the dark space. Relief flooded through Finn. His father was here. Everything would be fine now.

"Whatever you need," Hugo said to Mr Glad, "we can sort out for you."

"No, Hugo," said Mr Glad, steadier now, as if he had regained control. "I'm the Fixer, remember? I'm the one who does the sorting out. Me. Running. Fetching. Get this for me, Glad. Pick that up for me, Glad. Fix this, Glad. Well, this is one final fix. And, when the Legends reward me, it will not be with a scrap of paper to hang on my wall."

Holding Finn's mother, Mr Glad took another step

towards the gateway.

"No!" shouted Finn.

"Clara has nothing to do with this, Glad," said Finn's father, an edge of pleading in his voice.

"You're wrong, Hugo. You see, we ended up with three crystals, but two did fine for this device. That left me with one extra crystal as a means of escape."

Mr Glad pulled Finn's mother closer again, the light of the gateway almost lapping at them. "But I see now that I can send something far more valuable through there. You have always pledged yourself to this town. Sworn to protect it, to defend it, at all costs. But take away the armour, and the weapons, and the ego and I always wondered how far you were really ready to go, how much you're really prepared to sacrifice."

Finn's father moved forward a touch, the scarred breastplate of his armour catching the soft light of the gateway. The steel in his voice sliced through the air between them. "I will do what it takes."

Mr Glad held his gaze. "Let's see about that."

He pushed Finn's mother at the gateway's centre and let go. Her eyes widened and caught the reflection of the light. She fought the force of the push, but stumbled, unbalanced by the restraints on her arms and legs.

Finn ran forward and tried to catch her, but he was too late.

The light enveloped her. She disappeared completely.

Hugo had already reacted, covering the distance between himself and the gateway in a few strides. Without pause, he leaped straight after Clara.

The gateway swallowed them both.

Gone.

Finn stood frozen, concussed with shock. He waited for his parents to re-emerge. They would surely be back as quickly as they had gone. But there was nothing except a ripple across the deep yellow light of the gateway, like a pebble had been tossed into a pool.

Tick-tick-tick. The blue liquid in the canister burbled.

There were thirty seconds left on the timer.

"Well," said Mr Glad, bursting into a delighted smirk, his arms and gun hanging by his side. "Wasn't that something!"

Finn's rage propelled him towards Mr Glad. In the half-second it took to reach him, his mind flicked through the nights of training, the endless hours of repetition, the dozens of possible moves, all there to be plucked out at the precise moment he needed them. This moment.

Then he simply barrelled himself at Mr Glad's stomach,

hitting him hard and sending him flailing towards the gateway.

One leg already out of view in the glowing portal, Mr Glad managed to regain his balance. He steadied himself and stopped, a foot in both worlds, as he glared at Finn. "That wasn't very clever, was it?"

But Finn saw the change in the gateway before Mr Glad.

It trembled, wobbled.

Its glow deepened.

It collapsed, its jaws biting down on Mr Glad, who crumpled, dropping his gun and wriggling and fighting until he was horizontal, his lower half lost in a ring of hungry light.

Mr Glad screamed.

Around him, the gateway pulsed and gulped and strained, trying to close but blocked by the thrashing body in its mouth. Mr Glad reached out in a futile search for something to hold on to. Light began to flood through his body, pouring through his nose, his ears, his eyes.

On the floor, the liquid in the canister began to boil. The timer went *ting*.

Then a most surprising thing happened. Mr Glad stopped fighting his fate. Instead, he matched Finn's stare, grinned and looked to his wrist. Finn and Emmie followed his eyeline and saw a trigger poking out from his sleeve. Mr Glad pressed it.

As he did, the gateway's pressure finally overcame him. He convulsed as brilliance flooded through his body and blew him into a million points of sparkling light.

The bomb woke up, its metal exterior turning as the canister of bubbling blue liquid rose from the centre. A white flash ran along the wires, sparking the crystals where they sat and sending a shiver through the entire device.

Then nothing.

From outside on the street, they could hear screaming, the panic of a mob under attack. But inside there was silence once again.

"Maybe it isn't working," said Emmie.

The bomb exploded.

57

The blast turned the room blue before subsiding into a fine mist that drifted across the library and settled slowly on the floor, on the shelves and on Finn and Emmie.

They sat up from where they had dived, layered in blue, spitting warm liquid from their mouths, their hands sliding on the now damp floor.

In one of the jars, on the edge of a shelf high on the wall, a desiccated ball rattled. The same thing happened in a jar lower down. Then another. The shelves began to shake under a clatter of vibrating glass as it spread from shelf to shelf, from jar to jar.

"That's not good," said Emmie.

Finn opened his mouth to reply. Nothing came out but a dribble of blue.

The library was cacophonous with waking Legends, the oncoming march of an invading army being roused from a coma.

Finn jumped to his feet and ran towards the device. All around him, jars began to fall from their heights, smashing to the ground, where their desiccated spheres rolled free, the last spasms before Reanimation. He stood at the device and stared at the computer screen. It was filled with lines he didn't understand. Something very significant suddenly occurred to him. "I don't know what I'm doing!" he screamed at Emmie.

She slid over to him, shouting over the noise. "Do what looks right!"

Amid a shower of breaking glass, balls began to expand and scream, a howling chorus of reanimating Legends.

Finn thought of his mother and father, somewhere on the other side of the air, a whole world away. He heard the chaos of the street outside, a town in tumult.

The machine had been labelled with yellow sticky notes at each end of the large light switches. One had D scribbled on it and the other R. The switch was currently in the R position. His dad liked simplicity, Finn reminded himself. Even in disorder. The notes had to mean *desiccate* and *reanimate*. They had to, otherwise they were all about to die.

He pressed the switch to the D position. He figured

that if the device could reanimate all these Legends it should still be able to desiccate them all too, like his father had originally intended.

Maybe.

The dial was a third of the way up. Finn hesitated over it, but a *smash* as something large fell from a height encouraged him to turn it up high.

His finger hovered over the large red button and the awful things that might happen rushed through his mind.

He could destroy the house.

He could accelerate the waking of the Legends. Who would destroy the house.

He could desiccate Emmie.

He could desiccate *himself*.

"What if I desiccate the whole town?" he called at Emmie, his heart pounding, the enormity of the decision beginning to crush him, narrow his vision. *I could always just run for it*, he thought.

"Just do it!" yelled Emmie. "We're all going to be dead anyway in a minute."

Finn smashed hard on the button.

A shockwave tore across the library, knocking Finn and Emmie off their feet as the blast burst through the walls and swept out to the street outside.

Back in the library, all was quiet. Finn prodded himself to make sure his body was still in one human-shaped piece. He looked at Emmie to see that she was all there too, then lifted his head and saw the floor was calm. The Legends were spheres: shrunken, hard, unmoving.

"You did it, Finn," said Emmie, punching the air with delight.

On the floor in front of them, a single hard ball twitched lightly. It rocked forward. Then it hopped a little, began to expand with a growing, guttural scream.

Finn grabbed Mr Glad's abandoned weapon from the floor beside him. "We'd better go," he suggested.

Emmie already had.

58

The wave pushed quickly across the street, across the town. As it struck each Manticore out there in Darkmouth, they froze wherever they were, mid-attack, mid-chase, mid-riddle, and imploded one by one, shrunk into little spheres.

Whooop.

Whooop.

Whooop.

The blastwave travelled on, rippling up lanes, rolling into the remaining open gateways, slamming them shut. On it went just beyond them, quickly weakening, failing and then dissipating completely, well short of the edge of Darkmouth.

On one of those streets, Emmie's father stood, breathing hard, surrounded by a carpet of desiccated Manticores.

And, as yet unknown to the people of Darkmouth, every goldfish within 1,000 metres had vanished from its bowl.

On the street outside Finn's house, people emerged from behind walls and cars, picked themselves up off the concrete, limped in search of assistance and tended to the wounded. Sergeant Doyle stood in the centre of the road, panting heavily, a baton in one hand and a small can of pepper spray in the other, alert to any new chaos. There must, he thought, be a psychopath somewhere who needed escorting; a dangerous gang that needed infiltrating. *Anything* to get away from this place.

Those who could moved towards the house once again, picking up stones, shoes abandoned in the panic, anything they could find. One man lifted a desiccated Manticore, weighed it in his hand and judged that it would make an excellent missile. He lifted his arm to launch it.

From the house, there was a sound not unlike a roar.

The crowd went mute.

Some kind of crunching echoed from deep inside.

The crowd shuffled forward a little to hear better.

There was another roar. Closer this time.

Having hidden there throughout the Manticore attack, the man who had broken down the door in the first place reappeared, tumbling backwards, bouncing his way out of the door. He turned and barged a path through the crowd.

After watching him run all the way across the street and round the corner, the mob's attention again turned to the house. From inside came a bowel-shaking growl.

Finn and Emmie burst out through the doorway.

They stopped at the wall of people spilling out over the garden and on to the street. Finn waved his weapon at them, its barrel bulging. "Go!" he shouted, but even the pistol didn't seem to shock the crowd from its stunned stupor. "Now!"

He grabbed Emmie's wrist and pulled her through the crowd.

"That's the boy!" shouted someone.

"Grab him!" demanded another.

"You do it. I've had enough," insisted someone else.

There was another great roar from inside.

A shadow passed behind the door.

A very large shadow.

And then a Minotaur appeared, bending through the frame, unfurling itself in the flickering light at the front of the house. It raised itself up to its full height. Once again, the crowd screamed, shouted, panicked, flailed, fled in all directions, falling into one another, clambering for an escape.

Finn and Emmie were dashing away when Emmie tripped. Finn tried to help her up, pulling her arm round his shoulder, imploring her to keep moving. All around them, the mob was in pandemonium.

"Come on, Emmie!" Finn yelled. "Please!"

As the Minotaur loomed closer, Finn pointed the pistol, found its slim trigger and aimed squarely at the Legend, telling himself, *You can't miss, you can't miss, you can't miss.*

Just as Finn pulled the trigger, a fleeing local clipped him in a panicked dash to safety. Finn missed, flying backwards under the force of the shot, a red glob firing into a tree and sucking it inside out, exposing light, crumbling wood where there had been dark bark. The local standing beside it at the time was briefly the luckiest woman in Darkmouth.

Finn lay winded, clicking the trigger uselessly. Evidently, Mr Glad hadn't designed it to fire more than once.

The Minotaur moved towards him, sweeping within centimetres of Sergeant Doyle. Finn watched as the policeman searched his belt for something to stop it. It was as if he could see exactly what was going through Sergeant Doyle's mind: his baton would be useless; a squirt of pepper spray would hardly reach the creature's chest, never mind its eyes...

Doyle ran to his car, sprang open the boot and began rummaging through it.

As the creature strode closer, Finn searched for something else that might be useful as a weapon, pulled the helmet from round his neck and threw it at the giant. It bounced pathetically off the Legend's skin and on to the road.

Steam pumping from its nostrils, each eye a deep and merciless well, the Minotaur reached him.

"Hey, you big lump, over here!"

Finn peered round the Legend's thick leg to see Sergeant Doyle waving a hi-vis jacket about his head. "Come on. Pick on someone your own size!"

The creature ignored Sergeant Doyle and refocused on Finn, fixing its bleak eyes on him, great snorts of anger rattling above vicious teeth.

Finn gulped.

Then there was a pop and a fizz as a blinding light burned itself into the Legend's skin. The Minotaur roared in anger and pain as the white light died out, revealing

Sergeant Doyle aiming a smoking flare gun.

The Minotaur moved away from Finn and Emmie and towards this new threat. Sergeant Doyle backed off and fled to the safety of his car. The Legend grabbed the underside of the vehicle and heaved it off the road, where it gave a small turn of its siren and tipped helplessly on its side. Sergeant Doyle, meanwhile, made a break for the wall at the front of Finn's house, half falling over it into the garden. He lifted his head to see the creature coming for him, vibrations shaking him with each pounding step. Sergeant Doyle's hands quivered as he reloaded and gripped the flare gun. *Wait*, he ordered himself. *Wait*.

The Minotaur loomed over the wall. Its horns appeared first under the street light, followed by the deep, wet nostrils, chipped tusks sprouting from a foaming open mouth. Sergeant Doyle pulled the trigger.

The flare had no time to light before it was launched straight down the Minotaur's throat. The Legend swallowed it, shook its head and belched. From within its gullet came the muffled fizz of ignition. A burst of white phosphorous shone through the creature's ears, nose and mouth.

It stumbled backwards and Sergeant Doyle raced towards the house. As he reached the doorway, he felt the strangest sensation, a numbness through his chest. It was odd to him that his legs moved, yet he was not moving.

He looked down at a large claw piercing through his ribs. The Legend withdrew it, and Sergeant Doyle's world went sideways.

Slumped on the front step, his right cheek pressed against the concrete, Sergeant Doyle watched the Legend stalk back towards the children. But Finn and Emmie were gone. Sergeant Doyle had bought them some time at least. The Legend scanned the area for them, before bounding off towards the far end of the street.

At the front of Finn's house, Sergeant Doyle hauled himself up against the door frame and examined the hole in his uniform. A dark stain was seeping through his shirt and coat. His breathing grew shallow, his eyes heavy.

He thought of the stain that would never come out.

He thought of Tahiti.

59

Escaping round the corner, Finn and Emmie collided with two bikes, and four bodies hit the ground in a heap of limbs and metal.

"Watch out, monster boy," complained Conn Savage, picking himself up as Manus tried to untangle himself from his pedals. Finn heaved Conn's hefty body back, then lifted his bike and gave it to Emmie. "Get on."

As Manus struggled to his feet, Finn took his bike too.

"What are you doing?" Manus demanded. "Give that back or even your girlfriend won't be able to stop me from wrecking you."

"We need it," snarled Finn. "And you need to run. Now."

"You're not exactly scary in your fancy-dress costume."

"It's not me you should be scared of." Finn stood up on the pedals and pushed off, Emmie following.

There was a ground-shaking thud.

Slowly, Manus and Conn turned to look behind them.

A long shadow fell on the twins as the Minotaur blotted out the street light. Manus grabbed Conn out of the way just in time to stop him being comprehensively squashed.

Finn led Emmie through the maze of laneways into the heart of Darkmouth. "We have to shake it," he shouted at her.

They kept checking over their shoulders, standing up on the pedals to peer above walls, trying to keep track of the Legend.

They spotted the Minotaur pounding through a parallel lane at the same time as it saw them. Finn and Emmie turned sharply on to a side street. The Legend tore through a garden and crashed over a wall, a line full of clothes wrapped round one thigh.

Finn braked, skidded, navigating the maze of laneways as Emmie struggled to keep up. They needed to escape; he just didn't know where to. He yearned again for his father to appear with a plan, his mother to return and calmly—

His mother. That was it.

The Minotaur appeared again, blocking their way; Finn spun the bike round. "I've an idea," he shouted as he hared past Emmie. "My mam's place."

She turned sharply after him. The Minotaur followed, stopping only to tear a water hydrant from the ground and toss it towards them. It smashed off a kerb and bounced on, narrowly missing the front wheel of Emmie's bike. She wobbled, but managed to stay upright.

They arrived at full pelt on Broken Road, jumping off the bikes at Finn's mam's dental surgery.

"What now?" asked Emmie.

They got their answer when a postbox skimmed Finn's ear and punched a hole straight through the front door. The surgery's alarm responded by hammering out a deafening duet of siren and bell.

Scrambling through the door and into the dark hallway, Finn searched for his mother's room, eventually finding it just as there was a crunch of a giant fist on glass at the front of the building.

Emmie screamed into her radio. "Dad. The dentist's. Now."

In the dark of the room, a fraught Finn patted the walls until he found the hook on which his mam hung her keys. He dropped to his knees to find the keyhole. There was another smash outside. He told himself to be calm. To take deep breaths. To focus. But he couldn't manage that. His hands shook. And trembled. The gloves of his fighting suit made gripping the key awkward. Blind luck slid the key into the door. It turned with a welcome click.

Grabbing what he hoped were two bottles of anaesthetic, Finn handed one to Emmie.

"What do we do with this?" she asked.

A minor quake shook the room, equipment falling from trolleys as the Minotaur pounded at the front of the building.

"Knock it out hopefully," said Finn. "But I don't think there are syringes big enough," he added, abandoning his search through drawers and cupboards.

More blows shook the building. Finn ran back through the surgery, his eyes growing used to the dark. Through the window he could see the silhouette of the creature out on the street, pounding at the building. The front window had caved in.

Every instinct was telling Finn to run far, far away. But he wasn't going to do that.

He was going to do the opposite in fact.

He was going to run *towards* the Minotaur.

Finn took a deep breath, then went for it, vaulting on to a chair, out of the window and stumbling on to the pavement.

Seeing Finn, the Minotaur bellowed with such ferocity

it set off a row of car alarms. Finn faced the giant. Inhaled. Exhaled. As soon as the Legend dug a clawed foot into the concrete and lunged, Finn ran straight towards it, feeling as if the world was moving in slow motion.

At the last moment, he slid between the Minotaur's legs, twisted and popped up behind it.

As the Legend lurched towards him, Finn took one stride on to the bonnet of a car, a second on to its roof and then leaped high towards the Minotaur. As he flew through the air, he threw the bottle of anaesthetic at its gaping mouth.

He missed.

60

The bottle of anaesthetic bounced off the giant's fat, blistered lips and shattered on the ground. Finn crumpled on to the tarmac, pain shooting through his leg, and clawed at the hard ground, trying to escape.

The Legend towered over him, the tufted blotches of its skin like the surface of a hostile planet, its hot breath ruffling hair already rigid with fear. Finn could see his face reflected in the dark pools of the Minotaur's pupils: a vision of how brittle he was.

He wanted his father so desperately; longed for him to come to the rescue again, to calmly blast this creature into Desiccation and walk away with a quip.

It wasn't going to happen this time.

The Minotaur reared up, fists tight, its roar in chorus with the thunder booming above. Finn braced himself. Closed his eyes. Tensed for impact.

It didn't come.

He opened his eyes to see the giant grabbing at the back of its neck, searching around its shoulders. Gripped on to it, scurrying about its head and shoulders as he evaded the giant's claws, was Broonie.

"Female child!" he shouted to Emmie. "Give me the vessel."

Emmie steadied herself and threw her bottle to the Hogboon. Juggling, he managed to catch it, rip off its cap and drop the bottle straight down the Minotaur's gullet.

The Legend gripped its throat. It gave its head a shake, then took another step towards Finn.

"I hope that's not just water," Broonie said to Emmie.

"So do I," she responded.

The giant stopped, shook its head again, took another step. Its knees buckled a little, but it regained its balance and loomed over Finn, who was on all fours, trying to pick himself up even as pain shot through his knee. A deep gurgle ran along the vast tracts of the Minotaur's innards as it collapsed across Finn, its face wedged against the wall.

Steve's van screeched into view at the top of the street and accelerated towards them as Emmie ran to Finn and pulled him out from underneath the fallen Minotaur.

The van skidded to a halt and Steve jumped out. Seeing the Hogboon, he raised his weapon.

"Don't, Dad," said Emmie, stepping in the way. "Finn's alive because of him."

She laughed a little in disbelief and relief. Her dad pulled her close and hugged her, smearing her fighting suit in damp blood.

Finn stood now, the shock seeping through his body, a shiver spreading through his chest. He felt cold, alone.

"I didn't have to do that, you know," said Broonie.

"How did you survive the Desiccator wave?" asked Finn, a rattle running through his teeth.

"The Desiccator what?" said Broonie.

"There was a… a sort of bomb, that shrank all the Legends. Well, almost all of them anyway. I set it off," said Finn.

"I don't know," said Broonie. "I ran. You told me to run, so I did. I managed to get almost all the way out of town."

"You must have been outside its reach," said Emmie. "But why did you come back?"

"I was on a hill overlooking the town when I saw the Minotaur. And I saw who he was chasing. I've met Minotaurs. You don't want to be chased by one. Besides,

I owed the boy a debt. A Hogboon always pay its debts. Most of the time. But, if Gantrua ever knew what I did, he'd skewer me on those teeth he collects."

"I thought I was dead..." said Finn, shivering.

"Are you going to thank me for saving you? Don't forget that since I came here I have been beaten, shot, frozen, electrocuted..."

"Electrocuted?" asked Emmie.

"Don't ask."

"Thank you," said Finn. He looked at Emmie. "Both of you."

"You're welcome," said Broonie, then pointed at the Desiccator. "Anyway, if I was you, I'd perform your little magic trick on that Minotaur and worry about the details later. Whatever it's just gobbled is unlikely to be potent enough to keep it quiet for long."

Emmie's father raised his Desiccator, but, before pulling the trigger, changed his mind and handed it to Emmie instead. "It's time you had a go," he said.

She took it willingly, but hesitated to shoot. "It seems sort of cruel to do this when it's just lying—"

The giant snorted angrily into life.

Emmie pulled the trigger.

It was Emmie who first noticed the dust eddying in the breeze, a dull sheen reflecting in the glare of the street lights. It settled in a fine layer on the cars, their alarms still screaming. It fell gently on the broken bricks at the front of the dental surgery. With her foot, Emmie rolled the desiccated Minotaur and it carved a small path through the lightly dusted pavement.

Broonie held his finger out to catch some of the dust, licked it and spat it out. "Tastes of home," he said.

Finn stood, shoulders slumped, hands hanging by his side, feeling utterly lost. The sky had closed up again. The gateways were gone and his parents were lost somewhere in that terrible beyond.

"Come with us, son," said Emmie's father.

But Finn stayed where he was, resisting Steve's gentle pull on his shoulder. He took his phone from beneath his fighting suit, dialled his mother's number and hoped forlornly for a connection.

A stranger's recorded voice told him: "*This number cannot be reached at present...*"

Emmie stepped forward. "Finn..." For once, the words that usually flooded from her had dried up. She simply reached out, squeezed his wrist and kept hold.

Broonie hopped about anxiously. "Are we going to stand here much longer? I am very far from home, you know. Maybe someone could acknowledge that."

Steve took the Desiccator from Emmie and waved it half-heartedly at Broonie, who cowered immediately.

"I have warmed to the young humans," Broonie murmured, "but you deserve to be fed to the death larvae."

Emmie's father picked up the desiccated Legend and walked back towards the van. Emmie tugged a little at Finn's wrist, encouraging him to follow, and he trudged slowly over to the vehicle, stopping briefly to nod at Broonie.

The Hogboon looked around and, having weighed up his options, followed them. Emmie put out her hand to open the van door. Finn paused. "They're gone. Mam and Dad are stuck there on the Infested Side and there's nothing I can do about it."

Beside him, Broonie crouched by the door. "You're not

the only one who's lost everything, you know. Without a crystal, there's no way home for me. I've a bag of beetles needs feeding." He jumped into the van.

"What did you say?" asked Finn.

"I said I've beetles to feed. They'll start eating each other and then I'm done for."

"Not that. The other thing. About the crystal."

"Well, unless you happen to have one lying around, I'm stuck here."

Finn leaped into the back of the vehicle, slammed the door shut and ordered Steve to take him home as quickly as possible. The van screeched away, Broonie protesting in the most vigorous terms as he was flung around in the back.

62

Broonie reached as high as he could. The crystal Finn had found in the aftermath of the Minotaur's first attack was no longer in his underpants drawer: it was in Broonie's outstretched hand and the Hogboon was standing in the middle of the library. The little Legend moved the crystal around, trying to find a snag in the air.

"Are you sure you know how to do this?" asked Finn as politely as he could.

"Don't insult me," snapped Broonie. "Of course I do. But it's not simply a matter of holding it up and letting it go. It requires patience, finesse, and if you could pass me that chair it would be a great help too."

Finn obliged and Broonie stood on the office chair, almost losing his balance as it swivelled round in a full circle. "Really," he barked. "This place..." He resumed his hunt for the snag in the air.

"Having you all stare at me while I try isn't very helpful either," he complained. Finn, Emmie and her father kept staring.

The Hogboon cursed under his breath, then quietened as he appeared to find what he was looking for. He slowly unwrapped his fingers from the crystal and dropped down off the chair. The crystal stayed where it was, impossibly but firmly attached to the air.

"You should stand back," he said, shuffling away from the crystal. "It can sometimes frazzle your ear hair. I knew a fella once who lost an entire—"

The gateway exploded into the room, sending them all reeling. Broonie landed on his bottom. Finn fell on to Emmie, who caught him and held him up for a moment until he righted himself. He tried not to look too embarrassed, but failed completely.

They grouped at the flowing light of the narrow gateway, examined the shower of sparks dancing at its edges.

"You're sure my mam and dad will be there?" asked Finn.

"Every part of the Infested Side is linked to a specific place in the Promised World," answered Broonie. "If they went through *here*, they'll still be *there*. If you see what I mean."

He wasn't sure they did see what he meant, so he continued. "Imagine one world is on top of the other. Open a gateway in this room and it will always lead to the same place in the Infested Side. Open a gateway on the other side of town and you could end up on Gantrua's lap, for all I know."

"So we wait?" asked Finn.

"We wait," confirmed Broonie.

They waited. No one came through.

"You had better not be lying," said Steve through gritted teeth.

"Right, my time here is over," said Broonie, indignant. "*This* was supposed to be the Promised World. Not worth losing a finger over, if you ask me."

He stepped towards the gateway.

"Wait," said Finn.

"I've opened the door," said Broonie. "It's not my fault if no one walks through it. I'm not waiting for it to close."

"I want to come with you," said Finn.

"Over there?" said Broonie. "I don't think you do."

"You're not going," said Steve.

"My parents are in there. I'm going to get them back."

"That gateway will close soon," said Steve.

"Then I need to do this now." Finn stepped up to the

gateway, its aura raising goosebumps that pushed against the inside of his fighting suit. Then he stopped, suddenly aware of what he was about to do. His father hadn't hesitated to jump in there, he told himself. Neither should he. It was time to become the Legend Hunter he was expected to be.

He just didn't want to do it on his own. "I could… actually… do with some help," he said.

Emmie skipped forward. "Then count me in too," she said.

Her father placed a hand on her shoulder and stopped her dead. "He doesn't mean you, Emmie."

"I can't let Finn do it alone, Dad."

"He won't. I'll go with him. You stay here and if you don't I'll put your fighting suit through the shredder. This is not a game, either of you. And Finn, before we go in there, here are the rules: if we don't see your parents, we leave. If I say we leave, we leave. If I leave, we both leave. And, if I get killed, I will never let you forget it."

Steve lifted his Desiccator and approached the gateway. For the second time, Finn put his hand into the light and let it pool round his wrist, like he was checking out the temperature of the sea before diving in.

"What about the prophecy?" asked Emmie.

Finn pulled his hand from the gateway, which remained vivid and strong for now.

His death on the Infested Side. Finn had forgotten, those lines becoming buried under the shock of losing his parents and the need to get them back. But he felt again the full weight of the prophecy, stared at the gateway, golden and beckoning, but which he knew was a torrent ready to sweep him away.

"See you soon, Emmie," he said.

"Right, enough talking. Time is running out," pleaded Broonie, a lilt of panic in his voice. He barged between Finn and Steve into the gateway and was at once devoured by the light.

"A bit of spying, they told me," muttered Steve. "Nothing dangerous, they said." He dipped and stepped boldly into the light.

Finn raised his chin, held his breath and followed.

63

For a moment, Finn was nothing but light.

64

Then Finn experienced a sensation like the jolt between waking and sleeping, like the last embers of a dream. It was his consciousness being scrambled for a nano-moment and put back together in almost exactly the right way.

It was exhilarating.

Then he reached the Infested Side and spent his first seconds there being violently ill, bent double with the shock of the foul air. Steve was standing beside him, peering into the grim light, his helmet still on and his visor down, offering protection from the wretched atmosphere.

As Finn recovered, he wondered what Steve was looking at. Then he saw the two bodies lying in the scrub.

65

Finn and Steve ran to the bodies, crumpled in a hollow among spiked reeds.

"Fomorians," said Steve. He examined the two large prostrate figures, each with a crescent scar branded into their forehead. "Even uglier than we've been taught. And still alive, it seems. They'd be pretty hard to kill with your bare hands, so I'd say your father's done well to do this much damage. Assuming it was him, of course."

Finn stood and looked around. Behind them, Broonie was standing by the light of the gateway, which seemed far more piercing here, its radiance contrasting with the almost complete lack of charm anywhere else in this world.

"It's wonderful, isn't it?" squealed Broonie with sincere delight. "Oh, I didn't think I'd miss it so much, but it tastes as sweet as slugwine." He did a little jig of happiness.

Finn gagged, then composed himself enough to shout, "Dad!"

"No one out there," said Steve. "Not that I can see."

"Mam!"

"You shouldn't hang around," warned Broonie. "There are bandits on these roads and, whatever price a Hogboon skull would fetch as an ornament, you don't want to find out what a human's would be worth." He took a couple of seconds to assess the boy, until he dismissed the dark idea forming in his head. "No, I shouldn't. It wouldn't be right. Honour above wealth. Always. Even if wealth *and* honour would be nice…"

Ignoring Broonie, Steve added his voice to Finn's and their shouts carried across the hard grass towards the gnarled, leafless trees that bordered the clearing. The field stretched away from them, up a hill, beyond which the land dipped and then sloped upwards again to the foot of bare, forbidding mountains.

"Dad! Mam!"

"Hugo! Clara!"

In the distance, a squawk pierced the foul air.

"You can shout all you want," said Broonie. "I'm not waiting around to see who answers."

Steve, his voice still muffled by the visor, leaned down

towards Finn. "They could be gone by now. And our gateway isn't going to remain open much longer. We'll have to leave soon."

"I'm not going anywhere," said Finn. He called again for his parents, ending with more gagging.

There was another squawk from above, and nearer this time. Steve pointed the Desiccator at the sky. A shadow moved through the low cloud. Fast.

Finn took a couple of steps away from the still-open gateway and cocked his head towards the distant mountains. "Do you hear that?" he asked Steve. It was an almost imperceptible rumble through the ground.

"I hear nothing, Finn. And we have to go."

The shadow crossed over them. A high-pitched call stabbing through the cloud. Finn, Steve and Broonie turned their attentions skywards.

From the ground, they sensed the tiniest tremor.

The anxiety in Broonie's voice ratcheted up a notch. "Well, I have a hovel to attend to, so if you'll excuse me."

A creature bolted from the cloud. Serpentine, with wings scooping at the sky, it coiled its body, bared its fangs and shot forward towards the isolated Broonie.

The Hogboon screamed and ducked, hands over head. The mouth of the winged serpent enveloped Broonie's crown, his skin grazed by the tip of a fang.

Phzzzzt.

With a *whuuupfh*, the creature crumbled, half desiccated, its head and a wing mashed into a rough sphere, but its tail writhing on the ground, every flail of its undesiccated wing pushing it further round in a circle. Broonie peeked out from the gap in his hands as the serpent quickly exhausted itself and stopped still in the scrub, the gateway illuminating its horrific state.

"Interesting," muttered Steve, lowering his smoking weapon. "The Desiccator doesn't seem to work as well here."

Finn didn't hear him. He was again concentrating on the rumble, which was getting louder, closer. The gathering tremor in the ground now tickled at the soles of his boots.

The sparkling edges of the gateway dipped for an instant.

"The gateway's going to close soon," said Broonie, beginning to back away from the scene. "It was interesting meeting you. Let's never do it again. Goodbye." He sprinted towards the twisted forest.

Steve gripped Finn's shoulder and pulled him over to the gateway. "We're going."

Finn shrugged him off. Steve grabbed him again, hauling him to the edge of the light. "We will come back for them, Finn. Somehow, we'll come back."

Feeling the gateway's warmth against his skin, Finn looked back at the empty, bleak world, making a silent promise to return. He began to step into the hole between worlds. Then he heard it.

"Finn!" His father's voice reached them from the edge of the trees. Then two figures appeared. In the gloom, they were hardly recognisable, only dark shapes kicking up dust. Finn's mam's arm was slung round his dad's shoulder as they ran towards him.

"Dad!" He jumped forward a few paces. Steve shouted at him to stay where he was.

Hugo and Clara separated, both concentrating solely on Finn, but, even in just a few steps, Finn's mam had fallen behind and Finn watched as his dad stopped for a moment, grabbed her hand and then began running again.

The earth shuddered. The tremor worked its way up through Finn's armour, forcing a rattle through his fighting suit. He peered out at the hill.

Over its crest emerged an army.

Manticores and Wolpertingers to the front, giant

loping Fomorians following, and between them an array of other Legends. It was a crazy mass of shapes, scampering, lumbering, snarling, charging towards them.

"Hurry!" Finn screamed as loudly as he could.

66

Finn's parents ran hard, their gaze fixed on the gateway. Steve fired a volley from his Desiccator. The net traced a blue arc towards the hill, but fell short.

Behind Finn, the gateway groaned a little, beginning to collapse inwards. "Quick!"

Over the trembling earth, the army raced. At its head there were two figures riding on the back of enormous three-horned, four-legged beasts. One of the individuals was a giant, and even at this distance Finn could make out a jagged grille reaching upwards from his neck.

The other figure looked puny beside him, almost completely concealed beneath a hooded cloak.

Finn watched his father and mother race across the hard ground. Steve fired off another shot towards the onrushing Legends and this time the net landed in the front ranks, sending creatures sprawling and falling. The rest of the army ploughed through the victims and ever forward.

Finn stood at the precipice of the gateway. "Hurry. Hurry!"

The light bent again as a prelude to the gateway's imminent closure, just as his parents reached it.

Hugo grabbed Steve's Desiccator, thrust Clara towards him, then pushed them both towards the gateway.

"I suppose I have to thank you now," he said to Steve.

"Nah. Looks like you had everything under control here," said Steve before taking Clara's arm, the light swallowing them as they both vanished to safety.

Now only Finn and his father were left on the Infested Side.

The wall of cursing, ravenous Legends was almost on top of them. The two lead riders pulled hard on their beasts and halted as the hordes bore down behind them. The giant at the front snarled through the broken teeth lining his mask, pushing up the scars that criss-crossed his face, holding the beast below him in place with arms that were each wider than Finn's father's chest.

The Legend held Finn's stare, as if he knew exactly who this boy was. At that moment, Finn realised that this must be the Fomorian Broonie had talked about. This must be Gantrua.

Beside him, the hooded figure held tight against the bucking of the beast beneath him, face lost beneath the hood.

Finn refocused. He was standing at the rim of the buckling gateway. "Dad, we need to go!" he called. But, instead of leaping through the gateway, Finn's father aimed the Desiccator at the two leaders on their beasts before setting his sights on just one of them. His target pulled the hood slowly from his head.

Hugo recognised him instantly, at least as far as Finn could tell from the way he staggered back, horrified. It took Finn a moment longer.

The man's skin – because it *was* a man, not a Legend…

…the man's skin was drained of colour and terribly scarred, his eyes a burnt-out pink, but enough remnants of the face from the portrait clung on. Hugo lowered his weapon, his mouth hanging open in disbelief as a wry smile crept across his father's wizened lips.

Niall Blacktongue, the man who had tried talking to Legends and it didn't end well, Finn's father's father, the one who was lost, stared back at them until he was swallowed by the swarm of Legends clamouring to reach the intruders.

The gateway groaned. Finn screamed at his father to go, but Hugo didn't move at first, instead keeping his eyes glued to the spot where Niall had been before the Legends engulfed him. He finally turned to Finn.

"Tell your mam I love her and I'll see her soon," he shouted, "but I have to do this."

"Do what?" asked Finn.

"Go after my father."

"But—"

"You'll be all right. You'll find a way to get back here. You've already shown me that, Finn the Defiant." He looked behind them quickly, the clamouring wall of Legends now almost upon them. "Listen to me, Finn. There's a map somewhere. In room S3 in the house. Do you hear me? Find the map."

He pushed his son through the gateway.

Finn's last tumbling vision from the Infested Side was of his father turning away and charging into the oncoming army of Legends.

He lay on his back, the acrid breath of the Infested Side escaping his lungs. His mother crouched beside him, hacking while Emmie and Steve attempted to comfort her. Finn reached out and touched her hand.

The gateway snuffed out.

From A Concise Guide to the
Legend Hunter World, Vol. 7,
Chapter 42, from footnotes to the
introductory paragraphs on 'The
Great Unpleasantness'

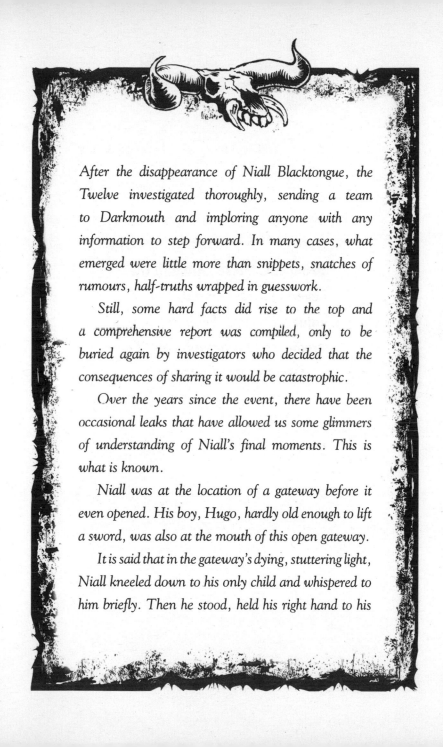

After the disappearance of Niall Blacktongue, the Twelve investigated thoroughly, sending a team to Darkmouth and imploring anyone with any information to step forward. In many cases, what emerged were little more than snippets, snatches of rumours, half-truths wrapped in guesswork.

Still, some hard facts did rise to the top and a comprehensive report was compiled, only to be buried again by investigators who decided that the consequences of sharing it would be catastrophic.

Over the years since the event, there have been occasional leaks that have allowed us some glimmers of understanding of Niall's final moments. This is what is known.

Niall was at the location of a gateway before it even opened. His boy, Hugo, hardly old enough to lift a sword, was also at the mouth of this open gateway.

It is said that in the gateway's dying, stuttering light, Niall kneeled down to his only child and whispered to him briefly. Then he stood, held his right hand to his

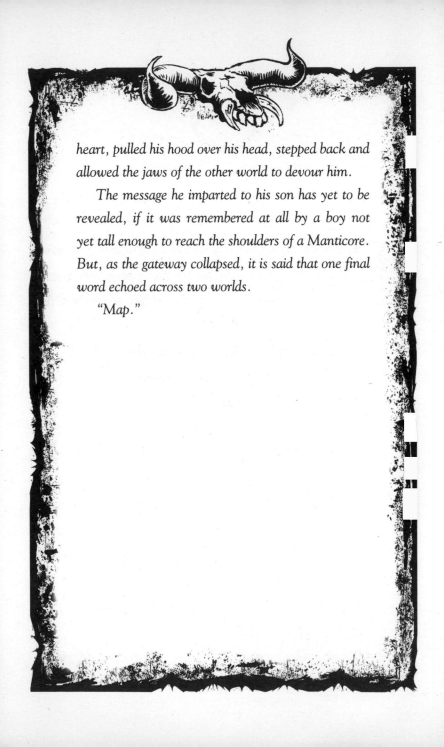

heart, pulled his hood over his head, stepped back and allowed the jaws of the other world to devour him.

The message he imparted to his son has yet to be revealed, if it was remembered at all by a boy not yet tall enough to reach the shoulders of a Manticore. But, as the gateway collapsed, it is said that one final word echoed across two worlds.

"Map."

67

The door swung open so suddenly that Finn almost sprawled across the floor. He righted himself just as his mother, Emmie and Steve pushed in behind him.

The room was S3 – a storage room down the Long Hall. Near the door to the main house, it had a thick wooden door, with iron rivets studded across it from top to bottom and a fat brass lock. It was sandwiched between E1, an equipment room, and A2, where some of the family's hundreds of years of archives were kept.

But otherwise it appeared unremarkable. Even the fact that neither Finn nor his mother had ever been in it was not unusual. There were many doors along the Long Hall. Many rooms they had never set foot in.

Steve tried the light switch. The single bulb in the room flared, sparked and died.

The room was narrow, with only a slit of a window

high on the far wall, through which a single stream of moonlight fell on the only object in the empty space: a tall thin table halfway along the right-hand wall.

On the table was a brown wooden box. Finn walked over to it and the others followed, his mother first, but slow in her movements, shock still dulling her senses.

Finn examined the simple box, which had no markings, no patterns, not even a keyhole, just clean, rounded edges. Dust scattered from it when he touched it, dancing in the pale light. Finn worked his fingers round the rim of the box, searching for a lid. Finding it, he gently prised it open.

Inside was a piece of paper, clean, folded. Finn looked round at his mother for consent to pick it up. Exhausted, frail, still suffering from the atmosphere of the Infested Side, she simply nodded.

He took it in his fingers, unfolded it gently. It was obviously stiff with age, fragile, and he was careful not to tear it at the folds.

He looked at it, then back to his mother, his uncertainty clear.

"What?" she whispered.

"It's not a map. It's a sentence. Just one sentence.

And it's not even in Dad's handwriting."

"What does it say?" asked Emmie.

Finn read it aloud: "Light up the house."

68

They turned on every light, every lamp, in every room and every corner of every room, illuminating the house in the early morning before the sun had yet peeked through the windows.

"Where do we even begin?" Finn asked Emmie. "Where would someone hide a map?"

"At least we'll get a day off school for this," said Emmie.

The corridor stretched ahead of them. Behind them, in the library, Steve was standing amid debris, examining the long curves of shelves while holding an atlas in his hand. "The good news is that there's a map here," he called out to Finn and Emmie. "The bad news is that there's another, oh, couple of thousand alongside it."

Finn's mother approached down the Long Hall, opening her mouth to speak when she reached them only to get caught on a cough. "I guess it'll take a few days yet," she said when she finally cleared her throat.

"You need rest, Mam."

"I'll rest when we find your dad." She placed her arm round Finn's shoulder and he snuggled into her, briefly forgetting to be embarrassed in front of Emmie. His mother gave him a kiss on the head and walked into the library.

"Clara, I know we've only just met," said Steve, "and you mightn't exactly trust me, but I want you to know—"

"Let's just find this map, OK?"

"OK."

Emmie leaned in to Finn. "Does your mam know about the prophecy?"

"I haven't told her. She has enough to worry about. You're not to tell her either."

"My spying days are done, I promise," said Emmie.

"No more secrets, please."

"Agreed," said Emmie, with a nod of her head. "Except for that one we're keeping from your mother obviously."

"Obviously."

Emmie looked at the long line of doors in the Long Hall. "Which room should we try first?"

"I don't know. The nearest one, I suppose," said Finn.

"And then?"

"Look for a pattern maybe. Anything that seems like it

could be a map. If it was obvious, Dad would have told me where to find it. It must be hidden somewhere."

Emmie hesitated. "Do you think he's going to be OK?"

"I do," said Finn. "I really do. Even when he was our age, he was doing incredible things, fighting Legends five times our size. Did I ever tell you about the time he—?"

"Yes."

"And the day he—?"

"That too."

"Well then, you know he's going to be OK."

"And what happens when we find the map?"

"Then we go after him," said Finn, with more confidence than he actually felt.

"I'm not sure I'll be much use," said Emmie.

"I don't know. I could teach you a couple of moves. Do you know MacNeill's Limb Severer?"

"Whose limb did he sever with that?"

"His own actually."

Emmie eyed Finn for a moment, then gave him a poke in the shoulder. "I told you, don't try and scam this city girl."

She moved to the first door and turned the handle.

Finn followed her. "But it's a real move, I swear."

Behind them, Niall Blacktongue looked down from his portrait, head bowed, eyes refusing to meet anyone who might look at him. Instead, fixed in crusted paint, he gazed downwards, towards a red table at his side, on which were scattered a few items: a compass, a feather in an ink pot, a magnifying glass, some coins, a couple of unnamed books and a small square mirror propped upright.

And in the mirror was the reflection of a piece of paper, no bigger than a thumbnail yet bright and detailed, at the centre of which was painted a tiny but very distinguishable X.

THANK YOUS

Thank you to my amazing agent, Marianne Gunn O'Connor, for the hard work, encouragement, support and hot chocolate. I am also grateful to Vicki Satlow for bringing *Darkmouth* around the world.

Enormous thanks to my editor Nick Lake for believing in *Darkmouth* from the beginning, and also to HarperCollins US editor, Erica Sussman, and Samantha Swinnerton at HarperCollins UK, for their invaluable guidance and advice.

Thank you to all at HarperCollins who have put so much into this book, including interiors designer, Elorine Grant, cover designers, Kate Clarke and Matt Kelly, Geraldine Stroud and Mary Byrne in publicity, Nicola Way and Hannah Bourne in marketing, Amy Knight in production, and Brigid Nelson and JP Hunting in sales. And thanks to copy editor, Jane Tait.

I am particularly indebted to Ann-Janine Murtagh, head of children's books at HarperCollins, for her great kindness and faith in me.

James de la Rue's illustrations are so good it's like he could read my mind, something which freaked me out for a while to be honest.

Thank you to my parents, Tim and Marie, who gave me books as fast as I could read them, and to my sisters, Niamh and Anne, who let me read theirs when I ran out.

Thanks to my children, Caoimhe, Aisling, Laoise and especially to Oisín, who told me he loved the book without any need for bribery.

Finally, my love to Maeve, who puts up with my grumpiness when I'm writing. And not writing.

SHANE HEGARTY

DARKMOUTH

WORLDS EXPLODE

On a list of things Finn never thought he'd wish for,
a gateway bursting open in Darkmouth was
right up there. But that's about his only
hope for finding his missing father. He's
searched for a map, he's followed Steve
into dead-ends, but found nothing.
And he's still got homework to do.

But soon Finn and Emmie must
face bizarre Legends, a ravenous
world and a face from the past,
as they go where no Legend
Hunter has gone before. Or, at
least, where no Legend Hunter
has gone before and returned with
their limbs in the correct order.

COMING
AUGUST 2015

SHANE HEGARTY